Epitaph 5: The Selkie
Karla Brandenburg

Acknowledgements: As always, thanks to Terry Odell and Steve Pemberton as my other sets of eyes who help point out what I miss throughout the writing process, and my editor, Kelly Lynne. Special thanks to Jay Brandt, Ed Presser, Kira Butler, and Cheryl Bouschard for helping me out with the injury (anything I got wrong is my fault, not theirs!)

Chapter 1

With the pre-season started, The Chicago Stockyard Cowboys Soccer Club couldn't spare their athletic trainer to check on the injured asset who'd been sent to the development league. Liam McCormick had been an all-star defensive player until he'd blown his ACL last season, and he was slated to make his return to the field at an international exhibition game in Ireland. As assistant trainer, Emma Parrish was nominated to travel to the away game to check on Liam's rehab and recovery.

The physical therapist intern working with the injured soccer players had falsified information, including McCormick's. If he'd missed his rehab, the injury that ended his season last year would potentially become career-ending.

The development league team based in the Chicago suburbs—the Rockford Mustangs—reported McCormick was moving well, showing up for training sessions, but the Cowboys' front office wanted a first-hand report.

Without an agenda her first day in Ireland, Emma opted to adapt to the time change by taking a tour. She'd assess McCormick at practice tomorrow. For now, she planned to stay away from anyone on the team.

The cab driver who drove her to Kinsale had been chatty, and when she told him she planned to do a walking tour followed by a stop at a local pub to get "the Irish experience," he'd told her to make sure she ordered a Murphy's rather than a Guinness. Apparently, it was a local favorite.

Clouds were gathering when Emma stopped at the tourism office to pick up a guidebook. Undaunted, she did the self-guided tour while the chilly wind blew through her hair, the sea air adding frizzy volume.

She stood on the Castle Park peninsula to look across the picture-perfect landscape, the harbor where sailboats dotted the water. She'd read about a triathlon route around the sites she'd visited, and although the hike was steep in places, she ached to test the running leg of the course. If she could fit in another visit to Kinsale while she was in Ireland, she'd come back, after she was more rested and after she'd assessed McCormick. For now, she'd visit the pub the cabbie had pointed out and have a pint.

For the first time in forever, Emma relaxed. She loved her job, loved the hectic pace, but looking out over the brilliant greens, the sparkling sea, she appreciated half a day of downtime.

Emma walked into Casey's Anchor and, as instructed, ordered a Murphy's.

"An American, are you?" the barmaid asked.

"Yes," she answered with a big smile. The Irish had been very welcoming, despite identifying her as a foreigner.

The bartender strolled up behind the barmaid. "Here after the legends?"

"I'm here for the soccer game in Cork. Thought I'd take in the sights while I had time," she replied. "I've been reading about your history, from Charles Fort to the sinking of the Lusitania."

The bartender cast a glance at the locals gathered at the bar, his friends, by the looks of it, and gave her a sly smile. "A pretty young thing like you, you've a lonely look in your eye. Thought you might be out in search of a selkie."

Lonely? Emma didn't have time to be lonely. She'd had enough of the wrong men to prefer her own company, but she'd take the bait. Maybe the Irish weren't used to seeing women on their own. "And what, pray tell, is a selkie?" she asked, knowing it would lead to a story. Everyone she'd met so far had a story to tell, and the bartender was clearly eager to share his.

He leaned on the bar as the barmaid set the glass of stout in front of her. "A selkie is a seal what's come ashore and takes on human form. A strikingly bewitching creature who calls to the first human it comes in contact with—a siren's call. Irresistible, so they say. Sure, it's mischief the selkie's after when it walks the land."

Emma handed the barmaid her credit card and took a swallow of her stout.

One of the patrons chimed in. "They say Frank found his da's skin, and that's how he was able to return to the water."

"His da's skin?" Emma repeated cynically, taking another sip. "They can exchange skins?"

The bartender turned to the man at the end of the bar. "Shush, and let me tell the story to our fine guest." He resumed his tale, the lilt in his speech adding to his flair for storytelling. "The legend tells that whether the selkie be a man or a woman, when they leave the water, they peel off their skin and hide it for safekeeping, and when they're ready to return, they slip back into it and swim away, but if someone on the land should find the selkie's skin, the selkie is imprisoned on the land by that person until their skin is returned to them, or until they find where its hidden."

He paused, for dramatic effect no doubt, and Emma took another swig. Had the barmaid refilled her glass? She didn't remember finishing her first drink.

"The selkie is beautiful to look upon, and the story tells that the object of their affection falls prey to their charms," he went on. "Many a man or woman has gone mad in the pursuit of capturing a selkie's skin. They say the selkie is attracted to those who feel themselves outside of society, those who don't fit in. While on the land, the selkie is loyal to that one person, but they are sea creatures at heart, and once they find their hidden skin, they will leave everything behind to return to where they belong."

There was something to be said for loyalty. Emma drained her glass and it was instantly replaced with a full one. She held up a hand to forestall another refill. "But you haven't answered the question about Frank and his father's skin," she said.

The bartender shot a glance at the barmaid, a twinkle in his eye. "A selkie can live on land for many years, and there are tales that go back generations." Muddy green eyes met Emma's as he continued his tale. "A woman sheds tears of loneliness into the sea and a selkie can't help but come ashore to ease her sorrow. They're empathetic creatures, selkies are.

If she manages to capture and hide his skin, he's bound to her until such time as he finds it again. They're rumored to be ardent lovers. Many a selkie has raised a large family, and often enough it's one of his own children who knows where the skin is hidden and inadvertently tells the secret what sends him back to his home in the sea."

As Emma sipped more of her stout, her head began to swim. How many times had the barmaid refilled her glass? Had the bartender answered her question? She didn't remember what she'd asked.

She was entranced by the story of a tantalizing man peeling back the black skin of a seal, a man who would seduce her and be loyal to her if she managed to steal and hide his sealskin. Could such a creature exist? He sounded like a better option than most of the human men she knew.

"'Tis said Frank's da was a selkie," the patron at the end of the bar said again. "A selkie who never found his skin and died whilst on the land. In such a case, it is believed the child of a selkie can take his place in the sea."

Right. That was what she'd asked. Except things were becoming more muddled in her head.

"True enough," the bartender said with a nod. "The dark ones are a bit odd themselves, as if they don't quite fit in."

"Dark ones?" Emma asked. Her voice didn't sound right. Had she slurred her words?

"That's how you know a selkie," the patron said. "By their dark hair and their dark eyes, like those of a seal."

Another full pint had appeared in front of Emma. "I'll take my bill now," she said, before another beer appeared. The air grew thick. She glanced at the window, at the clouds blocking the sun. "I need some air," she said half to herself. She signed the credit card slip and stumbled outside.

The chilly breeze did little to clear her head. Emma giggled at the story, a seal coming ashore and peeling off his skin to reveal a man.

A man. She flapped her lips. Her last boyfriend had been a huge disappointment. She'd let him con her into believing he cared about her. After two months of courting her into his bed, as soon as he'd succeeded, he disappeared.

Maybe she was lonely. How else could Cliff have fooled her so completely?

Emma found a wooden staircase from the street to the beach below and held tight to the railing, taking each step cautiously. Yes, she was drunk, and no, she shouldn't be walking steps, but she had an urgent desire to reach the seashore.

Bitter tears slid down her face. She didn't quite fit in, as evidenced by her inability to attract and keep a boyfriend. Emma shook her head. She didn't have time for a boyfriend. She had more important things to worry about.

When she reached the beach, she laughed at the legend once more while she wiped tears from her eyes and washed her hands in the surf. She imagined a seal emerging from the sea, peeling off his skin to take on the form of a man and looking at her like she was the only woman on earth. Attentive and loyal, he could make her feel special for as long as he remained on the land.

Two men splashed and laughed at the shoreline. "I'll race ya," one called to the other.

The now overcast sky blocked the late afternoon sun, making the world dim and gray. Emma tried to focus on the spectacle before her. Both men peeled off a layer of black—wetsuits? Or sealskin?—folded the layer and placed it under a rock, before they took off running.

LIAM MCCORMICK HAD a seventy-five percent chance for a full recovery. Then what? The last guy to have ACL surgery had come back from his injury too soon and re-injured his knee, as in permanently injured. Another guy had fully rehabbed and his ligament had torn a second time.

Statistically, one percent of college athletes made the cut to the pro level. Liam was one of the lucky few, until the collision on the field. A torn ACL was a stark reality check. One injury and your career could be over. What then?

He hoped he wouldn't find out for a few more years.

He'd ended up doing most of his rehab on his own. How well would his repaired ACL withstand prolonged game minutes? If he wanted his job back, he had to prove he was able to play with the development team first.

The exhibition game was in Cork, half an hour from Kinsale where his father had been born and later died, where the Irish relatives he didn't know still lived. Ma had given Liam her blessing to look them up. Did he want to? The McCormicks didn't all have to be like Da, and there were no guarantees any of them were still in Kinsale, but he was about to find out.

Liam's career was on the line, which is why he went for an open-water swim in the Celtic Sea with Shane Fahey, a midfielder on the Irish team and a fellow triathlete. Swimming was considered rehab, didn't hurt, and surely it would improve Liam's fitness to play soccer. If he bumped into a distant relative or two, well, swimming seemed like a good excuse to stop in Kinsale.

Shane drove Liam past brightly colored storefronts along narrow streets and angled to where sailboats and masts bobbed in the harbor. He parked near the marina and Liam glanced at the gray clouds in the sky.

"Will the weather hold?" he asked Shane.

"Looks calm enough."

Liam opened his door, turned to set his feet outside the car and pulled off his sweatshirt and jeans to the tri-suit he wore beneath. He grabbed his wetsuit from the gear bag he'd thrown in the back seat and struggled into it. "You think we'll hit rough currents?"

Shane grunted, doing his own shimmy into neoprene on the other side of the car. He reached across the front seat and handed Liam a yellow swim cap. "Worried? Here. Wear this so we can fish you out should you decide you can't make it." He donned his own yellow cap, got out of the car and pointed out landmarks. "There's a narrow channel that will take us to the end of the island over there. Mind the rocks I was telling you about. Then it's a swim around the other side. The ocean current is stronger there. Once we're to the other end of the island, we can swim to the beach with the tide."

"When we get done, I'll buy you a pint," Liam said. "Unless you'll be too tired to raise one."

Shane laughed. "It'll take more than a swim to stop me. You say you have family around here? Maybe we'll run into them, then?"

"Yeah, maybe," Liam said quietly.

"When's the last time you saw them?"

"Never met them. My da moved back, gotta be close to fifteen years ago, but he passed on a few years back."

"That's rough." Shane shot him a glance. "How will you recognize the relatives?"

"My ma says I look like a lot my da, and they're his family, so maybe they'll recognize me."

"God help us." Shane laughed.

Shane pointed out a wooden staircase that led to the street. "The pub is just there, above the beach. Once we hit the sand, I'll not be waiting for you." He grinned at Liam. "Ready, Yank?"

"I am." The distance from the beach to the steps was a short sprint. He'd been cleared for running, but the stairs might be pushing things.

Shane patted Liam on the back and guided him to the boardwalk—the slipway, according to Shane—that dropped into the water.

"We should be able to finish the lap in half an hour, well before the sun sets," Shane told him, "although if our pace is slower, we might keep to this side of the island. When they run the triathlon, they swim two circuits around. We'll stick to one for today?"

A polite way of acknowledging Liam might not be back to form. "One'll do. Let's go."

Liam adjusted his goggles as he slipped into the water. It was cold, but the wetsuit did its thing and kept most of his body warm. He took measured strokes and felt an overwhelming sense he'd come home, despite never having been to Ireland before. This was the land of his ancestors, the town was where his father had been raised.

Beneath the surface, seaweed swayed with the gentle swells of the ocean. Liam and Shane kicked side by side as white foam whipped against barnacle-covered rocks jutting from the water, marking their course.

Crabs scuttled along the bottom of the sea and fish darted around in schools. At the first checkpoint, the end of the island, Shane stopped and shot a glance at Liam. Liam motioned him on. A black seal joined them, darting between them, and they swam to the back side of the island.

Shane and Liam swam stroke for stroke. The sea buffeted them, occasionally knocking them into each other. Two more seals appeared, one undulating near Liam's head and the third bobbing and ducking beneath them. Liam continued to pull against the water, taking measured breaths between views of the sea life. Fatigue settled in, the muscles in his still-mending leg fighting the pull of the current.

When they rounded the far end of the island, the seals dived and curled playfully between Liam and Shane. Shane flipped to his back and Liam raised his head to ride the tide that carried them to shore.

Shane laughed. "Never had a seal escort before."

"They won't hurt us, will they?" Liam asked, even as he extended a hand to touch the slimy skin of the seal closest to him.

"The males can get aggressive during mating season, but we should be safe enough. Mind the beach. There's a strong current that runs toward the slipway. You'll have to swim hard to get through it."

Liam nodded, their seal companions nudging them toward the shore. The tug of the cross current grabbed hold and Liam concentrated on strong strokes again, swimming toward the beach in a race with Shane for who would get there first.

With the seals barking encouragement, Liam and Shane ran through the surf, tugging and hopping to be free of their wetsuits.

Outside the water, the air was cool, moderate for February in Ireland and warmer than in Chicago, for sure, but in his tri-suit and trainers, the chill raised gooseflesh.

"We'll leave our suits on the beach," Shane called out. "They should be safe enough."

They folded their discarded suits, left them beside a rock and broke into a run across the beach.

They climbed the steps and crossed the cobbled street. In the warmth of the pub, they both laughed between gasps for breath.

Liam's knee buckled, a streak of pain shooting down his leg. The restraint of the wetsuit had kept his knee straight, and the chill of the sea had held the pain to a minimum, but the steps were a bigger challenge than he'd anticipated and he was a long way from whole. He should have stopped to put on his knee brace. Bent over, he made a pretense of catching his breath.

Shane lowered his voice and lay an arm across Liam's shoulders. "First one's on me, mate. I remember what it was like when I had the same surgery."

Liam raised his head, met Shane's eyes, and nodded. "You sure our gear is safe on the beach?"

The pub door opened once more and a young woman charged in, her hair frizzed out like his sister Kathleen's on a humid summer's day. She was backlit by waning sunlight, her features muddy in the dimly lit pub. She wore a fleece jacket, tight blue jeans and high-heeled boots that went to her knees. "I've got your skin, selkie. You're mine to command."

Chapter 2

The bar patrons laughed when Emma held up her prize. She took a long look at the men she'd seen running from the water. The beer muddled her senses, and coupled with the story she'd heard, she wasn't sure what she'd seen on the beach.

Those guys had come from the sea on two legs. Men. Not seals.

What, exactly, had she seen on the beach?

She lowered the suit in her hands. Manmade. Not a seal's skin.

"It's your fault for putting such ideas in her head," one of the old men at the bar told the bartender.

A blond man tried to grasp the wetsuit from her— neoprene, not sealskin—but she yanked it back. The out of focus part of her wasn't ready to surrender to the facts.

"No," she said. "I found it, fair and square." What was she talking about? She didn't believe in fairy tales. Emma blinked, taking in the bright colors of the clothes the men from the sea wore. Tight shirts and shorts, yellows and oranges. Tri-suits like triathletes wore. They looked more like Tour de France riders than selkies. She turned to the man with the black hair. In the dark pub, she couldn't quite make out his features, but there was something familiar about him. "It isn't a seal's skin," the blond man said, a note of derision in his voice. "It's a wetsuit, and costly, at that. I'll thank you to return it."

Emma held the skin away from him and he backed off. She examined the wetsuit more closely, found the tag at the neck. A zipper. No. It wasn't a skin. She knew that, but for a moment in time, she'd wanted to believe the legend.

Maybe she was lonely. Why else had she gone to the sea in search of selkies?

"You can't blame the lass," another old man at the bar said, taking a swig of his stout. "If I'd seen the lads coming out of the water and taking off suits like that, I might have wondered myself."

She'd let a pub full of Irishmen fill her head with fairy tales along with the beer. No. She wasn't giving up the sealskin. Wetsuit. Whatever it was. The black-haired would-be selkie would be a nice consolation prize for one night. She'd even let him return to the sea. She didn't like the whole hide-their-skin-and-keep-them-captive-on-the-land part of the legend.

There was no such thing as selkies.

She tried for a 'come hither' glance. "You want it? Come and get it."

"I wouldn't if I were you," the blond man whispered to his friend. "Seems a trick."

"Anyone care to enlighten me as to what this selkie business is about?" the dark-haired one asked. He didn't have a telltale lilt to his voice. He sounded like an American.

He took a step closer, into the light of one of the tables. His face connected to his name like a wanted poster. Liam McCormick.

This wasn't good.

Emma dropped into a seat at the table and bowed her head, hoping he wouldn't recognize her, the wetsuit clutched in her hands.

"Seems you've filled her head with your nonsense," the blond man said to the bartender. "You might share your story with my friend, as well, since he seems to bear the brunt of your tales. That way he'll know what he's up against if he wants to get his wetsuit back."

Emma rested her forehead against her hands on the table, mortified.

The bartender retold the same tale, his Irish lilt drawing pictures of a lonely woman letting her tears fall into the sea, of seals who turned into men, the answer to her prayers.

She was holding a wetsuit, not sealskin. Not even the alcohol could alter that fact, but she couldn't give it up, not without Liam recognizing her.

"Hold off there, Declan," the barmaid interrupted the story. "This man might be descended from the selkies in truth." She stood before Liam with her hands on her hips. "You're American?" she asked, casting a wayward glance toward Emma. Guilt by association, no doubt. Now the poor guy was likely to be teased along with her.

"I am," Liam replied.

"What's your name then?"

"Liam."

The barmaid nodded. "Aye. Liam McCormick, I'd wager?"

Everyone in the pub seemed to hold their collective breaths.

He turned to his friend. "Time to go."

Maybe Liam wouldn't recognize her in the light of day, when he met her tomorrow. If she handed the wetsuit off to the blond guy, Liam would be none the wiser.

If she was lucky.

"THAT RESEMBLANCE TO your da must be stronger than you thought." Shane took hold of Liam's arm, preventing him from making his escape, although Liam's aching knee was deterrent enough.

Liam's pulse amped up. Bad enough he'd become the center of attention, now he'd been labeled a McCormick. Would they kick him out of the pub?

"I'm your cousin," the barmaid went on. "Moira Kincaid." She held out a hand.

Liam shook it cautiously. "I'm afraid I'm not acquainted with the family here."

"And you wouldn't be," Moira went on. "Your ma didn't have any people left, did she? And then when your da, Uncle Frank, took her off to America..."

"But he came back," Liam said, grinding his teeth.

She held his gaze. "Aye."

Moira opened her mouth and then pursed her lips. She glanced at the bartender before she pulled Liam to a table. Shane followed and slid onto the bench beside him, too eager to hear the grisly details of Liam's family history. So much for keeping a low profile.

"When's the last you heard of your father?" Moira asked.

Memories he'd thought he'd buried years ago erupted to the surface, but he didn't dare share them. These people were his father's family, and likely wouldn't take well to hearing adolescent horror stories. "Not since he returned to Ireland," he said.

"But you'll know he's dead."

"Yes. My mother told me."

Moira nodded at the drunk woman in the corner—why did that woman look so familiar?—the one clutching his wetsuit. "Since we're telling tales tonight. He came back a broken man. Sat on that barstool every night saying as how he wished he could return to the sea. Ramblings after too much drink, to be sure, and his da, your grandda, was a fisherman by trade, so no one thought aught of it, until a new neighbor moved to town, told of how he'd bought this house, you see. The same one your parents lived in when they were first married. He found something akin to tarpaper, or so he said, and your da nearly shook the man out of his shirt, demanding to know what he'd done with it."

Liam chuckled. "You're going to tell me this new neighbor found a seal's skin? That my da was a selkie and my ma trapped him on the land?"

Moira smiled. "Me? I'm not one for the old tales, but it does make for a good story, and it sounds better than saying your da went for a swim next night and never came back."

The close atmosphere of the pub pressed against Liam's lungs. He fought to even his breathing before he asked his next question. "He committed suicide?"

She cocked her head. "You don't know?"

"Ma only said that he'd passed on," Liam said.

"No one really knows what happened. He might well have walked into the sea and drowned, or he might have donned his seal's skin and swam away."

Shane laughed and slapped at the table. "Now that's how you welcome family back to the homeland."

Liam pushed away from the table. "I think it's time to head back to Cork."

Moira laid a hand on the table. "But I've only just met you, cousin. Stay. It's but a story that makes a tragic death sound less tragic. Stay and meet the rest of your family—your da's family."

"Let's at least have a beer before we drive back," Shane said. "We need the refreshment after our swim, no?"

Every nerve ending in Liam's body told him to get the hell out of this pub, out of Kinsale. Moira was right about one thing. Thinking his father had donned a sealskin and returned to the sea was a better story than suicide, a mortal sin for a devout Catholic.

His da might be gone, which was a relief to some extent—no fear of invoking wrath—and yet Liam had always hoped his father had sobered up, straightened out after he'd returned to Ireland. So much for pipe dreams.

"A couple of Harps," Shane told Moira, taking Liam's silence for acquiescence.

She brought them each a mug and sat at their table again. "Tell me about Auntie Eileen, and the rest of you. Your da did say there were five of you?"

His father had spoken of them? "There were," Liam said, fingering his mug and staring into the brew. "Mary, the youngest of us, died." He raised the beer and stared at Moira. "He told you about us?"

She nodded. "When a man drinks, he shares more than he ought. And if it's our legend bothering you, a true selkie remains loyal to his mate, at least until he finds his own skin. Nothing can keep him from the call of the sea." She smiled, reached across the table and patted his hand. "I'm that sorry he left your ma, but from the sounds of it, it was for the better that he did."

The pub door opened again to a chorus of voices calling for Moira, followed by, "Where is he, then?"

Liam heaved a sigh. Apparently it was family reunion time.

Chapter 3

Someone tugged on Emma. No. Someone was tugging her clothes. No, that wasn't right, either. She raised her head from the table and nearly lost her grip on the wetsuit in her hands.

"If you don't mind," Liam said.

Liam McCormick. The player she'd come to assess. Right. She'd been told a fairy tale and then seen something close enough to it that the line between fact and fiction had been blurred. She clutched the wetsuit to her chest. "Did you say you were going back to Cork?"

"Which is why I'd like my gear back," Liam said. He leaned closer. "Do I know you?"

She didn't expect to be unforgettable, but if he didn't know who she was now, he would tomorrow. Better not to answer.

He narrowed his eyes and she swore she could see the wheels turning inside his head. Might as well hitch a ride since it was available. He'd find out sooner or later.

"Would you mind giving me a ride?" she asked, stumbling to her feet. "I'm staying at the same hotel as the team."

"Not taking her if she's going to hurl in my back seat," his blond friend said.

As if this day could get any more embarrassing. "I won't hurl."

The blond man bent over the table to assess her eyes. "But we can't be sure of that, now, can we?"

"I only had a couple of Murphys."

He rolled his eyes and straightened. "Well, at least you drank the local brew."

"I'd like my wetsuit, if you don't mind," Liam said. "You know that's not sealskin, right?"

"Yes, I know it's not sealskin," she snapped. Which meant he wasn't a selkie, which meant the man of her dreams wasn't going to walk out of the sea, seduce her and ruin her for the rest of mankind. Did she want to hold a man against his will? "What kind of legend is that anyway?" she grumbled.

"Not a happy one, to be sure," blondie said.

She held out the wetsuit and Liam took it from her.

"Thank you."

"And you are?" she asked the blond man.

"Leaving," he said.

"It isn't as if it's out of our way," Liam said, squinting at her, as if trying to place her.

To be fair, he was meeting her out of context, and he'd been healthy when he was with the Cowboys, up until his injury.

"She does seem like she's had a rough day," he added.

The blond guy rolled his eyes once more. "Fine. I suppose we can abide her for thirty minutes."

She pushed away from the table and second-guessed her promise not to vomit.

"How much did you have to drink?" Liam asked.

"I'm not sure. I opened a tab and once the bartender started telling his story, I seemed to be getting automatic refills. I'm a lightweight, and they went down easy."

"Ah, that's fine. Just drink what they set before you," the blond one chided.

"I'm not talking to you until you tell me your name," she said, swallowing the urge to gag.

"This is Shane," Liam told her. "And who are you?"

Emma started to tell him, but she wasn't prepared to have this discussion. Not here. Not now. He'd find out soon enough, hopefully after the earth stopped rolling like a fishing boat on the ocean.

She'd gone to the sea looking for a fairy tale. This was not the way an athletic trainer was supposed to act, especially a female one trying to prove herself to male athletes.

Liam didn't wait for her answer, thankfully. He led the way into the chilly night air and toward the beach.

The locals had set her up for their practical joke. She was done with Ireland. The Cowboys had gone to a lot of trouble to fly her over here, an investment in Liam's future, and on her first night, she'd ruined all credibility.

She flapped her lips. What a mess.

"Something funny?" Liam asked.

She shot him a disgruntled look and followed them down the wooden stairs to the beach, hanging tight to the railing to keep her balance.

Shane retrieved his wetsuit. She should have paid attention when she'd picked up Liam's. Seals didn't need holes for their extremities.

Speaking of seals... a herd of them, or passel, or whatever you called a pack of seals together, bobbed at the edge of the surf, barking. One bounded its way to Liam and tripped him. He went down with a groan and was quickly surrounded by the others.

Emma resisted the reflex to drop beside him and assess his condition. Instead, she watched curiously. The seals seemed to want to comfort him.

"Looks like you've made some friends," Shane teased.

Five seals. Each of them resting its head on Liam's legs. "You sure you're not a selkie?" she asked.

Liam scowled. "Did you say something about aggressive males?" Liam asked Shane.

"They're not hurting you," Shane replied. "You got herring in your pockets or something?"

"I think I've had enough of the legend for one night," Liam said, pushing to his feet gingerly.

But he didn't walk away from the seals that surrounded him. Instead, he reached down and stroked each of their shiny heads. Like puppies, they leaned into his hand. If they'd have been cats, Emma would bet they'd be purring. One by one, they slipped into the harbor.

"Let's go then, selkie," Shane teased.

Together, they walked to the parking lot without another word.

Shane unlocked his car and they climbed in. Liam slipped a sweatshirt over his head and Shane did the same. For the most part, Liam and Shane ignored Emma, which suited her fine.

Could she have made a worse impression?

"You a tourist or are you in Cork for the soccer game?" Shane asked.

"The game," she muttered sullenly.

"Rooting for the Mustangs, I'd wager."

"I might be." She folded her arms. "I'm guessing by your accent you're not on the Rockford team."

"No," he replied. "I'm on the team what's going to beat them." He laughed as he drove up the hill, toward the lighted windows that dotted the countryside, and onto the motorway.

"How's the knee doing?" Shane asked Liam.

Emma's ears perked up. Liam had obviously gone for a training swim, so she had to believe he had done some rehab.

"Well enough."

She wanted to ask all the trainer questions, like his pain level and where it hurt, but she'd save that for tomorrow, when she saw him in her official capacity.

"Maybe that's why the seals were tending to you. They could sense you were hurt," Shane said. "Never seen anything like it."

"I'm fine," Liam said more emphatically.

They rode in silence for a few miles before Shane sang, "What shall we do with a drunken sailor." His voice trailed off and he snuck a glance in the rearview mirror, along with a cheeky smile. "Why'd you get all langered tonight?"

Her head hurt trying to decipher what he meant to say. "Might you translate that to English for me?"

"It means why'd you drink so much," he said.

"I already told you I didn't order all those beers. I wanted to get out of Cork and someone suggested I might like the sightseeing in Kinsale."

"Didya?"

"Yes."

"And the pub?"

"Poor judgment on my part." She hoped it wouldn't cost her her job.

Chapter 4

Liam sat on the bench inside the practice arena and donned his knee brace. Until last night, he'd been sure the rehab he'd done on his own was enough to make him as good as new, but running the steps from the beach reminded him he was a mere mortal.

Could he make it back to the big league?

On top of that, he'd woken in the middle of the night to the realization the woman from the bar was the assistant trainer for the Cowboys. What was she doing in Ireland? Would she give him hell for drinking while he was in training? While he was rehabbing? She'd had more than a few drinks herself.

He walked to one end of the field to start sprints. His roommate with the Mustangs, Cody Voigt, the team's striker, met him at the end line. No pressure. Liam knew he should jog the first lap, warm his muscles up before he tried to run, but Cody would test him, challenge him. Cody had a chip on his shoulder that he hadn't been drafted to the bigs and he meant to prove he was better than Liam despite the fact Liam played defense.

If Liam didn't keep pace, Cody would make sure the rest of the team knew.

Liam went through a series of stretches, hoping Cody would take off without him, but Cody stayed close. Finally, Liam smiled at Cody and started for the opposite end line at a slow jog. Cody fell in step beside him.

"Knee ready for the game?" Cody asked.

"As ready as it's going to be."

"You're a step behind," Cody said, picking up the pace.

With Cody pushing him, he felt compelled to prove himself. He matched Cody's stride. Achy, but no pain. He was going to be all right. Liam grinned at Cody and pushed him a step faster. They reached the other end line, touched it and turned to run back.

Without the brace, without the recent surgery, Liam would have beaten Cody by several yards. Instead, they ran nearly the same pace. At the opposite end line, Liam dipped down to touch the line again and the extra exertion to his knee sent a burst of pain through his leg.

He wasn't going to let Cody beat him, not as long as he was still standing. One more lap. He could go one more lap.

With Cody at his shoulder, they ran the length of the field one more time. Liam crossed the line a step behind Cody. Liam turned, slowed, and jogged down the sideline.

"Quitter," Cody called after him as he took another lap.

If you're in pain, pay attention to what your body's telling you. Certainly he was capable of doing more, except he'd done more than he should have. Liam's ache had grown into pain.

The next drill was lateral moves.

He shouldn't have run those steps with Shane last night.

He shouldn't have let Cody push him, but competitive edge was what got him into the big leagues to begin with. If Liam couldn't keep up, he might as well hang up his boots.

He could do this. He'd been doing the drills for weeks. Liam joined the defenders for the lateral drill. "McCormick," the coach shouted.

He hadn't been limping, had he? Liam looked up and Coach Clarence waved him in.

Liam concentrated on proper form as he jogged to the bench, conscious not to favor his knee.

"Status," Coach Clarence barked.

"I'm fine."

The coach scowled. "I heard you were one of those guys, the kind who pushes too hard, but you do realize you'll do more damage if you don't rehab properly?"

"I've been rehabbing," Liam told him. "Including an open water swim yesterday."

"So I've heard."

He'd heard?

"There were concerns about the physical therapist you worked with after surgery," Coach went on. "Coach Simmons wondered if you might have something to add to the story."

Liam had an uncomfortable feeling. What had Daphne said about their encounter? "What concerns?"

Coach Clarence raised his eyebrows, inviting Liam to share, but Liam wasn't about to tell him his physical therapist had made a pass at him—and he'd turned her down. Had she spun a different interpretation of what happened?

When Liam didn't offer anything more, Coach Clarence leaned closer. "They walked in on her with one of your teammates," he said. "It's a good bet he wasn't the only one, and your rehab isn't where it should be." He waved over his shoulder. "Coach Simmons is eager to get you back. They sent a trainer to check on you. I take it you know Emma Parrish?"

She appeared beside Coach Clarence. In the daylight, Liam got a better look at her. She'd tamed down her hair, sort of. An ashy shade of brown, it no longer had the electrified look she'd sported when he'd first seen her in the pub in Kinsale. Today her hair looked expertly tousled, short ends finger-combed into a casual style. Pale skin and squinting bloodshot eyes told him she was struggling with a hangover.

"You lost a step on that last lap," Emma said. "Anything pop when you touched the line?"

He wasn't about to tell her anything. "No."

"I think you were smart to stop when you did." Emma folded her arms. "I'm here to see how you're progressing."

Liam shot a side-eye to the coach. They were kidding, right? Daphne might have been unprofessional, but Emma? She'd believed Liam was a selkie, a seal who'd taken on the form of a man. He snorted.

"Something wrong?" Coach Clarence asked.

So many things, but before Liam could say anything, Coach wagged a finger at him.

"If you hope to return to the Cowboys, you'll do whatever this lady tells you and no distractions. Understood?" Coach cast a glance at Emma to assure her compliance with his dictates as well.

"Yes, sir," Liam said.

"Are you ready to play tomorrow?" Coach asked.

"Yes, sir."

Coach squinted at him. "I saw you limping on the field."

"Still working out the kinks."

"Water therapy is good for that," Emma said. "I'd suggest another open-water swim."

She might be a trainer, but after last night, he wasn't sure what to expect from her. "Whatever you say."

Coach nodded. "You can skip the side-to-sides, but I want you to tackle some balls." He turned to Emma. "You can have him after practice."

"She can have me? I thought Yosh was the Mustangs' trainer." Liam turned to Emma. "The Cowboys can't be ready to recall me yet, are they? Or are they? I haven't played a game with the Mustangs yet."

"I'm here to observe," Emma told him. "The concern stems from the physical therapy you missed, and what you've been doing to supplement."

Why did he suddenly feel like a five-year-old who'd been caught misbehaving? "Wouldn't it be easier to ask Yosh than to send you?"

She tilted her head and raised her eyebrows. "You don't want me to assess your progress?"

A loaded question. "Whatever it takes to get me back to the Cowboys."

Coach nodded to the field.

Right. Liam had drills to do.

"See ya later," Liam said, jogging to the field.

WHAT WAS LIAM DOING to get game-ready other than the open-water swim?

Emma was here to do a job. No more fieldtrips on her own, and no more stops in the local pubs. Lonely? She was too busy to be lonely.

She scrambled to find Shane Fahey's contact information. If he'd been willing to swim with Liam last night, he might take Liam out again. She wasn't an experienced swimmer, and open water was not something she was willing to undergo. Shane also provided a third party to avoid any appearance of impropriety, another sucky part of being a female trainer.

As much as she'd tried to take her free time in Ireland yesterday as far from the team as she could, she'd made one doozy of a mistake. If Liam wanted to make trouble for her, he certainly could, and then she'd be back to teaching self-defense and physical fitness at the health club.

Emma stood beside Yosh Tanaka, the Mustangs' trainer, to watch the team scrimmage. "He looks ready," she said. "You said he hasn't asked you for any assistance?"

"Nothing aside from an ice pack or kinesio tape. He's usually in the training room an hour before report time, on a bike or on a treadmill."

From watching him on the field, Emma got the idea Liam was holding back, not playing full strength. Scrimmages were one thing, but the opposing players in a real game would seek out his weaknesses and attack.

"He doesn't seem to be limping now," she said.

"He won't. Not when he knows someone's watching him," Yosh replied.

"But when he doesn't think anyone can see?"

Yosh nodded. "Yeah. I've caught him a time or two."

"Which wouldn't be unexpected." Liam appeared strong. In control. Either he knew what to do or he had a personal coach helping him. That was good news, but what about the emotional side of things? Questioning their ability to come back after an injury wasn't unusual for athletes, especially when they had personal issues. He'd discovered family last night, family he didn't know he had, and he'd discovered his father's death might have been self-inflicted. How would that impact his mental toughness?

Her phone vibrated with a text, Shane Fahey confirming he'd pick them up after practice for another swim. She'd ride with them to Kinsale to do more observation.

Chapter 5

"Athletic trainer, ya say," Shane said while they waited for Liam. "You'll not be following us everywhere we go, will you now?"

"No, but I would like to discuss his plan to return to the Cowboys, and the car ride will give us time to do that."

"Why'd they send you?" he asked.

"Liam skipped part of his physical therapy."

"Did he now?" Shane looked past her, to where Liam exited the players' entrance. "So they sent you as part of his punishment?" He cocked an eyebrow at Emma.

"They sent me to make sure he doesn't re-injure himself."

Liam climbed into the car and she figured she'd better clear the air right away. "I wasn't at my best yesterday. I hope we can forget that little episode."

"If you choose to sit in a pub all day and drink yourself silly, that's your problem," Liam replied. "Are we ready to go?"

"I'm here to do a job," she said. "I intend to fulfill that obligation." Emma fingered the heart on the chain around her neck, fuming. "As for last night, I stopped to get a taste of the local culture and was talked into 'a pint.'" She shook her head, wishing she could shake off the embarrassment as easily. "Mistake one was giving them my credit card. Once they started in with the stories, someone—your cousin—" she said, spearing Liam with a pointed look, "kept refilling my glass. I should have been paying closer attention. That won't happen again."

Shane sputtered.

"There's a question regarding your physical therapy," she went on. "The intern who worked with you falsified the records regarding her sessions. The Cowboys want to make sure you've been training, that you get the care you need. I'm here to assess your progress, physically and mentally, and get you back to the Cowboys—or guide you to someone who can help you plan for an alternative career."

"Now wait," Shane said. "I had the same surgery, and I'm back on the field."

"How many years in the development league?" she asked.

Liam laughed. "Ouch."

Shane shot her an angry glare in the rearview mirror.

"I guess I should be grateful the team is willing to invest in me," Liam said. He turned to Emma once more. "I've been training. You can check with Yosh. I don't need your help."

"Is that why you were limping around the field today?" she said. "And I did check with Yosh."

"I was fine until I ran the stairs from the beach yesterday," Liam told her. "I'm sure it's a minor setback."

"My fault," Shane said. "I should have realized, but look at me. Good as new." He darted a glance toward Liam. "You will be, too."

Emma retrieved her notebook from her messenger bag. "Can you tell me about your diet?" she asked Liam.

"I keep up with my nutrition. I do take my job seriously, whether you believe me or not."

Professional athletes were highly competitive, and if there was part of his regimen that was missing or if he had concerns about his ability to return, he wouldn't confess in front of another athlete.

"Tell me what other training you've been doing besides swimming."

"Stationary bike. Running. I'm used to doing triathlons, and I've been working with some of my old friends, hence swimming the water leg of the triathlon course here in Ireland."

"That's good to hear," she said. "Any difficulties? Pain?"

"Nothing out of the ordinary."

They'd arrived at the beach. The sun was shining, and the temperature was warmer than yesterday. While Liam and Shane tugged on their wetsuits, Emma sat on the beach to wait.

Wetsuits didn't look anything like sealskin.

She needed to refocus her own mental energy, to set aside the cringe-worthy moments of her meeting with Liam last night.

The men walked the wooden ramp into the harbor, adjusted their goggles, and swam away. Emma took the opportunity to practice tai chi while she waited—a moment to center her own energy.

You choose how you will respond to your challenges.

Did they all have to present themselves at one time, those challenges? Emma tried to concentrate on her form.

The tai chi wasn't working. She'd made a bad impression, and that was going to be hard to overcome. Was there time to go for a run while they were in the water?

She checked their progress. Liam and Shane swam stroke for stroke toward the island that separated the harbor from the Celtic Sea.

Emma should have paid attention to how much she'd had to drink, but she'd been captivated by the stories the bartender had told. He had a gift, for sure.

No more fairy tales.

The guys had reached the end of the island and were about to disappear on the other side when several black heads popped up in the water, swimming beside them. Seals. No wonder the locals had their legends. A herd of friendly seals could do wonders for an active imagination, and she'd certainly been susceptible to the legend last night, with the help of too much alcohol.

Emma pulled out her tablet and typed her preliminary notes. He appeared strong mentally, determined to succeed, and he'd coordinated a workout with Shane yesterday. Even if he hadn't had the full benefits of physical therapy, he didn't seem the sort to slough it off and shortchange his recovery.

"Watching for more selkies?" a woman asked.

Emma nearly dropped her tablet, then turned to Moira, the barmaid. "You surprised me."

"Ah, I see what you're watching for now," Moira said. "Wanted to prove to yourself that they're truly men and not beasts?"

Shane and Liam had rounded the island—along with several seal escorts.

Emma watched, fascinated by the entourage. "Is that normal? Having the seals swim with them?"

"No," Moira said, "but then, Liam is one of the dark ones. They'll be looking out for one of their own."

Emma scoffed. "You're not going to try to tell me he's a selkie again, are you?"

"No, but the stories do say there was one in our family. The seals'll be watching out for him. Can't you see the way they tend to him as he swims?"

Shane had flipped to his back and floated toward the beach, while Liam lifted his head and rode the tide, smooth and sleek.

And moving too fast. He laughed and flipped as a seal swam out from under him.

Moira spoke softly. "You see it, no? The way they take to him as one of their own?"

Yes, she saw it, but she wasn't going to be drawn into more fairy tales. "How many others in your family are 'dark ones'?" she asked. "Do you come from a whole family of seals?"

"Laugh if you will, but once a generation comes one such as Liam, with dark hair and soulful eyes. We'd actually thought it might have missed this generation had Liam not come home."

Emma watched Shane and Liam playing in the water, until they both resumed swimming, taking hard strokes toward the beach.

Yes, she might have been drawn into their stories in a dark, atmospheric pub, but in the light of day...

A seal waddled onto the beach, wiggling its back end onto the sand. It stopped, raised its head, and Emma swore it looked right at her. It barked, and then slipped into the water.

On the island, a shadowy figure—a man who looked a lot like Liam—materialized. "What's on the island?" she asked Moira.

"Naught but goats," Moira replied.

Emma swore she'd seen a man, not a goat. Had she misunderstood? More legends? "Did you say ghosts?" Emma turned toward Moira, but Moira had gone as silently as she'd come.

AFTER MAKING SURE THE seal hadn't hurt Emma—she assured them it had merely startled her—Liam suggested going straight to Cork, without a stop at the pub. He'd prove to her he was serious about his job.

Caught up in conversation with Shane, Liam hadn't noticed Emma hadn't spoken again until they'd returned to Cork. Had the seal frightened her more than she'd let on?

Shane dropped them at the team hotel with reassurances his team would better the Mustangs at the game tomorrow, and singing *Emma, Emma bo-bemma* as he drove off.

Before Liam had a chance to ask *Emma, Emma bo-bemma* why she was so quiet, she jumped in to fill the void.

"I want a journal of everything you're eating," she said, leading him into the hotel lobby. "I'll meet you in the training room ahead of the game tomorrow to assess your physical condition."

"Tell me again why Yosh can't do that?" he asked.

"He could, but he might release you too soon to lighten the roster, or keep you too long to help the Mustangs. He doesn't know what your physical condition was before the injury, doesn't know your personality. He doesn't have a baseline."

"And you do?"

"Yes. I do. Or at least the parts that matter. We're going to assess whether you recognize when you should back off and when you're strong enough to push harder. You were holding back during practice. Who have you been training with?"

"Listen, Emma..."

"I have a job to do. You can work with me, or you can get cut." She raised her chin to show him she wasn't going away.

Well that was clear enough. "I've been training on my own."

"Do you want to tell me why you stopped going to physical therapy?" she asked.

Chances were she already knew. "Because her idea of PT and mine didn't agree."

"I'm here to help," she said gently. Emma cocked her head toward a pair of chairs. "Let's sit down for a few minutes."

He followed her to the wingback chairs, waited for her to sit, and then sunk into the one across from her.

"From what little I've seen, your physical condition seems solid. There are also psychological effects when you sustain a potentially career-ending injury. I have to consider the development with your father, and what effect it might have on your recovery, also."

The small hairs on Liam's arms stood up. She might think she was trying to help, but she was going about it the wrong way, especially when he didn't want her help. He waved a finger between them. "We don't know each other."

"I know you're hurt..." she said.

Liam rose to his feet. "You don't know anything about my father."

Her eyes grew large. She pushed up from her chair, her head cocked to one side, her intentionally-tousled hair standing at odd angles. Realization dawned. She hadn't been referring to his father when she'd said he was hurt. He glanced at the brace on his leg. "Or what I've done to rehab," he added belatedly.

Cody Voigt stepped off the elevator and strutted through the lobby. "Making friends with the locals, McCormick?" he asked.

Emma took a step backward. "Why don't you take it easy tonight. I'll see you at the game tomorrow."

Cody grabbed her by the arm. "What's the hurry? If you want to meet the Mustangs, I'm the star. Cody Voigt. Striker. Wouldn't you rather get to know me than a washed-up has-been?"

A has-been? At twenty-three? Before Liam could step up and beat the hell out of Cody for irritating him one more time, Emma held up a hand.

"I'm sure the trainer for the Mustangs can help you with whatever your problem is," she said.

"Trainer, huh?" Cody said. "Nah, but I do need a good luck charm. Why don't you come up to my room and let me rub you?"

Liam stepped between them. "That's not a very polite way to address a woman."

"Stay out of this, McCormick," Cody said quietly, "or your injury might get a lot worse."

Emma patted Liam's arm. "I can handle this."

He wasn't reassured. His ma would give him hell if he didn't do his duty to protect a woman from an ape like Cody. Cody was at least six inches taller than Emma, and that was a conservative estimate. Cody was a trained athlete. She wasn't stick thin, but if Cody decided to press his advantage, she didn't look like she had the body strength to fight him off.

Cody wrenched Emma's arm, twisting her to face him. A second later, he lay sprawled on the lobby floor, a look of shock on his face. Emma stood over him. "You don't touch me without my permission ever again. You hear me?"

Liam's mouth hung open. He took a second look at Emma, more than a little turned on.

"Talk to you tomorrow," she said to Liam, and walked away.

"Didn't see that coming," Cody said, regaining his feet. "You, on the other hand..."

"Your beef's not with me," Liam said, watching the sway of Emma's hips. "You deserved what you got. Didn't your mother tell you to respect women?"

"Tell me you're respecting her," Cody said, nodding after Emma.

Liam smiled. "Oh, I respect her. Even more now that I know she packs a wallop."

Chapter 6

Emma had to prove to Liam she could help, which meant not getting distracted by his sleek, dark hair, or those soulful eyes Moira had pointed out. The patrons in the bar had made Liam appear a sexy folk legend.

He was a mortal man.

A professional does not get involved with her clients. That was reportedly the issue for Liam in the first place—a starstruck physical therapist.

Nothing to worry about there. Watching her throw Cody Voigt down probably ruined any chances she might have of Liam making a pass at her, even if she wanted him to. Which she didn't. He was a client.

A client who had appeared to her as a seductive legend.

If she hadn't been in such a suggestible state, thanks to the locals, she wouldn't be objectifying him.

Portia would straighten out her wayward thoughts. They'd been best friends since junior high. They'd nursed each other through their first broken hearts. Portia had been there for her when her mother abandoned her—okay, she didn't abandon her the way Emma accused her of doing, but she had moved away and told Emma she was on her own.

Emma checked her phone, calculated the time difference. Lunchtime in Chicago. Portia would be at her desk, most likely.

"Hey, girlfriend. How's Ireland?" Portia answered.

"Scenic. A little creepy, and a lot distracting."

"Uh-oh. What's going on?"

Emma pulled the curtains aside in her hotel room and looked across Cork, at the city lights reflected in the harbor, at the church spire against the horizon. "I made a fool of myself my first night here, and by coincidence, I met the player I came to assess while I was being an idiot."

"Well, that sounds interesting. Pray, do tell."

Emma told Portia about her tour, subsequent trip to the bar and the Irish legend.

Portia giggled. "I think I'm starting to get the picture. Does the rest of this story turn into 'a man walked into a bar?'"

"Actually, it turns into a girl walks out of a bar, sheds a tear into the ocean to call the seal forth and witnesses two men stripping off their wetsuits."

"No. And what were they wearing under their wetsuits?" Portia's giggle turned into a guffaw. "Gotta tell you, Emma, so far it still sounds like fun, to me."

"They were wearing tri-suits, which I didn't actually note at the time, as I had been overserved."

Portia gasped. "Please tell me one of those men was not the player you went to assess."

"One and the same."

Portia lowered her voice. "Is he irresistibly handsome, like the legend says?"

"I'd like to think I wouldn't have paid attention if he hadn't walked out of the sea and stripped off a wetsuit like a seal might strip off its skin." Emma put a hand to her head to wipe away the embarrassment.

"Oh, honey, I don't mean to laugh, but the way you tell it..."

"And then one of his teammates on the D-League tried to make a pass at me."

"Was the teammate cute?"

Emma laughed then. Portia provided the balance she needed right now. "They're all dumb jocks. I threw the guy down. In front of Liam."

"That should resolve any worries you might have about getting too close to Liam, then, am I right? Flattening a guy will scare most men away. Sounds like you have nothing more to worry about."

"Maybe, but wait. There's more," she continued, like a late-night ad announcer. "The people in the bar told Liam another story, about his father. The assumption is his father committed suicide. That has to be hard to hear."

"I like the other story better."

"Right. Did I tell you about creepy? I think I saw the probably-dead father standing on an island in the harbor."

Portia gasped again. "Goosebumps."

"It's my imagination, right? Like imagining seals walking from the ocean on two legs?"

"Did anyone else see the guy on the island?"

Emma let the curtain fall across the window. "Liam's cousin might have. But she disappeared when I went to ask her."

"Disappeared? Another ghost?"

"No, she's flesh and blood, but she is sneaky."

Neither of them spoke for a minute.

"When you coming home?" Portia asked.

"The game's tomorrow. I'll be home the day after."

"So, Monday."

"Right."

"You want my advice?" Portia asked.

"I want you to tell me I'm not crazy."

"You're sleep deprived. Jet lagged. Stay away from the jock, and avoid the island. I'm assuming you've already done your assessment?"

Emma plopped down on her bed. "Yes, although the game tomorrow will be the defining moment. Will he compete or will he favor his injury?"

"Irresistibly handsome?" Portia asked with a teasing tone.

"Black hair, soulful eyes," she repeated Moira's description. "Body of an athlete."

"Who's to say you couldn't indulge in one night of pure lust?"

Emma scoffed. "I could lose my job. The reason I'm here is because of a groupie masquerading as a physical therapist intern."

"But you want to," Portia said.

Ever since she'd seen him walk out of the sea and strip off the wet suit. She hadn't seen him as Liam McCormick, she'd seen him as a legend rising from the mist, muscles bulging and sleek hair flying in his wake as he ran across the beach. "He'd make one hell of a legend," Emma whispered.

"You know what they say about hunger. If you can deny yourself for a couple of hours, the desire goes away. You're a long way from home," Portia added, "and you said it was a suggestive environment. Given what you've told me about the players you've encountered in the past, you'll lose your appetite by the time you get home. Dumb jocks, right?"

That was the thing about Portia. She always saw past the emotion and got to the heart of the matter. "You're probably right. Hey, thanks."

"What are friends for? Oh, and by the way, my mother says it's been too long since she's seen you and you're probably working too hard. I told her I'd talk you into coming with me next time I visit. Did I tell you my sister Natalie's getting married? That guy she's been dating proposed last week on her birthday. Mom'll be too distracted by that to make a fuss over you."

"I'll try," Emma promised, "but now that the team is in season, I don't have as much free time to run out to the suburbs and back. She knows that."

"We'll talk more, my friend," Portia said. "I have to get back to work. See you when you get home."

LIAM WOKE WITH A START, ducking behind his raised arm to avoid the blow that was coming at him.

"What the hell, McCormick?" Cody mumbled.

Had he called out in his sleep?

Liam wiped a hand over his face and sat up in bed, glancing around the hotel room. Today was game day. He was in Ireland. His da was dead. Nothing more to fear.

The dream must have come after the stories he'd heard from Moira and the rest of the clan, the memories of his father. Except they didn't know his father the way he did.

Cody opened an eye and sneered. "Game day jitters?"

"Screw you," Liam retorted.

Cody chuckled, threw back his covers and paddled to the bathroom.

While Liam's heart rate returned to normal, his phone chimed with a text from Emma.

Meet me in the trainer's room at 10.

He chuffed and texted back.

Do we really have to do this?

"Let me guess," Cody said, walking back to his bed. "Your trainer?"

At the same time, Emma's response came through.

Yes, if you intend to play for the Cowboys again. They won't let you come back until I say you're good to go.

Right. He had to play nice or she would end his career. "At least they care enough to invest in my future," Liam replied. "You keep working at it and maybe you'll get an invitation to practice with the Cowboys. Problem with strikers is everybody wants to be the one who kicks the goals. Lots of competition."

"Put in a good word for me?" Cody asked in a rare moment of vulnerability.

Liam got out of his bed and slugged Cody in the shoulder as he passed to the bathroom. "If I make it back to the team."

That was a big "if." What had Emma told him? Part of her job was to help him plan for an alternate career if he couldn't get back to full strength, and he needed to be full strength to play in the big leagues.

Today was game day. The proving ground.

The alarm on Cody's phone rang out. "At least you didn't deprive me of too much sleep. Hurry up. I want to get down to breakfast before it's all gone."

Fifteen minutes later, Liam and Cody filled plates in the banquet room. The team was subdued for a pre-game feast, a quiet buzz instead of a boisterous buildup. Even Cody, when he took his seat, leaned across and spoke to the person beside him with a low voice.

A moment later, someone's cell phone chimed with a text. Liam cast a casual glance toward the coach's table and found the reason for the mood in the room. Emma sat beside Yosh, someone the rest of the team didn't know. Except Cody, and he appeared to be spreading what he knew like peanut butter.

One by one, the members of the team sent Liam a curious glance, and then one to Emma. As much as he hated everyone knowing she'd come to report on his progress, apparently her presence also gave him a sense of stature. He was valuable enough to the Cowboys that they'd sent someone to check on him.

"I heard she decked Cody," the guy on Liam's left whispered.

Liam was embarrassed to admit he couldn't remember the guy's name. He was a midfielder who didn't get much playing time. The whispered opinion was the midfielder would be released from the team sooner rather than later.

"Yeah," Liam said. "You won't want to mess with that one." She was a surprise, for sure, and the fact she could take care of herself gave him a rush all over again. The memory of her standing in the pub door that first night, backlit by the sunset and claiming her due, had him revising his initial assessment of her. Yes, she'd been overserved, but she'd stood there like a warrior holding her prize.

With his career on the line, he'd do whatever the warrior princess told him to, and once his fate was decided, he just might give her his wetsuit to hide until she was done with him.

EMMA TAPPED LIAM ON the shoulder and cocked her head to invite him to join her outside the breakfast room.

"Everything okay?" she asked when the door closed behind them.

"So far, so good," he said.

But there was something different about his whole attitude, starting with the way he looked at her. He'd had trouble remembering who she was that night in the pub. Today, the fire in his eyes could light an Olympic torch.

"Something's changed," she said.

"Game day," he said, holding her gaze.

Good. Intensity.

And dark, soulful eyes. Why couldn't she get that legend out of her head? She set her jaw and raised her chin. "I can see you're eager to get back out there, but you need to be mindful of your body." Her mouth went dry. She was all too mindful of his body, but then again, so was the intern who'd caused the problem in the first place.

Emma was not a groupie, and Liam was not a selkie, but the sensual smile on his lips had her heart fluttering.

He raised his eyebrows, challenging her? "I feel good. Won't know until I get out on the field how well I'll hold up, but the knee feels strong right now."

"How about a couple miles on the bike to warm those muscles up." She pulled her clipboard from under her arm. "Anything you want to talk about? Worries about your performance?"

The look he gave her sizzled. No, he didn't seem to be suffering from any lack of self-confidence, at least not personally. Professionally...

"What happens if you miss a tackle out there?" she asked. "Will it inspire you to work harder or will you suddenly wonder if you've lost your mojo?"

His expression shifted to something less self-assured.

"Want to talk about it?" she pressed.

"No." His answer was immediate. Not surprising.

"You had an unexpected family reunion in Kinsale. How will that affect your game?"

"It won't."

"Finding out how your father died?" The words raised gooseflesh on her arms. Who had she seen on the island? She paused, giving him an opening to speak, but he remained silent. "That's not easy news to hear."

"Then you also heard my father hasn't been part of my life for more than fifteen years." He leaned in, his eyes narrowed. "There's nothing there. Unless you think he's going to magically reappear and slip off his sealskin."

The warmth of embarrassment crept up her neck. No, they weren't going to get past that night in the pub. How drunk was she that she'd imagined Liam was part of the legend? "To be fair, the bartender does tell a good story," she said. "And I'd had too much to drink."

"So you've said." Liam's eyes twinkled with mischief. His lips twisted with a smirk, but he didn't say anything more.

"I'll meet you at the stadium," she told him, feeling too warm. "We'll talk more when I have a chance to assess your knee. Any concerns you have, physical or emotional, I'm here to help. Understood?"

"I don't need help. Physical or emotional."

He wasn't getting off that easy. "If you'd have done the work instead of banging that PT, I might believe you."

He leaned close, his voice low enough to send ripples across her skin. "I did the work, with or without the PT."

Why was it suddenly hard to breathe? She nodded, not trusting herself to speak. She understood the appeal, why groupies threw themselves at professional athletes. Something about their swagger, their peak physical condition, but there was no depth.

She wanted more from a man than raw animal magnetism.

Chapter 7

Even though Emma had pronounced Liam game-ready, Coach Clarence hadn't started him. No reason he should have, but Liam ached to run the field. He paced beside the bench.

Liam struggled to think of this as his team, even if they were the development team for the Cowboys, and they weren't playing for a home crowd.

He pointed out a missed tackled to the defenders marooned beside him, taught them what he'd learned while playing with the Cowboys about anticipating moves.

Cody Voigt went down after taking a shot on goal, courtesy of an illegal tackle that earned him a penalty kick. Liam sat on the edge of the bench, his legs bouncing.

"McCormick!" Coach Clarence shouted.

His heartrate jumped. He was going in. Liam took the sign the coach handed him and waited for the referee.

On the field, Cody lined up, let loose, and missed the goal.

Liam shook his head. One reason why Cody was still in the development league.

The referee waved Liam in. He handed off the substitute sign to the outgoing player and took his place on the field.

The adrenaline rush that coursed through him made the ache in his knee disappear.

The kickoff went to the opposite end of the field. Liam took a quick glance around the stadium, a packed house filled with banners, and fans who'd painted their faces and bodies in team colors.

The Irish team pressed down the field toward Liam and the goal, venturing into Mustang territory. Liam met the forward dribbling the ball and challenged him, keeping pace with him. He attempted a tackle, and then the forward passed the ball. The pass was returned to the forward and Liam intercepted it, booming the ball down the field into Irish territory.

His leg vibrated like a bell after it had been rung. Liam trod lightly, testing his knee. Yes, it hurt, but he could bear weight. Everything seemed stable.

"Okay?" Emma shouted from the sideline.

He raised a hand without looking at her. He wasn't going to give up his place on the Cowboys without a fight.

Another voice echoed inside his head.

"Liam."

He glanced around the stadium. Where had that come from? It sounded just like...

His da. Standing in the second tier against the railing. Holy hell.

Liam stood flat-footed, staring. The man wore jeans, a long Henley shirt and an open vest. The only thing missing was his da's usual paddy cap atop his head. Instead, he had a shock of white hair.

"Quit chasing butterflies, McCormick," the keeper shouted. "Get the ball!"

Startled, Liam looked around the field. The forward had nearly run past him. Liam darted toward the ball, stuck out a leg to tackle and both he and the forward went down.

His head swam with the pain this time, but he refused to stay down. The referee appeared beside him and held up a yellow card.

"For what?" Liam argued.

The referee gave him a stern look and blew his whistle. "Fine, then," Liam muttered. His leg hurt, but it hadn't buckled. He limped as he went to challenge the throw-in. Before the ball was returned to play, he took another glance at the stands.

The man who looked like his da had disappeared.

EMMA HELD HER BREATH, waiting to see if Liam bore weight on his injured leg. With the ball on the opposite end of the field, he had his hands on his hips, wincing and limping as he tested his knee.

"You have to take him out," she told the coach.

"He just went in," Coach Clarence replied.

"He's clearly in pain."

Coach pointed to the scoreboard. "I have a limited number of substitutions, which I think you know. Besides, he's got something to prove. Seven more minutes to the half, plus stoppage time. He can make it that long."

This was the part about her job she hated. What if he'd re-injured himself? They'd wait until he went to the ground, and professional athletes with something to prove tended to be stubborn and play through the pain.

"Unless he goes down first," she muttered.

"Then you'll have your answer, won't you?" He took a step toward the field, cupped his mouth and shouted to the striker to move up.

The game was still scoreless, but the Irish knew where the weak link was. They'd go at Liam until they knocked him out of the game. Another hit could end his career, and they weren't above a penalty to put him down.

The players on the field swarmed the ball along the sideline near where Emma and the coach stood, Shane Fahey among them.

"Can't ya help him?" Shane called to Emma, alternating glances between her and the ball.

"Up to the coach," she replied.

He nodded as he blocked the ball out of bounds. One of the Mustangs rushed to pick it up and threw it back into play. Emma checked the scoreboard again. They'd reached forty-one minutes in the half. Four more minutes to go, not counting the extra time tacked on to replace stops in the action—stoppage time. How much stoppage time would they add?

Liam wasn't even pretending anymore. He bent at the waist, stared at the ground, hobbled toward the action. Adjusted.

The ball came at him and he ran around to his good side, tackled the ball away from the forward and passed it to the Mustang striker. Telling that he hadn't used his dominant foot, but a good decision, by Emma's reckoning.

"Open field," Liam yelled.

The striker dribbled the ball to the other end, darted around the defenders and passed the ball ahead.

The referee blew his whistle. The striker had passed offside, a penalty that gave the ball to the Irish.

Emma checked the clock. Forty-four minutes into the first half, plus the as yet unknown time to be tacked on.

The scorekeeper rose beside the sideline and raised the post to display the added time. A minute and a half. Thank heaven for small favors.

The game clock stopped and Coach Clarence hit his stopwatch to keep track of the extra ninety seconds. The Mustangs pushed the ball to the Irish side of the field, giving Liam a much-needed respite. When the halftime signal sounded, Liam hobbled to the bench.

Dumb jocks.

Emma rushed to his side. "How bad is it?" she asked, handing Liam a water bottle.

"It'll be fine."

"Don't lie to me."

He met her gaze, the determination evident. "It hurts, but not like it did when..."

She slapped an ice pack on his knee. "Do you need help to the locker room?"

Liam bowed his head, and in the first sign of weakness she'd seen from him, he nodded.

She signaled Yosh, who looped Liam's arm across his shoulders and helped him off the field.

The keeper shouldered past. "Too many meds, McCormick? What the hell were you doing out there?"

Liam winced and stalked away.

What had she missed? "What happened?" Emma asked the keeper.

"It's like he blanked out for a minute."

"I saw something in the stands," Liam called over his shoulder.

"Yeah, well save chasing the skirts for after the game." The keeper barreled ahead into the locker room.

Emma hurried beside Liam. "What did you see?"

Liam shook his head.

"What distracted you?" she asked again.

Liam reached for her arm, a haunted look in his eyes. "A man. He looked just like my da."

Emma shivered as gooseflesh broke out across her skin.

Chapter 8

Liam's head was clearly not on the game. Emma lent him an arm while he hiked his butt onto the table. She shifted into trainer mode. "Did you hear anything pop?" she asked.

His face was set into a stoic mask. "No."

"Does your knee feel the same as when you tore your ACL?"

"No."

"Rate your pain on a scale of one to ten."

Liam shifted his eyes to Emma's, maintaining the stubborn set of his jaw. "Maybe a five."

She was about to tell him she couldn't help him if he didn't level with her when one of the Mustangs trailed them into the trainer's room and sat on a stationary bike. He shot a curious glance at Liam.

Emma lowered her voice, nodding to Liam's leg. "Where's the pain level when you bear weight on it? One to ten."

Another of the Mustangs came in and asked for an ice pack, although he, too, seemed more focused on Liam.

Liam leaned forward on the table. "When I kicked the ball downfield, it was like kicking a rock. My whole leg vibrated. It felt sort of tingly after that, and when I made that hard tackle, I felt a streak of pain right before it went numb, but it's not the same as when I went out last year."

He seemed to be working with her.

"He gonna be okay?" the guy on the bike asked Emma.

"That's what we're trying to assess," she replied.

The second Mustang, the one who'd come in for the ice pack, stopped beside Liam as if to be included in the prognosis. Emma put her hands on her hips and fixed him with a glare.

"You've got your ice. Get going," Yosh said, pointing to the training room door.

"Right," he said. "Good luck, McCormick." He tossed the ice pack he'd come for on a shelf and returned to the team room.

"All right," Emma said gently. "Lie back and try to relax." She watched Liam's face to see if he would flinch and positioned her hands on his legs as she manipulated his knee for range of motion and excessive gaps between the joints. So far, so good. "Any pain?"

"More like throbbing."

She bent his legs at the knees, sat on his foot, and tugged. Everything seemed tight, and he hadn't yelped.

He held her gaze, unflinching.

"Okay, tough guy. Everything seems normal. I am going to recommend you sit out the second half and ice the knee, and when we get home, you should get an MRI to make sure there's nothing more going on."

Liam closed his eyes and practically melted into the table. "I can play."

"There's no reason to. Ease back into it. In the meantime, the team will likely recommend more physical therapy," she cocked an eyebrow, "and you'll want to consider asking for a man this time."

He narrowed his eyes but withheld comment. She sensed he had an epithet ready.

Emma wiped her hands on a towel. "As for your father, in a moment of personal crisis, memories tend to resurface, and you've had several reminders of him since you've been here. It's normal to pull out comforting memories. I wouldn't make too much of it."

Liam sputtered. "Comforting? You have no idea what you're talking about."

Emma crossed her arms. "So you believe he killed himself?" She couldn't blame him for not wanting to acknowledge he'd died intentionally.

"Even if he wasn't dead, if you knew anything about my father, then you'd know he would be the last person I'd want to see."

Unfortunately, she hadn't heard much of their conversation at the pub.

Fifteen years was a long time. That would have made Liam on the shy side of ten years old. What memories did he have of his father?

"Do you want to talk about it?" she asked.

"I do not."

She huffed. "Your emotional state is as important to your recovery as your physical state. Clearly, something's bothering you if you've imagined seeing a man you haven't seen since you were a child." Her words echoed in her head. Was his father the man on the island?

"There's nothing wrong with my emotional state," he said, his voice a low growl. "I've done the rehab. I will continue to do the work, and my father be damned."

His attitude piqued her own temper. "If you hadn't dallied with that intern, you might be further along. Have you thought of that?"

"I didn't *dally* with anyone." He hit his chest with an open palm. "This is my career. I've been working my ass off to return to the team. Are we done here?"

Coach Clarence stuck his head in the training room. "We're headed to the field. Is he coming?"

Emma retrieved an ice pack and slammed the freezer closed. "As soon as I have his knee wrapped, but he won't be playing the second half."

WELL THAT DIDN'T GO well. Liam shouldn't have to defend himself against unwanted attention. Was that why Emma had benched him?

She could. Permanently. Worse, she could recommend his release from the team. Fighting with her wasn't going to help him achieve his goals. She hadn't made a pass at him the way Daphne had, but women had a way of being irrationally jealous. Why else would she keep bringing up his one and only PT session with Daphne?

She walked beside him when they left the locker room, a show of medical concern, no doubt. Liam made sure he stood straight, walked heel to toe, and used every muscle in his damn leg to show them he was fine. Fine, dammit!

He grabbed the scorebook from the assistant coach and took a seat on the bench. He'd be the model benchwarmer, doing his part to support whatever team he played with.

He would not sacrifice his career because one silly groupie had thrown herself at him. He'd worked too damn hard to come back from this injury.

Damn woman. If Emma meant to condemn him for whatever rumor Daphne had spread, he could tell people how gullible Emma had been. She'd believed he'd walked out of the sea like an old Irish legend.

That line of thinking wasn't productive.

With more work in the training room, he should be able to play the regular season when they got home. He'd come back to the Cowboys better than before.

He started the stopwatch as they kicked off the second half and watched the Irish advance the ball up the field, toward the Mustangs' goalie. Liam charted a defensive block and a moment later, a member of the Irish team went down. A yellow card went up.

After making notations in the scorebook, Liam glanced into the stands, at the place he'd seen the man earlier. A mirage. It had to have been his imagination.

Ten minutes into the half, Emma spoke behind him. "How's it feeling?"

"I'm fine," he answered curtly.

"We should take the ice off."

"I'm busy."

The assistant coach tapped him on the shoulder and held out a hand for the scorebook.

Liam reluctantly handed it over, motioned to the stopwatch on the bench and turned around.

"Happy?" he asked her.

She smiled sweetly. "I take great pleasure in pissing off hurt athletes." She knelt and unwrapped the icepack bound to his knee. "Let me see you walk."

He glared at her.

"Don't make me push you," she threatened jokingly.

"You gonna drop me like you dropped Cody?" The memory brought with it an unexpected flare of heat. She didn't look strong enough, but he'd seen her in action. This was no frail little girl.

Her eyes grew wide with surprise. "You want me to drop you?"

No, but he liked knowing she could, liked knowing she was a strong, independent woman who was able to take care of herself.

She pointed. "Walk," she said again. "To the end of the bench and back."

His mind wandered to other orders he'd like to hear from her, and that surprised him more than anything else she'd said to him in the last two days. Liam saluted her and marched behind the bench, proving to her he could.

When he returned, he stopped one step inside her personal space. Why?

She didn't back down. This was why he'd taken that extra step. To be closer to her. He wanted to be closer still. Her eyes reflected the heat coursing through him.

Emma's presence in Ireland proved he was being monitored after what they'd discovered about Daphne. Hitting on the assistant athletic trainer for the Cowboys was a bad idea. Liam took a step back. "Do I pass the test?"

Her throat bobbed and her nostrils flared. Good to know he wasn't the only one who felt this thing between them.

Emma didn't answer. She turned and joined Yosh at the other end of the bench.

He couldn't sit and watch. "Coach, I want to go in."

Coach gave him a once over, looked for Emma and then turned his attention to the field. "Sit down, McCormick. You should know I can't put you back in once you've been substituted."

Yeah, he knew. But he'd forgotten. Once again, the trainer got the last word.

Chapter 9

Really? He'd actually asked to go back into the game? Emma's blood raced. Unfortunately, it wasn't indignation that had her humming. Liam McCormick was lethal at close range. Maybe the legend was true and he was part seal—a selkie. The irresistible to lonely women kind.

She was *not* lonely.

She also wasn't dead, and the way Liam had looked at her not only underscored that fact, it added an exclamation point at the end.

"He's your problem once the team goes back to the states," she told Yosh. "I've completed my assessment."

"What have you concluded?"

The crowd roared as the Irish scored a goal, one Liam might have diverted had he been in the game. Assuming he was whole. Which he wasn't.

"Well?" Yosh asked.

"He still has work to do."

Yosh nodded. "I'll keep him doing squats, and put him on the bike."

"He's more likely to listen to you than a PT, by the looks of things," she said. "The Cowboy trainer wants to talk to him when he gets back, too, but Liam's not ready to rejoin the team, yet."

"Agreed." Yosh lowered his voice. "Tough call, telling a premiere athlete his body can't keep up."

"Hopefully, his body will catch up."

Liam's physical setback could be overcome, and he didn't seem to be hampered by a lack of confidence, at least not from what she'd observed, but something had manifested itself during the game. She glanced to the stands, looking for an older version of Liam.

A man who had stood on a strip of land inhabited only by goats.

The crowd roared again. Another goal.

Liam stalked to Emma's side. "I could be in there. I could be helping the team."

She gave him her best are-you-kidding-me look.

"I can kick left-footed," Liam said, looking between the two trainers.

"You could hardly walk when you came off the field at half-time," she reminded him. "Don't you think the other team knows you're injured? That forward would challenge you, and when you went to tackle the ball, he'd take you down. Hard. How many seasons have you played? Two? Is that all you want to play, McCormick? You want to be out for good?"

Liam clenched his teeth. "You said everything looked normal."

Yosh stepped forward. "It's your first game back, and it's only an exhibition game. Save it for when we'll need it."

Liam guided Emma to the end of the bench with a hand to the back. "Coach would have kept me in if you weren't here."

"I don't think so."

He threw his hands out at his sides. "I hate sitting here and watching the team lose."

"You can't beat the Irish all by yourself."

"So, what? You're going to ruin my career?"

Emma drew a fortifying breath. "No, I'm not going to ruin your career. Are you?"

"Aren't you here to assess if I'm ready to rejoin the Cowboys?"

"I'm here to make sure you're getting the proper training to return, training you missed."

He cast a glance toward the sky. "Daphne, again. I told you nothing happened. A male trainer wouldn't be giving me such a hard time about a woman throwing herself at me."

She leaned in, her temper riled. "A male trainer sent me down here, not to mention Yosh just backed me up. My being a woman doesn't make any difference. You've proven, not only to me, but also the male trainer standing over there, that you are not physically ready to rejoin the Cowboys. Take this opportunity and make the most of it. As for your problem with me being the one to assess you, after tomorrow, Yosh is the one you have to impress."

Liam huffed. "What am I supposed to do?"

She'd given way to temper, but what Liam needed was reassurance that he could overcome his injury. "Another open water swim before you go home?" she said gently, and then added, "Selkie."

His mouth twisted into a smirk.

"Maybe your seal friends can magically fix you." She gave him a finger wave and headed for the training room.

LIAM SAT ON THE BEACH at Kinsale, staring across the harbor. The boats bounced in the waves, white caps splashing against their sides. The air was considerably cooler than it had been on his previous two trips. He wrapped his arms around his knees and tucked himself against the biting wind.

Da couldn't have been in the stands. It wasn't possible, but he'd certainly distracted Liam from the game. If he wasn't really dead and he had something to say, if his Irish relatives meant to shield Da from the family he'd left behind, this was the most logical place to find him, and this was Liam's last night in Ireland. He'd make it easy for the old man and set the record straight about Da's mysterious disappearance to rejoin the selkies.

Liam had never seen a seal outside a zoo before. Black heads bobbed in the deeper water, as if they were watching him, but none of them ventured to the shoreline.

Emma had believed the legend. She might have been under the influence, but wasn't that when people let their guard down?

The legend said a woman called to a selkie when her tears fell into the sea. Had Emma been crying that night?

He shouldn't have taken his frustration out on her, but she was wrong when she said being a woman didn't make a difference. It did. Not because of how well she could do her job, but because of his response to her. Of course, she thought he responded to all women that way, or at least the women who were assigned to help him rehab. She probably thought he'd seduced Daphne to get out of doing PT, when that couldn't be further from the truth. When Daphne had climbed onto the table and straddled him, he'd firmly set her aside and walked out.

Emma had had that same "let's do this" look in her eye when she'd held out his wetsuit in the bar.

He wasn't that kind of guy, and if Emma *was* lonely, he was the last thing she needed.

But when Emma had tossed Cody...

No, he hadn't wanted to take advantage of Emma when she was drunk and confused, but when she stood toe to toe with him, got in his face for being an idiot, his thoughts went to all those places they weren't supposed to go with someone who held his career in her hands.

Her voice carried on the wind, as if he'd conjured her. "Where's Shane?"

Liam half-turned, needing to make sure she was really there after a day of seeing phantoms. "Celebrating the win with his team."

"You're not thinking of swimming alone, are you?" she asked.

"I'm not that stupid." He brushed the sand from his jeans and pushed to his feet. "Especially not in this kind of weather."

Her shoulders softened, as if she'd been afraid she'd have to go in after him.

"You don't swim?" he asked.

"No. What are you doing here, then?" she asked.

"I thought you'd washed your hands of me at the game."

She shrugged. "I wouldn't say I've washed my hands of you."

"Look. I'm sorry about what I said. You're right. Being a woman doesn't make you an inferior trainer."

Her lips twisted into a funny expression. "Thanks for that, I guess."

He couldn't help ribbing her. "So why are *you* here? Still hoping to catch a selkie?"

"I wanted to make sure you were all right." She brushed her hair off her face, a wasted gesture when the wind whipped it back.

"That's thoughtful of you," he said sarcastically.

"Listen, Liam, I sent an email to Ray, let him know you'd been training on your own. That's fairly evident. I assume you've avoided PT because of what happened. Am I wrong?"

Okay, so she was strong, independent, and smart. "No."

"The problem with that is you've missed some important strengthening, which is what showed up when you took the field today. You need more PT." She gave him a sly smile. "You can request a man, you know."

"What if I requested you?"

"My job is to treat your injuries, not rehabilitate you. I'm not a therapist."

"But you *could* do it."

She raised her eyebrows. "I could. You'd trust me?"

He chuckled. "I'm joking."

"Then you don't want me to help you rehab?" She held her hair out of her face, her cheeks pink from the wind.

"No."

"Why not?"

"Didn't you just say...?" he shook his head and looked across the water, toward the island.

"What?" she asked.

He narrowed his eyes, trying to bring a spot standing out against the horizon into focus. Probably a goat.

Emma took a step closer. "One minute you suggest I train you and the next you say you don't want me to. What's going on, Liam?"

He continued to squint toward the island.

"What is your problem, McCormick?"

His problem, which was growing rapidly, forced him to look at her. At the challenge in her eyes. "You gonna take me down?" he asked, his voice husky.

Her brows winged up. "That's twice you've asked. Do you want me to?"

"Maybe."

Her hands went to her hips and her head tilted. "Maybe?"

He couldn't. He'd never rejoin the Cowboys if he made a pass at Emma, and yet he couldn't seem to stop himself.

Liam cupped Emma's face and kissed her. She grabbed his arms and took one step between his legs to disrupt his balance, and then her grip loosened. Instead, she fisted the front of his jacket and pulled him closer, deepening the kiss.

Liam backed away and stared into her dark brown eyes. "I'm still standing."

"Is that a problem?"

"This is why I can't have you train me," he said.

"Problem controlling yourself around female health practitioners?"

He concentrated on her lovely face. "No. Just you."

"What about the therapist?"

"Already told you. Nothing happened."

Movement on the island caught his eye again. Stark. Solitary. Isolated. The shape on the island came into sharper focus and Liam tensed.

"What do you see?" Emma asked beside him.

No. He wasn't going to tell her he saw his da. She'd tell the Cowboys he was mentally unprepared to return.

"Tell me," she said.

He shot a glance at her. She was staring toward the island, too. "Do you see him?"

She nodded.

His da's voice echoed in his ears like a whisper on the wind. "You've grown to be a fine man, Liam McCormick."

Chapter 10

She'd only been in Ireland a couple of days, but it was enough to confuse her body clock. While her flight had departed Cork at seven o'clock Monday morning, at seven p.m. Chicago time, she'd been awake for nearly twenty-four hours and her eyelids were growing heavy.

Dinner with Portia her first night home made Emma's life feel more normal, even if Portia insisted on all the gory details.

"Then what happened?" Portia asked Emma, elbows on the table.

The waitress arrived and Portia straightened while their food was placed in front of them.

"Can I get you ladies anything else?" the waitress asked.

"I think we're fine for the moment," Emma replied.

When the waitress walked away, Portia picked up a fork. "Still waiting here."

"Nothing happened," Emma said, not meeting Portia's eye.

"No rendezvous at the hotel?"

"We shared a silent cab ride back to Cork, he went to his room, I went to my room, and we haven't spoken since."

"Did a taste of Liam McCormick satisfy your appetite?"

Emma looked up, met Portia's amused expression. "Actually, no. If anything, it made me hungrier."

Portia laughed. "Oh, girlfriend, you got it bad."

Emma set her fork on the table with a thump and took a sip of her wine. "I am not a groupie. I am a professional. I'm not about to go throwing myself at Liam McCormick."

"You said he kissed you, though, right? So you wouldn't be throwing yourself at him." Portia lowered her voice. "Nobody has to know."

Emma scoffed. "That's probably what the intern said, right before they kicked her out of the program."

"So, what are you going to do?"

"With Liam? Not a thing."

"Okay, then what about the ghost?"

Emma picked up her fork again. "That's weird. Right?"

"No argument."

"What would you do?" Emma asked.

"Blind, deaf and dumb. Didn't see it, can't hear it. What ghost?"

Emma chuckled. "Right, except I already told Liam I saw him."

"Deny, deny, deny. Tell him you were humoring him."

Emma scowled. "That's not what he needs from me right now."

"No, what he needs is another kiss, and maybe more." Portia took a sip of wine. "Tell me, is he sexy? Hard body? Easy on the eyes?" She set her glass down and put her palms on the table. "Take a bite of the proverbial apple, Emma. Get it out of your system."

Portia's idea wasn't *terrible*, but sleeping with Liam was the wrong thing to do. "No thank you. I like my job," Emma said.

Portia shrugged. "Hey, if he's still on the D-league team, technically, he isn't your problem, he's someone else's. You have one degree of separation, right?"

The thought had crossed Emma's mind. "But here's the thing," she said, glancing around to make sure there were no nosy eavesdroppers nearby. "This is one of those fields where women aren't taken seriously. I'd be doing a disservice to all womankind by crossing that line."

"You don't think female athletes with male trainers dip their toes in every now and then? I bet I could name you a dozen ice skaters who ended up marrying their coaches or their trainers. I can even think of one very famous diva who married her manager. Relationships happen, and sometimes they're meant to. As long as you're both on the same page, what harm can come of it?"

Emma shook her finger at Portia. "You are a bad influence."

"You said yourself the intern got fired for falsifying medical records, for saying she'd given them PT when, last I checked, sex doesn't qualify as PT. Am I right?"

"Falsifying the records primarily, but also for throwing herself at the players," Emma said.

"So don't throw yourself at him, but next time he kisses you, try to enjoy yourself."

Oh, she'd more than enjoyed it. She'd kissed him back, and if the ghost hadn't have shown up to distract them, no telling what might have happened next. Divine intervention?

"No," Emma said. "He doesn't need any more distractions. He's already grappling with whether he'll ever feel normal again on the soccer field, and then there's the whole dad thing—I'm not even sure what that's all about. He's got enough going on without the questionable ethics of sleeping with the trainer."

"But you still want to."

Emma gave way to a grin. "Got me there, but to quote a famous rock and roll song, we can't always get what we want."

LIAM STOOD INSIDE THE covered front porch, waiting for his brother, Kevin, to answer the door. Instead, his three-year old niece looked up at him with adoring eyes when the door opened.

"Unca Yum!" she said, holding out her arms.

Liam picked her up and held her over his head. "How's our little Chloe doing?"

She pointed inside the house. "Mama, mama, Unca Yum!"

Liam set Chloe on the floor and took her hand as she tugged him toward the kitchen, where Kevin's wife, Amy, was making dinner.

"Sorry to send Chloe to greet you instead of meeting you at the door myself," Amy said wiping her hands on a dish towel. "The timer was going off and I didn't want the sauce to boil over." She took a step toward Liam and hugged him, her belly swollen with her second child. "Kevin ran downstairs. He'll be right back."

"Need help with anything?" Liam asked.

"Not at the moment. Kevin says the Mustangs lost the exhibition game?"

"Yeah. I still think I could have stopped at least one of those goals."

"I'm sure if they believed that, they would have let you play," Kevin said, coming through the basement door. He set a box of spaghetti on the kitchen table, took hold of Liam's hand and pulled him into a hug. "How's the knee?"

"Holding up."

"Horsey, horsey," Chloe chimed in.

"Not right now, sweet pea," Liam said. "Uncle Liam's knee isn't strong enough to be a horsey yet."

She pouted and clung to Amy's pants leg.

Liam turned to Kevin. "Shouldn't Chloe be able to say Liam by now?"

"What? You don't like being Uncle Yum?" Kevin teased. He affected an Irish brogue. "Perhaps you'd rather be Uncle Lame?"

Liam scowled. "Not funny."

"I think Uncle Yum is cute," Amy added.

"So what's on your mind?" Kevin asked. "You said you had something you needed to talk to me about."

Liam shot a glance at Amy—Amy who'd heard their sister Mary's voice calling for help from beyond the grave. Should he tell Kevin about their father in front of Amy? In front of Chloe?

Kevin saved him from making a decision by nodding and waving toward the living room. He waited until Liam sat before he asked him again.

"I take it you met some of our Irish relatives while you were over there?" Kevin asked.

"I did."

"And?"

"Friendly folks."

"So what's wrong?"

Liam tensed. "Did Ma tell you how Da died?"

"No, and frankly, I don't care."

"I didn't think I cared, either."

Kevin raised his eyebrows. "And now?"

"They said he took a swim in the sea, drunk, and didn't come back."

"That doesn't sound too bright," Kevin said. "So he drowned."

"According to the family there, he found our grandda's sealskin and returned to the sea in his place," Liam continued.

Kevin blinked, furrowed his brow, and then laughed. "Seriously?"

"Are you familiar with the tale of the selkies?"

"Am I familiar with the legend? Yes. As it pertains to our family? No." His forehead wrinkled again. "They actually said that?"

"They did."

Kevin's eyes went to the top of Liam's head. "Or were they pulling your leg because of the color of your hair?"

"Well, there is that." All of Liam's siblings had red hair, but not him. No, he had the dark hair and eyes of a selkie, if his Irish family was to be believed. "But the alternative is to consider he committed suicide. Rejoining selkie ancestors seemed less disturbing."

"I get it now. Have you told Ma?"

Liam shook his head. "She has to know, right? I mean she's the one who told us. She's moved on with her life. There's no reason to mention what I found out, do you think?"

"I suppose not, although she will wonder about who you met while you were there."

"That's where this gets weird." Liam leaned over his knees. "I think I saw Da."

Kevin cocked his head again. "You don't think he's really dead?"

"This is going to sound strange."

Kevin laughed. "Buddy, you don't even know what strange is."

"I do now."

Kevin narrowed his eyes. "Go on."

"I did some training while I was there, swam a triathlon course in the sea that goes around an island." He considered how much he should tell Kevin, and decided he might as well relate everything. "Okay, so first, a family of seals thought it would be fun to swim with me and my buddy. That was odd, even if it was fun, but the really strange part..." he hesitated, checked Kevin's expression for skepticism, but Kevin appeared to be listening intently. "Actually, I saw him at the stadium first. I was on the field and I heard a voice inside my head. I looked up, and I swear I saw Da watching in the stands. I went back to Kinsale, where the family is. I figured if he's alive, I'd stand a better chance of seeing him there, or if he's dead..." Liam stopped to gather his thoughts. "I saw him on the island. An island in the middle of the harbor inhabited only by goats."

"Maybe he's doing a Robinson Crusoe thing. Swam to the island to be alone."

"Island's not that big, and it's not that far off shore." Liam shook his head. "No, he called me by name, and then he vanished like an Irish mist."

Kevin put a hand to Liam's arm. "He's dead, he can't hurt you."

"I don't think he intended to," Liam replied. "I'm not sure what to think. He's been dead for years, right? So why is he haunting me now?"

Kevin leaned back and folded his arms. "I'm not much of an expert on the afterlife. Jared, on the other hand," he said, reminding Liam their brother-in-law was a ghost whisperer of sorts.

"But you saw Mary. You and Amy. After Mary died. Right?"

"It's a shame your dad died so far away," Amy said from the kitchen doorway.

Liam rose to his feet. As much as he loved his sister-in-law, the stories Kevin had told him about Amy's ability to hear the dead were creepy.

She gave him a patient smile. "I don't know much more about the afterlife than Kevin does. I can hear them speak, but it's more like tuning into a radio station. If your father had something more to say, I imagine I'd be able to hear him if I stood near where he died, or where he's buried."

"I wouldn't put it past him to fake his death to avoid seeing family," Kevin said.

"He's a ghost all right," Liam said.

"Come eat," Amy said. "And since you're here, I need to talk to you. Kevin said you've been giving financial advice to some of the Cowboys. Can you give me suggestions for setting money aside for Chloe and Baby Boy McCormick?" She patted her stomach.

"Doesn't baby boy have a name?" Liam asked.

"We're thinking Randall, after Amy's father," Kevin said. "Can you help us with the college funds or not?"

"I can try. Your situation isn't quite the same as what I do for the guys on the team."

Kevin shoved him in the shoulder. "What? Because we don't have piles of money to throw around?"

Liam ducked away. "Something like that. You're also smarter than the average athlete who gets overwhelmed with a big payday and thinks he'll never spend it all."

"Put your finance degree to use. That is why you transferred to State University, isn't it? Wouldn't want you to forget everything you learned in college while you're chasing balls around a soccer field."

"Think you can keep up, tough guy?" Liam joked. "You wouldn't last five minutes in a scrimmage with the team."

"Don't I know it." Kevin wrapped an arm across Liam's shoulder and squeezed as they returned to the kitchen. "Nor would I want to. Take advantage of your opportunities while you can."

"I intend to." Liam smiled at Amy. "Thanks for dinner, by the way. Since this meathead made you stand over a hot stove, when we're done I insist you go put your feet up. I'll do the dishes before I head home."

"You don't have to do that," Amy said. "But you do have to tell me what I need to do to set up college funds for your niece and nephew."

"I'll see what I can do." He took a seat at the table and made a face at Chloe, which sent her into a fit of giggles.

Chapter 11

When Emma reported to the Cowboys training room on Wednesday, Ray, the head trainer, was in his office, seated behind his computer. He looked up when she knocked on the open door and waved her in.

"You get the results of McCormick's MRI?" she asked.

"Looking them over now. Everything seems to be okay. A few more games with the Mustangs to rebuild his strength and stamina should help. Anything to add after personal observation?"

She slid into the seat across from him. "He did stop going to his physical therapy appointments, apparently to avoid a second encounter with Daphne, but based on what I observed, he's been training on his own."

Ray sat back and stared over the top of his reading glasses. "You said all that in your report. What about his mental toughness? Is he going to favor the knee? Be afraid of going down again?"

Emma considered the way he'd run around the ball on the field after the forward had rung his bell in the exhibition game. "He didn't look to be afraid. In fact, after I pulled him from the game, he complained about being subbed out for the second half. No, he's determined to get back out there."

"Good." Ray checked his watch. "He should be here in about half an hour. Figured I'd check him over myself and have a chat with him. Confirm your findings."

"How many athletes were affected by the Daphne scandal?" Emma asked.

"Three that we're aware of. She's been released from the program, and the therapist overseeing her has received a formal reprimand for not supervising more closely."

Emma shrugged. "I suppose determined groupies will always find a way in."

"I guess."

"For what it's worth, McCormick says he turned her down," she said.

"I'd believe it," Ray said. "He isn't the type. I'm not surprised to hear he decided to train himself, but the front office was worried he'd given up when they'd heard he'd quit going to physical therapy."

The door to the locker room slammed shut. Emma checked the clock on the wall. "That's probably him now. I'll get out of your way. I have some paperwork to catch up on, and then I'll inventory supplies after he leaves."

"Good to have you back, and thanks for the report."

Emma disappeared into her office, doing her best to stay out of sight. No, she hadn't gone groupie on Liam, but her interest in him had definitely eclipsed a professional concern. She should have thrown him down, the way he dared her to when he'd kissed her on the beach, except there was something about him. The dark eyes. She'd enjoyed the kiss far more than she should have. What had they said about selkies? They were irresistible?

She laughed at the notion. She was no better than the intern.

Emma wasn't easily impressed by a flirtatious soccer player with a hard body. Why had she let Liam kiss her?

Then there was the specter on the island. A ghost?

She was letting the Irish legend get to her again.

Her own father had been a soldier, killed in Iraq when she was eleven. She'd give anything to have had more time with him, but her father loved her. Liam's father was a different sort of man, by all accounts.

Emma's hand went to the heart around her neck, the last gift her father had given her before his last deployment, a reminder of happier times when they'd been a family.

Seals. A handy legend to ascribe to a suicide.

She heard Liam's voice in the training room and her body warmed in response.

"Well, when a pretty girl puts her hands on you, well—you're a guy. When she noticed she'd gotten a response, she slipped her hands—That's when I told her to get off and walked out." Liam laughed. "My first groupie experience. Not my cup of tea. I thought it would be better to avoid any additional encounters. Training was easier without worrying she was going to try to jump me again."

"We had to make sure," Ray said. "Sometimes when a player gets injured, he thinks differently. His focus shifts."

"Uh-uh. I worked too hard to make this team. I plan to be back."

"That's what Emma said. How about this? Does this hurt?"

"Maybe a three on your stupid scale."

"And this?"

She shouldn't be eavesdropping. Her fascination with Liam had to be based on the fantasy his cousin had created in the pub. The more she thought about it, the more ridiculous she felt envisioning seals shedding their skins instead of swimmers peeling off their wetsuits.

Emma turned on her computer. A reflection on the screen made her turn to look behind her. She'd sworn she'd seen a man's face, but there was no one behind her. If she closed her office door now, Liam would know she was in there, would know she'd overheard his conversation with Ray. She turned to her computer again and gasped.

The man had creases in his face and his hair had gone white, but his dark eyes held the same soulful look as Liam's. He wore an Irish hat, similar to the flat caps the men in the pub had worn.

His voice, a whisper in her ear, sent shivers down her spine. "Take care of me boy."

Emma pushed away from her desk and jumped to her feet, sending the chair into her filing cabinet with a crash.

"YOU OKAY IN THERE?" Ray called out.

"Fine," Emma replied.

Emma?

Liam winced and rubbed his forehead. What had she overheard?

Why did he care?

She appeared in the office door, a sheepish smile on her face and gave him a nod. "McCormick."

"Emma," he said.

She had one hand on her door. "How's the knee feeling today?"

"Stable."

She glanced at Ray. "Let me know if you need anything." She closed the door.

What was it about Emma that was so darn appealing?

She'd been sent to evaluate him. If he asked her out and things went sour, she could end his career, or at least cast enough shadow to keep him on the sidelines. No. Better to avoid any potential issues.

"Problem?" Ray asked.

That was the difference between a man trainer and woman trainer. Approach. Women insisted you talk to them. Men threw it out as a suggestion. "No problem," Liam replied.

Ray shot a glance at Emma's closed door. "She can be a bit gruff. She give you any trouble in Ireland?"

"Nah. Just aggravating not to be in the game."

"You played minutes in the first half, didn't you?"

Liam nodded. "Until she sidelined me."

"So that's it. Don't take it personally. Better to work your way back gradually."

"I have been working through it gradually," Liam complained. "I've been cleared to play."

"How did that go?" Ray asked. "Your first game?"

Liam frowned. "Rough."

"Listen. We want you back as much as you want to be back. We also want to avoid re-injury."

Liam nodded.

"The MRI looks good. Everything seems to have healed nicely. Let's keep it that way. Are you working with the Mustang trainer?"

"Mostly working on my own."

Ray frowned. "The Cowboys will want to be sure you're doing the work. Put some time in with Yosh. Let him help you. When he says you're good to come back, we'll keep up with the training here. In the meantime, if you need anything, don't be afraid to call." He nodded for emphasis.

Liam hopped off the trainer's table. "To summarize, you want my rehab training documented. Right?"

Ray made an approving cluck in his cheek and pointed at Liam. "Now you got it."

Liam cast a glance at Emma's closed door. He couldn't see her through the window, but he swore he saw a man—a man wearing a paddy cap. "Think I'll stick my head in to say goodbye," he said absently to Ray and approached Emma's door.

No man in her office. Emma sat at her computer with her back to the door. Had the shadow he'd seen been his imagination? Liam rapped on the wood frame and turned the knob.

"Just wanted to say thanks," he said.

She turned toward him, her face pale.

"You okay?" he asked.

She nodded.

"I thought I saw..."

She nodded again.

Liam took a step into her office. "My da? Here?" He glanced over his shoulder at Ray, who appeared to be engrossed in a file folder spread out on the trainer's table. He lowered his voice. "You're not going to try to tell me this is a manifestation brought on by my insecurities about my injury, or some other nonsense, are you?"

"I saw him," she said quietly.

"We need to talk," he said. "Not here."

Chapter 12

Emma wrapped her hands around her coffee cup and watched for Liam through the Starbucks window. Commuters headed toward the busses and trains. Men in business suits hailed cabs. The tail end of rush hour in the city.

Starbucks. Quiet, but not intimate. A good place for a conversation, right?

Liam crossed the street, head down, collar high. She'd become intimately aware of his athletic build. He stopped, a startled look on his face as a woman extended her hands to him, reached into her purse, put her palms to her cheeks, all before she handed him a pen and a piece of paper. He smiled, scribbled an autograph and handed the pen and paper back to her. The woman bounced on her toes, stared at the paper and then at him.

Liam turned his head and met Emma's gaze. His expression brightened and he gave her a smile.

No, she wasn't going to be a fangirl or a groupie. She worked with these guys every day and none of them struck her as anything remarkable.

Until she'd met Liam.

She didn't want to squeal or shriek, but she did want to touch him, like the woman on the sidewalk who couldn't seem to take her hand off Liam's arm.

He extricated himself carefully, tipped his fingers to his forehead and continued into the coffee shop. He placed his order and walked over to Emma's table to wait for the barista to call his name.

"Is she going to send all her best friends after you?" Emma asked.

"We can go somewhere else," he said.

Emma waved a hand in the air. "I'm kidding. She probably has a train to catch, or some other form of public transportation."

"Leem?" the barista called.

Liam grabbed his cup and returned to the table, his back to the door, melting into his clothes as if to appear invisible.

"How was practice today?" Emma asked, searching for a neutral subject.

"Don't report until tomorrow. Besides, it's a two-hour drive out to Rockford from my place in the city, and I was scheduled with Ray today."

"So you would have missed it? Does that mean you're in pain?"

He fixed her with a dark stare. "You're off the clock. You agreed to meet me *after* work. I don't want to talk about my knee."

"Then what do you want to talk about?" The minute she asked, she wanted to take it back. The heat in his eyes flamed through her.

He didn't answer immediately. When his brows lifted ever-so-slightly, she was transported to their kiss on the beach in Kinsale. The one she hadn't been able to resist. One she would give anything to repeat.

Maybe he was a selkie.

Good choice, Starbucks. He wouldn't kiss her with a world full of commuters walking past the window, nor would she kiss him. Or worse.

"I want to talk about why my da is haunting you," he said. "Bad enough he's haunting me."

Oh yeah. That. Emma swallowed a slurp of hot coffee. "I've only seen him when you and I are together, or at least in close proximity. Are you sure you've seen him? Or are we both imagining things?"

"A shared hallucination?" he said.

"You haven't forgotten my night at the pub so easily, have you? I'm the one who was half convinced you and Shane were selkies. I'm a sucker for a good story."

His lips curled into a sensuous smile and Emma had to lick her own lips, which had suddenly gone dry.

Liam waggled his eyebrows. "I sort of understand how you might have misinterpreted two guys peeling off wetsuits for selkies."

Why did he have to be so attractive?

"The ghost is just an extension of the legend, isn't it?" she said.

"Except he keeps turning up. In the crowd at the stadium in Cork. On a tiny island in Kinsale. In your office today. Why?" He pointed a finger at her. "And don't tell me it's a manifestation of my injury."

She shook her head. "Like you said, we've both seen him."

Liam took a sip of his coffee. "Emma, let me tell you something about my dad. He was not a nice man. The world is a better place without him."

She squirmed in her seat, unsure if she should try to comfort him or reassure him. "Maybe he wants to make it up to you, whatever bad stuff he did."

"Part of me wanted to find out he'd changed his ways when I went to Kinsale, had become a better man, but it sounds as if he was the same son of a bitch who terrorized us. When my ma sat us down to tell us all he'd died, all I felt was relief."

Emma nodded.

"Whatever we're seeing now, how am I supposed to deal with that? You saw me at the exhibition game. I'm no good to the team if I'm spotting spooks in the stands."

Was he asking her professional opinion? Or was he confiding in her? Why couldn't she separate the professional from the personal? Her attraction to Liam wouldn't be such a big deal if the intern hadn't made a mess of things. Now management would be viewing all women like predators, although Portia made a good point. As long as Liam was on the Mustangs...

She shook her head again to rejoin the conversation. Panting over Liam wasn't going to help with his problem, professionally or personally.

"I'm not sure how one rids themselves of ghosts," she said, trying to make light of the situation. "It isn't as if he could hurt us. Ghosts are insubstantial, aren't they? If we ignore him, will he go away?"

Liam studied her a moment. "What's the old saying? In for a penny?"

"In for a pound," she finished. "You've told me this much?" she asked, assuming his meaning.

"A few years back, my youngest sister had an accident, or so we thought. Then my brother met someone who told us a different story."

Emma's heart sank as if he'd loaded it with rocks. "I'm sorry."

"Apparently, my sister was reaching out from beyond the grave. She wouldn't go away until someone knew she'd been murdered, until the murderer was brought to justice. If my father is manifesting himself to us, I'd have to guess he isn't going away until he has his say."

Emma swallowed down the lump in her throat.

LIAM SCRUBBED HIS FACE with his hand. If the ghost had stayed in Ireland, he could have dismissed the experience as closure, his father saying goodbye, or some other ridiculous notion. Maybe in his own way Liam was looking for a way to let go of the bad memories.

His cell phone vibrated and he read the display. Ma. Liam held up a finger to Emma while he answered the call.

"Jesus, Mary and Joseph," his ma said.

That couldn't be good. "What's wrong, Ma?"

"You're back?" she asked.

"I am."

"Why is it you haven't stopped by to see me yet?"

He had no intention of telling her about his run-in with the ghost. In fact, he'd been avoiding going home for exactly that reason. "I've only been back since Monday, and I had to report to the trainer this morning. Why are you Jesus, Mary and Joseph-ing me?"

"I'm on the train, Liam. Are you home?"

"I'm not."

"Can you meet me at the station. Will you do that?"

She was coming into the city? To see him? "Yeah. Are you going to tell me what's wrong?"

His mother hesitated. "I'll be expecting you to tell me everything that happened to you in Ireland. I suspect there's much."

Liam gulped. "You saw him."

"That I did, and I'll not return to that house until he's gone for good. Duncan and I will be staying with you for a bit, I'm thinking."

"Me?" Liam asked, glancing at Emma. So much for inviting her over to 'see his etchings.' "What about Kathleen? Or Kevin?"

"Kathleen's house is a war zone. How she and Sebastian can live there while it's yet under construction is beyond me. Besides, they're newlyweds. They won't want parents underfoot. The same with Kevin. While Amy's breeding, she doesn't need a meddling mother-in-law to fire her already out-of-control hormones. You've no one else to bother at your place, and you're never home—unless something's changed?"

Liam winced and massaged his forehead. "I'll meet you at the station." He wrote down the time on a napkin and hung up.

"I take it that was your mother?" Emma asked.

Liam nodded slowly, staring at the misspelled name on his coffee cup.

"More family drama?" She held up her hand. "You don't have to answer. You've already told me more than you're probably comfortable with."

"In for a penny," he repeated. He raised his gaze to meet hers. "She's seen my da."

Could things get any worse? He'd met Emma here to find out what she'd seen, make sure he wasn't losing his mind. She was the last person he should be baring his soul to. Emma had the power to have him released from the Cowboys permanently. Hadn't she told him she'd come to Ireland to check on both his physical *and* emotional state? He didn't sound rational at the moment. What if she was humoring him?

He needed to shut up, starting now.

"You know what?" he said. "Let's forget this conversation. Let's forget everything I've told you about my family. I learned to deal with my baggage years ago. I'm sure it's the shock of learning how my father died." He crossed himself. "God rest his soul."

Emma's eyes flashed and she grabbed his hand. Her voice dropped an octave. "Don't do that."

"Don't do what?"

"There may be a logical explanation for all of this, but don't you dare pretend it didn't happen. I know you're not a selkie. I know that's little more than an Irish legend, but by the same token, I know we've seen your father."

Oh yeah. This was the other reason he'd asked her for coffee. Emma had a toughness about her, something that made him want to ask her to be his bodyguard. Personal bodyguard. Very personal. How much time did they have before his mother's train arrived?

She backed away as if she'd been burned.

"What now?" he asked.

"This." She pointed first to him and then to herself.

He raised his eyebrows, inviting her to continue.

Emma lowered her voice. "You get that look in your eye."

"What look?" he asked, leaning over the table, daring her to put the tension between them to words.

She smirked. "The look you got when you asked if I was going to deck you in Ireland. You like getting beat up or something?"

"Not necessarily beat up." He liked her strength more than he dared to tell her.

"You're a weird guy, Liam McCormick."

"But you didn't deck me. In fact, you let me kiss you. Can't be that weird."

Her cheeks flushed and he pointed to her face. "Admit it. You like me," he teased.

"I'm not sure this conversation is helpful," she said with a break in her voice.

"I disagree." He reached for the hand she'd pulled away.

Their fingers touched and he laced his with hers. He stroked the back of her hand, holding her gaze. "You're the type of woman who sets her own terms," he said. "Not a pushover. Not someone to be trifled with. Am I right?"

"What's your point?" she asked.

"You kissed me back." The heat of her touch flamed through him. "You didn't deck me."

"So?" she whispered.

No, he didn't want to trifle with her. He wanted her to come to him on her own terms. He wanted to feel her strength. "What if I told you I wanted more than a kiss?"

She gave him a sly smile. "How do you know the reason I didn't throw you was so I wouldn't aggravate your injury?" She extricated her hand, leaned over the table and raised her eyebrows. "I can still drop you to the ground if need be." She straightened. "I'm not one of your groupies, McCormick."

"I don't play with groupies, Emma." He was fairly certain she'd overheard his conversation with Ray. She would have heard him say the same thing to the head trainer, someone he might have bragged to if he was a different sort of man. He wasn't that kind of guy, and she knew it.

Emma licked her lips.

"Something sent you to the sea in search of a legend in Ireland. What do you want? A devoted lover? A loyal boyfriend? Someone who's biding their time with you until they can return to the life they know? Seems to me a selkie isn't likely to hang around. He'd be waiting for his chance to return to the sea."

"I think I expressed my opinion on selkies when we were there," she said. "I don't want to hold anyone captive."

"Too late." She held him captive. He'd never been so drawn to a woman. "Are you lonely, Emma?"

Emma laughed. "I am not. I'm sure you could walk away from this."

"Could. Don't want to."

"I suppose you expect me to go home with you, now." Her voice was breathless. As much as she protested, he got the impression she would.

"No, I don't expect that," he said evenly. She was the type of woman who would appreciate an honest answer. "Although I'd be lying if I said I didn't want you to. Unfortunately, my mother is on her way into the city. She and her husband are planning to stay with me for the foreseeable future. Almost like fate is taking a hand, wouldn't you say?" He leaned over the table once more. "Which means you'd have to invite me to your place. A woman who prefers things on her own terms." He grinned. "Then again, I'm not particular. Tell me where you want me, as long as you tell me you want me."

Her lips parted and her cheeks were flushed. Emma's eyes sparkled with mischief. What he wouldn't give to be able to read her mind right now.

She rose from the table with her cup of coffee in hand and walked out.

Chapter 13

Emma unlocked her apartment door, took one last look over her shoulder, darted inside and leaned against the door after she'd closed it.

If she hadn't left Starbucks when she did, she would have invited Liam home. Selkie or not, he was hard to resist.

Her heart raced as she glanced around the sparsely decorated room. She imagined Liam sitting on her overstuffed floral brocade sofa, or in one of the ladder back chairs beside her plain IKEA dining table. She'd have to avoid going into her bedroom for at least the next thirty minutes, until her pulse slowed and she had a chance to forget the way he'd angled for an invitation.

She kicked off her shoes, set them neatly on the rug beside the door, then skated in stockinged feet across the hardwood floors to the kitchen. Emma set her purse on the counter and retrieved her ringing cellphone from inside.

"Tell me you're home," Portia said when Emma answered.

"I'm home."

"But are you really?"

Emma smiled. "Yes."

"I'm coming over. I need to borrow your LBD for a cocktail party tomorrow night. You don't need it, do you?"

Her little black dress? Not anytime soon. "No." Emma shot a glance toward her bedroom. Surely Portia would exorcise any fantasies of Liam that might present themselves. "How soon can you be here?"

"Walking down Chestnut now. Five minutes."

"See you soon." Emma let out an exaggerated sigh as she set her phone down.

Liam was just a man. The fact he made her legs rubbery and her boobs throb didn't mean anything.

Why were her lips so dry?

She picked up the remote control and pointed it at the television mounted to the wall. The oldie station she was tuned to flashed to an image of Mary Tyler Moore throwing her hat in the air.

A different image flashed to mind, her mother on the sofa shaking a finger at Emma and telling her if Mary could make it on her own, so could Emma. "You can do whatever you set your mind to. You don't need me." Emma hadn't had a choice when it came right down to it.

A knock on the door signaled Portia's arrival. Emma checked the peephole before she let her friend in.

"Have I ever mentioned how much I hate cocktail parties?" Portia said, heading straight to Emma's bedroom and her closet.

"Once or twice." Emma followed hesitantly until she was sure no fantasies of Liam had found their way to her bed. She breathed a sigh of relief.

"Vance told me if I could land this sponsor for the last skybox, he'd give me a big fat bonus, so naturally, the greedy monster inside me accepted the challenge." Portia slipped off her heels and shimmied out of her dress pants before she unbuttoned her silk blouse. She took the dress from the closet and pulled it over her head.

Portia huffed. "I was afraid of this. Three days of lunch meetings and breakfast meetings. Do I look like a stuffed sausage?" She held out her arms inviting a comment from Emma.

No, Portia looked curvy and sexy and beautiful, her sleek blonde hair curling around the décolletage. "I wish I looked as good as you do in my dress. It hangs on me like a bag."

"Nice. Rub it in, why don't you?"

Emma laughed, painfully aware of the khakis and polo that consisted of her work uniform. She ran a self-conscious hand through her short hair, rearranging it from the desired moussed mess to the straight mess it naturally took on. She'd never been much of a girly-girl. The little black dress she and Portia more or less shared was the only dress in her closet. One dress for all occasions.

Portia set her hands on her hips. "Do I look that bad? You're cringing."

Was she? "You look fabulous. You always look fabulous."

"Then what's bugging you?" Portia narrowed her eyes. "You're blushing." She gasped. "Oh, I get it. Something happened with that soccer player. Liam?"

Emma rolled her eyes. "Maybe."

"Let's hear it," Portia said while she changed back into her work clothes.

"I met him for coffee after work in a nice, safe Starbucks. He propositioned me, or at least I think he did. I'm not totally sure. Creepy? Or hot?"

"Didn't you tell me you kissed this guy? I've known you long enough to know you don't let anyone inside your personal space without your permission, which means you kinda like this guy, even if you did tell me you're not sure its kosher." She reached for her phone. "Liam McCormick, did you say?"

"What are you doing?"

"Googling him, of course."

Emma reached for Portia's phone, but Portia turned away. "Oh, definitely hot." She turned her phone to show Emma the picture she'd found of Liam, his team headshot. "I say you go for it. What have you got to lose?"

"My job?" Emma walked out of her bedroom with Portia close on her heels.

"You said he's on the development team, right? That means you aren't currently working with him, right? Which makes everything okay. This is the perfect time."

Emma walked around the counter that divided the kitchenette from the living room to put distance between her and Portia. The idea seemed so simple when Portia laid it out like that, and yet...

Portia put her hands on the counter. "I haven't seen you think this hard about a guy in a long time. I'm not even sure you thought this hard about Cliff. He never got to you like this. If your soccer player is this interesting, I think you need to give him a chance. What's the worst that could happen? Good sex?"

Emma laughed nervously. "I'm not good at casual sex, which is why it took Cliff so long to get that far."

"You're not going to throw Liam down if he makes another pass at you, are you?"

Emma put her hands on the counter, too. "He seems to like knowing I could."

"Huh?" Portia's eyes bugged out.

"He watched me drop the Mustang's striker and I swear his whole attitude changed. Maybe he sees me as a challenge." She pursed her lips. "I almost threw him when he kissed me. Had him in position."

"But?"

Emma closed her eyes and turned away. "There's something about him."

"Tell me more about this maybe-proposition."

"His mother called to say she was coming to stay with him for a while, so he said he couldn't invite me over, but he said that was probably best since he figured I preferred things to be on my own terms."

"He's right about that. Perceptive."

"Do you want to hear this or not?" Emma asked.

"Go on."

"So then he suggested I invite him to my place. My terms. Wherever I wanted him, as long as I wanted him."

Portia grinned. "Definitely hot. He said all that without making a pass at you?"

Emma nodded.

"Props for laying it out there?"

"I suppose." Emma rounded her shoulders. "He made it sound like he wanted more than—well, you know."

Portia walked around the countertop and hugged Emma. "You're afraid you'll end up giving him a piece of yourself."

Emma nodded when Portia pushed her to arms' length.

"You are so fearless in everything you do, except when it comes to letting your guard down." She shook Emma gently. "It's okay to have a little fun. Take what you need. It sounds like you have wicked chemistry with this guy. No one says you have to give away the keys to your heart. If he pisses you off, walk away."

"That's not me," Emma said.

"I know, but you can't hide forever. Who knows? This guy might be 'the one.' Weren't you willing to give yourself up to an Irish legend?"

Emma sputtered. "Yeah, but I was drunk and I would have gone into it knowing he had somewhere else to go, somewhere else he'd rather be. Something more important to him than me."

"So you don't want to get attached," Portia said gently. "And then have him disappear. Like your dad. Like your mom. Like Cliff."

Tears stung Emma's eyes as she nodded.

"Physical need is a lot different than emotional need, girlfriend. I think you could do with a little physical contact of the male variety, but if you want to be a lonely, shriveled old lady, that's up to you."

Emma punched Portia's arm. "Hey! I'm not lonely."

"You don't fool me. I know why you put in all those hours at work."

Maybe she was lonely, somewhere deep down. Emma did miss having someone to talk to when she came home, but that didn't mean she had to fill the void with the first hot. Sexy. Man. Who propositioned her.

But it might ease the fire burning in her womb.

LIAM WAITED INSIDE Union Station, by the doors that led to the platform where his ma's train had arrived. He saw Duncan first, his step-father who, by all accounts was a good guy, but Liam still had a hard time getting used to the idea of his ma being married again. Ma walked alongside, at least nine inches shorter than Duncan, but a giant in her own right. She was the bravest woman Liam knew, at least until he'd met Emma.

Duncan shook Liam's hand. "We can go to a hotel," he said apologetically.

"If that were true, you wouldn't be here," Liam replied.

"And where did you go while you were recovering from your surgery?" Ma asked. "Did I not take you in? You're my son and it's your duty to take me in."

"Did I say you couldn't stay with me?" He leaned down and hugged his ma.

She shook a finger at him, then broke into a smile. "It's that good to see you."

"You, too, Ma. Come on. We can get a cab on Adams Street."

They rode the escalator up to street level and found a taxi. On the ride to his apartment, Liam told them about the relatives in Kinsale, about how once Moira had discovered who he was, she'd invited the McCormick relatives to meet him at the pub.

He saved the part about his father until they got to their destination.

They walked into his condo—investment property in case he got traded, and home while he lived in Chicago. For the time being, Liam had temporary quarters in the players' hotel in Rockford with the Mustangs. Until he was reassigned to the Cowboys, his ma and Duncan had the place to themselves. He showed them into the spare bedroom.

They regrouped in the living room. Ma and Duncan took a seat on the brown leather sofa.

"Can I get you something to drink?" Liam asked.

"I'm sure we can help ourselves," Ma replied. "You'll tell me the rest?"

Liam sat back. "Are you going to tell me what happened? What you saw?"

Her lips disappeared into a fine line. She smoothed her white hair with a shaky hand. He couldn't remember seeing his mother unsettled. Even before Da left them, she'd stood face to face with him despite the punishment she knew he'd mete.

"A face in the mirror," she said quietly. "When I turned, he wasn't there. A voice inside my head." She sat on the edge of the sofa. "It was Frank. Not my imagination."

"What did the family tell you about his death?" Liam asked.

"That he'd drown. I didn't ask for details, nor did they offer any." She made the sign of the cross.

"They said it might have been suicide, although he'd had quite a bit to drink and might not have known any better."

She stared at him, waiting for him to continue. Well, if his mother was confident the ghost wasn't her imagination, he might as well share the rest. She didn't blink an eye when he told the tale of the selkies, didn't twitch so much as a muscle when he told her he'd seen the man in the stands during the game. When he relayed the apparition on the uninhabited island, she merely nodded her head, and when he told her about the ghost in the training room, she settled against Duncan's arm.

They sat a few moments in uncomfortable silence.

"Did you know the story about the selkie?" Liam asked.

She waved a hand before her face and snorted. "Just like those McCormicks to excuse his behavior with a legend. Your da spoke of the selkies often enough. When we yet lived in Kinsale the seals were about him whenever he was near the water. They were always in the harbor looking for cast-offs or droppings from the fishermen's nets."

"I can't figure—," he cringed, "I thought maybe his spirit isn't at rest, or he doesn't know he's dead. Maybe by going to Ireland... maybe he was waiting for a member of the family— our family."

"Nonsense," his mother said.

"It seems I have brought him home if you've seen him, as well," Liam said. "Should I warn the rest of the family to expect a visitation from their father?"

"Best not," she said quietly. "Perhaps they'll be spared."

"I thought the same of you." Liam said. "That's why I haven't been to see you yet. That, and I've had appointments to keep here in the city."

She nodded. "I know the Mustangs lost. How did you fare—your knee?"

"Sore, but it's holding up so far. They sent a trainer from the Cowboys to check on me." He took a deep breath, his thoughts of Emma nowhere near those he should be having about a trainer. "I still have work to do before the knee's a hundred percent."

"Likely, it'll never get back to a hundred percent," Duncan added.

Duncan. The doctor.

Liam didn't need to be reminded that he'd never get back to 'original condition.' "As near as I can get."

"You're young and healthy," Duncan went on. "No reason you can't continue to play as long as you take care of yourself."

Liam was good and tired of doctors. He gritted his teeth, but smiled politely. "Have you had dinner? Are you hungry?"

Ma jumped from the couch and headed to the kitchen, opening the door of the stainless steel refrigerator.

She tsked. "You've nothing in here to eat."

"I've been away."

She put her hands on her hips. "You'll tell me you would have food otherwise?"

Liam fought a grin. "When I'm staying here, which I'm not while I'm with the development team. Eggs. Milk. The essentials. There might be fish in the freezer."

"What are we to eat, then?" she asked.

"There's a nice steakhouse around the corner."

"First thing tomorrow, I'm going to the grocery. You'll waste your entire fancy paycheck going out to eat every night."

"You know that's not true." Liam smiled at Duncan. "I don't have food in the house because I'm staying at the team hotel in Rockford, remember? I do cook for myself on occasion and even if my paycheck was as fancy as you envision, you know I have the sense not to fritter it away. I did learn something in college." He took hold of Ma's shoulders. "I talked to Kevin when I got back. And Amy. We could call Jared. He's a ghost hunter, isn't he? I'm not sure what to do about Da, but from what I've seen of him, I don't think he means us harm."

A tremor shook his mother's body, a reminder his father had already done more harm than any of them could ever repair.

"At least if you don't have food about, you likely don't have a lady friend living with you that I don't know about," Ma said, veering away from more discussion about Da.

He wanted to point out how Duncan had spent the night at Ma's not long after they'd met, but decided that might not be the prudent course. She needed reassurances, not judgments. "I paid attention. To every word you taught me about how to treat a lady, Ma." She smiled when he crossed his heart.

Ma reached up and patted his cheek. "I know you did. You and your brother, the same. I know the two of you aren't saints, but I'm that proud of you. You'll make some girl a fine husband one day, Liam McCormick."

Until Ma and Duncan went home, or to a hotel, he wasn't likely to get the chance to pursue his current option, a very appealing woman in the form of one Emma Parrish. Assuming he hadn't offended Emma past the point of ever speaking to him again.

Chapter 14

Emma finished taping a sixth player's ankle, patted his shoulder and watched him hop to his feet. Most of the team had found their way to the practice field. Ray followed to keep an eye on them. She had the training room to herself for five glorious minutes, enough time to prepare the ice bath before she rolled the Gatorade cart onto the field.

"Liam?" a quiet voice asked.

She wondered for a moment if she'd imagined it.

"Will he be strong enough to play again?"

"I'm not at liberty..." she began, turning to address whoever had found their way in, and then she stopped cold. A man stood beside the table she'd just wiped down, clutching a cloth hat in his hands. He had thick white hair and wore a vest over a Henley shirt, but that wasn't the oddest part of his appearance. He wasn't quite solid. As much as he looked like a person, the outline of the table was visible behind him. Every hair on her body electrified.

His mouth didn't move when he spoke, and his voice came from inside her head. "You are the lassie what treated him, are you not?"

A shiver went through Emma. "What do you want?"

"He's the one came to find me." The voice was deeper than Liam's.

She wasn't really talking to a ghost, was she? Emma cleared her throat. "Um, Mr. McCormick?"

He grinned Liam's grin, except with ghostly chipped teeth. "He'll be okay? My boy?"

"As long as he follows protocol," she found herself saying as a matter of routine, but the man asking the questions wasn't real. "Why are you here? How...?"

He winked, touched one finger to his nose and then pointed at her before he dissolved into nothingness.

Emma gasped and checked the trainer's room for anyone else—living or dead. No. She hadn't actually had a conversation with a dead man, had she? And yet he'd stood before her.

She could see through him.

She had a job to do. With a fortifying breath, she took hold of the drink cart and pushed it onto the field.

Ray stood with the college interns, assessing the players on the field. Emma pulled out her cell phone and dialed Liam to tell him about her encounter. The call went to voicemail, no surprise. He was likely on the practice field in Rockford.

"When you hear the beep, tell me what you want," his voice said.

As long as you tell me you want me.

A different kind of shiver went through her and she disconnected the call. He'd definitely gotten to her. If she took Portia's advice, she'd take her bite of the forbidden fruit and be done with it. The teams traveled in opposite directions, so she wouldn't have to worry about the awkward "how do we act at work" scenario. With the degree of separation—him being on the development team—sleeping with him wasn't a conflict of interest, was it? Or was Portia contaminating her thought processes?

It was a matter of time before she gave in. Sooner would be better than later, before he rejoined the Cowboys. If he rejoined theCowboys.

"Emma?" Ray stood beside her, giving her the 'trainer eye.' "You okay? You look pale."

Her heart was beating too fast and her skin was clammy. "Not feeling quite myself," she answered truthfully.

He took a step back. "Why don't you go home? Don't want to pass along anything to the boys."

"I'm okay." Home? Or a quick drive to Rockford? No, that would be a waste of time. Liam was in team housing there, sharing a suite with three other players. Not the place to go for what he'd proposed, and yet he'd said anywhere.

They'd find a place.

"Now you're flushed. Take the rest of the day off." Ray turned his back and rejoined the interns on the sidelines.

Emma nodded.

She was on the expressway to Rockford before the first doubts crept up. What was she doing? She wasn't usually so impulsive. Emma imagined all the conversations she might have with Liam in her head, from "I saw your father," to "All right, let's do this," to "Just checking on your progress. How's the knee?"

What was she doing?

Portia was right. Until Emma got this out of her system, she was going to be hopelessly distracted. Maybe she didn't do casual sex, but it wasn't too late to learn.

Why was Liam's father haunting her?

Emma was going to make herself crazy going over all the scenarios for the two hours it would take her to get to Rockford. She flipped on the radio, and at the same time, her Bluetooth told her she had a call.

Liam's sultry voice seeped through her like a warm cup of tea on a cold night. "I saw the missed call," he said. "Professional call or personal?"

She swallowed her nerves. "Personal."

"I like the sound of that, but you do know your timing isn't very good, don't you? My mother was one thing, but I have three roommates here in Rockford, unless you're inviting me over."

"Your father came to see me," she said. Not what she wanted to lead with, but it had to be said.

"Where?"

"In the training room."

'THIS THING' BETWEEN him and Emma was more than the apparent chemistry. Was she part of his father's hauntings? Liam didn't believe in coincidences as a rule, and if the ghost was showing up for Emma, he should invite her along on his expedition with Kevin.

"Liam?" she said. "I'm driving to Rockford now. It'll take me another hour to get there."

To see him? Another spark shot through him. Did he know Emma well enough to invite her to his mother's house? She was fearless, braver than he was. Then again, she didn't share all the bad memories associated with his father, memories born in that house despite all the good memories his mother had sought to replace them with.

Something about her drew him in—her fearlessness. She'd never be weepy or clingy.

"Get off at Edgarville. I'm meeting my brother at my mother's house."

"Ghost hunting?"

"Yeah. You okay with that?"

"What's the address?"

Liam gave it to her and checked the clock on his dashboard. His drive would be about forty-five minutes, and based on where she said she was, they should arrive within ten minutes of each other. As much as he wanted to talk more, to find out about her visitation from his father, he figured in person would be better, when he could see her face, the glimmer in her eyes.

He disconnected the call and thought about the Irish legend Emma had pursued. Why would she go in search of a mythical being? Yes, the selkies were supposed to be seducers, but they also represented empathy. Selkies sought to comfort, much the way the seals on the beach had comforted Liam.

According to the barman, the male selkies were called by the tears of a woman. What would make Emma cry?

She'd had a few beers and gotten wrapped up in the story, that's all.

Another call kept him from dwelling on the matter further. "Talk to me," he answered.

"Hey, little brother. Sorry to back out last minute…"

"Oh no you don't," he said to Kevin. "I'm not going in there without you."

"Something's up with Amy. Might be contractions, might be Braxton-Hicks, but we're going to the hospital."

"What's a Braxton-Hicks?" Liam asked.

"False labor," Kevin told him. "Listen, if you're going to hang around town, we can go later if this turns out to be nothing."

Liam wiped his face with his hand. "As it happens, one of my trainers asked to meet me and I told her to go to the house."

"The same one who saw Da in Ireland?"

"Yeah. Apparently, he appeared to her again."

Kevin's breath became a quiet whistle. "You going to be okay? I mean, he can't hurt you if he's dead, right?"

Liam hoped not, but with Emma there, his father would make an effort to control himself. "You go take care of Amy. Who's watching Chloe?"

"Kathleen."

All the years growing up, Kevin had been the one to protect them when Da got it into his head one of them had done something wrong. Kevin might have taken over the role of father figure after Da left, but he had his own life, his own family. They weren't kids anymore. "I got this. Call me later, and good luck. Tell Amy Uncle Yum is rooting for her."

Kevin chuckled. "Will do. Later."

It helped to know Emma was coming, but a shiver coursed through Liam.

He'd already seen the ghost. Nothing bad had happened. All he had to do was figure out why Da was haunting him— and why he was appearing to Emma.

Liam exited the expressway and wound his way into town. He stopped in front of the house—home, the place he'd grown up. Why did it feel like the Amityville Horror?

He wasn't going to let his father destroy the peace of mind his mother had so carefully cultivated. Liam steered into the driveway, got out of his car and slammed his door shut. "I'm not afraid of you anymore," he whispered. Liam walked to the back door, slotted his key and pushed the door open.

Chapter 15

Emma double checked the address she'd put into her phone. Yes, this was it. A paved walk led to the front door, with mulch-filled gardens waiting for spring flowers on either side. Windows peeked out from the roof, which wrapped around the second story. One car was parked in the driveway. Liam's?

When she mounted the porch steps, the front door swung open slowly.

"Liam?" She walked inside, expecting to see him, but there was no one in the small living room. The walls were painted a pale shade of yellow, and flowered curtains hung at the windows. Lace doilies protected dark wood tables. The kitchen appeared to be straight ahead, a big country kitchen, and an arched opening to her left showed a staircase to the second floor. On her right was another small room.

Where was Liam? "Hello?" she called again.

"Holy hell!" Liam gasped, appearing from the kitchen. "I didn't hear you come in."

Emma glanced over her shoulder, at the now closed door. "Your brother must have let me in. Someone opened the door."

Liam glanced at the front door. "Not my brother."

"Then who?"

Liam cocked an eyebrow, inviting her to take her best guess. The gesture sent a shiver up her spine.

"Are you sure it wasn't your brother?" she asked.

"He's not coming. He took his wife to the hospital."

"I hope nothing's wrong?"

He managed a smile. "They think she's in labor."

Emma glanced behind her. "Please tell me the door isn't a practical joke."

Liam shook his head and wrapped his arms around himself. "I wish it was that simple. You said you saw my da? In the training room?"

"He asked if you were going to be able to play again, or at least that's the way I understood it."

Liam rolled his eyes and returned to the kitchen. Emma followed, taking in the large room.

Liam ran the tap for a glass of water. "Something to drink?"

"No thanks." The fascia between the cupboards and the ceiling was stenciled with words—*Bricks and mortar make a house, but the laughter of children makes a home.* "You grew up here?"

He nodded.

"And your mother said she saw the ghost here?"

Liam drained the glass and set it in the sink. He leaned back, palms against the counter. "Why me? Why not my brother? Or one of my sisters? Why come back here, after all this time?"

"Are you the oldest?"

"No, I'm the youngest. Now."

Emma had a few questions of her own, like why his father's ghost was appearing to her. "There has to be a reason. Maybe it's connected to your trip to Ireland. Have you seen anything in the house?"

"No, but I've only been here a few minutes, and to be honest, I'm not eager to see him."

She reached for his hand. The contact flamed through her. How could a simple touch affect her so much? "How about you show me around? Give me a tour?"

"Are you afraid of *anything*?" he asked with a chuckle.

The question caught her off guard and she took a step back. "Sure. What should I be afraid of here?"

Liam managed a smile. "Nothing. Come on. We'll see if he shows up." He tugged her by the hand, through the living room to the room opposite the staircase. The walls had pine paneling and a sewing machine was set up in one corner. A desk was pushed against the wall and a well-worn recliner was nestled into another corner. More of the shiny, flowered curtains hung at the windows, more of the lace doilies protecting wood surfaces.

"This was his study. After he left, Ma made it into her sewing room." Liam hung back, didn't step inside the room. "When he came in here, we made ourselves scarce."

"Why?"

Liam faced her. "This is where he did most of his drinking."

The tone of Liam's voice explained a lot. Drinking was clearly a bad thing. He'd mentioned his father was a bad man. The picture of an abusive drunk took shape.

Emma took a step into the study and surveyed the room. It was cheery and welcoming. Whatever Liam's father had done, it seemed his mother had worked hard to undo the unpleasant memories. No shadows haunted the corners, no ghost seated at the desk.

Liam tugged her hand and led her across the room to the staircase. They walked up the narrow flight single file, to a hallway at the top. He hesitated, as if deciding which room to check first. She watched a host of emotions cross his face, and then he led her to a bedroom at the end of the hall.

"My ma's room."

A sleigh bed with a matching oak dresser and an oval standing mirror dominated the room. The curtains at the window looked to be lace. The room had an en suite bathroom and two closets.

"Your mother has good taste."

Liam shrugged. "They redecorated when Duncan moved in. The house used to have wallpaper everywhere, but they took it down and painted. She used to have a brass bed..." He turned his head.

More bad memories?

"Did she say where she saw the ghost?" Emma asked gently.

"The mirror." Liam stood before it—looking for the ghost?—before he tugged her down the hall.

"Bathroom," he said as they passed the next door. "Boys' room." He pointed to the door at the other end. "Girls' room."

Emma stopped at the boys' room. Twin beds, each with a nightstand. "Yours and your brother's?" she asked.

Again Liam hung back.

A football helmet rested on one of the nightstands. The other had a wax figure that looked like a seal beside a stack of books. She fought the urge to laugh. "A seal?"

"Coincidence," he said quietly. "Souvenir from the zoo." He pointed to one of the two tall dressers. "There are others."

She crossed to his dresser. A gorilla, an elephant, a panther. She glanced at the bed she assumed was his. The bed he'd slept in as a child. Liam continued to watch her from the doorway.

"I don't see any ghosts," she said, a break in her voice.

"Lots of ghosts," he replied. "None of them my da."

"Memories, you mean?"

He nodded.

As she crossed to the door, the look in his eyes was much like a lion watching its prey. His intensity reflected the same pull she felt, but she wasn't very good at this relationship stuff. Would he make the first move? Did he want her to make the first move? She glanced at his bed once more, right there, waiting for them.

Anywhere you want me.

Emma laced her hands with his, meeting his gaze. Her heart pounded. "Kiss me?" she whispered.

He bent down and slanted his mouth to hers, gently at first, until their tongues met. Need consumed her as the kiss grew more heated. She pulled him into the room, toward the twin bed she assumed to be his. Her hands fumbled with his belt, brushing against the bulge inside his pants. Liam inched down to kiss her neck, his hands roaming her body, massaging their way to her chest. A sigh escaped her lips and he pushed her onto the bed. She tugged on his zipper and the bulge became more pronounced, held in by the thin layer of his cotton briefs. Liam covered her with his lean body, sliding his hand inside her polo shirt and under her bra, his hips bucking against hers.

"Please tell me you have a condom in your nightstand," she whispered, the haze of lust making it difficult to breathe.

The kisses grew feather-light as Liam pulled away. He sat on the edge of the bed and ran a hand through his hair. "Not here."

Not here? Emma glanced around the room. Had the ghost appeared? "Excuse me?" she asked, reaching for him once more.

He caught her wandering hand. "Not here." He tucked himself in and refastened his pants.

"You're kidding, right? Aren't you the one who said anywhere I want you, as long as I want you?" She reached for the bottom of her polo to pull the shirt over her head. "I want you."

He stopped her from taking off her shirt. "To be continued, but not here."

She tilted her head, frustration replacing lust.

"Some lessons can't be unlearned," he said. "My mother's house. My mother's rules. I also have curfew. I have to get back to Rockford. There's a game tomorrow, and if I'm late, they won't let me play."

Was he serious?

He leaned over and kissed her again, his eyes dark. "To be continued," he said in a low, seductive voice. "If you can understand."

She sat back, aching for release. Needing that release. "You might have said something sooner, like before you pinned me to the bed."

He chuckled. "Technically, girls aren't even allowed in the boys' room, and vice versa with the girls' room. Call it a mental block. Even though Ma isn't here, she made sure we knew what was and wasn't acceptable."

It made sense. "How much time do you have before you have to get back?" she asked.

"A couple of hours. We can find a room somewhere in town."

The absurdity of paying for a bed when they were sitting on one made Emma laugh. "You're something else, Liam McCormick."

"Likewise," he replied. "I've never met anyone like you. There's so much..."

The hardwood floor in the hall creaked and Liam jumped to his feet.

FOR ALL THE TIMES DA had beaten him for no good reason, surely Liam had it coming to him this time. For starters, he had a girl in his room.

But Da was dead.

Liam stepped into the hall and glanced around. No sign of the ghost.

"Do you see anything?" Emma asked at his elbow.

"No, but I'd bet he'll be waiting in his study to reinforce the 'no girls upstairs' rule."

Emma slid her hand into his once more. "He can't hurt you anymore."

His father had never stopped hurting them. All of them. They'd never forget the abuse.

Liam marched down the stairs, to the study. Sure enough, the ghost sat behind the desk.

"You've made something of yourself, then, have you?" Da said, his voice a hollow echo inside Liam's head.

Liam drew a deep breath. He was done being afraid. "What do you want?"

The ghost smiled. "I'm that proud of you, Liam. Doing the family proud. Showing the world the McCormicks are worth something." He leaned over the desk.

The words Liam held back all his life spewed out. "Ma doesn't deserve this, nor do any of the rest of us. What do you want from me?" Liam asked again. "Why are you here?"

"But you came to find me, did you not?" The ghost wavered in the dim light.

Did he?

Liam clenched his teeth. "If that's what you think, then I guess I found you, so you can go now. There's nothing more to be said. Nothing more to be done."

The ghost rose from behind the desk. "That's where you're wrong, boy." He vanished before the sound of his voice finished echoing in Liam's head.

Liam stood there for a moment, the familiar taste of fear in his mouth, and yet he'd spoken his mind to the bastard and not suffered because of it.

Emma's voice was soft beside him. "You okay?"

No. Not even a little. No one knew what he and his siblings had suffered at the hands of their father. Making friends had been difficult when they were kids, and they hadn't invited friends over. He was embarrassed she'd witnessed the confrontation, angry his father had made him look foolish once again.

"I have to get back," he said without looking at her.

Chapter 16

When she got to her apartment, Emma set her purse on the counter that separated the kitchen from the living area.

One minute Liam had said he had a couple of hours, and the next he had to go. Apparently, he'd changed his mind.

He'd turned down the intern. Ray didn't believe Liam was the type to take advantage, and today she'd seen for herself what kind of man Liam was. He respected his mother, as demonstrated by his unwillingness to break the rules he'd grown up with. He had a moral compass, in spite of the proposition he'd made to Emma.

Which made him that much more attractive.

Had she come on too strong?

Emma opened the refrigerator and took out a bottle of water and a salad. She pulled a bar stool up to the counter, retrieved a fork and sat down to eat.

Problem number one. The look on Liam's face when they'd parted wasn't the *can I call you* face. He'd had a *what the heck was I thinking* face. One minute he'd been proposing a hotel room, and the next he was running for the hills. Because of the ghost? Or because he'd come to his senses and the man of the moral compass realized this thing between them was only lust?

Lust which still burned inside Emma, hot and bright, more intense than she'd felt for any other man.

Projection. That's what it was. She thought of him as an Irish legend come to life.

Nothing a good workout wouldn't relieve. She'd finish her dinner and go down to the gym, get rid of the excess adrenalin on the treadmill, lift a few weights.

Emma wasn't a groupie and she wasn't going to throw herself at Liam again, especially after he'd changed his mind so quickly.

For a few moments, she'd remembered what it was like to be loved.

No, not love. Liam certainly had a way about him, but he didn't love her. He'd made his intentions clear.

And then changed his mind.

Emma pushed her salad away. She was overthinking. The Irish folktales had imprinted in her mind in a moment of weakness. He was a mortal man, complete with the needs and wants of a mortal man. He also had a demanding job that required his full attention if he expected to fully recover from his injury.

Another trait she'd seen in him was his drive to succeed. In spite of a useless physical therapist, he'd worked hard to regain his strength, but he wasn't done yet. Now that he'd been given the proper support system, he didn't need a hot and bothered trainer distracting him.

She might have acted impulsively today, but she'd control herself better in the future. No more unscheduled trips to Rockford.

She'd find another outlet for her excess energy.

Emma put her salad back in the refrigerator, changed into a t-shirt and a pair of shorts and laced up her trainers. She grabbed her phone and her keys and headed down to the gym with her bottle of water.

Half a dozen other building tenants were in the gym when she arrived, the same nameless faces she usually saw. She headed for the treadmill, set a program on the machine and tucked in her earbuds.

The exercise was like meditation, nothing but the music and the feel of her muscles. When the belt slowed half an hour later, she'd reached a state of Zen, peace with the world around her.

"You look like you were running away from something," the guy beside her said.

"Not very easy to do when you're on a treadmill," she joked. He was a regular in the gym. Nice looking. They'd exchanged smiles in the elevator although they'd never spoken. Had he been watching her?

"You ever run outside?" he asked.

"My job keeps me pretty busy. I don't get much chance to run during the day and I don't want to run outside at night. You never know what kind of people you might encounter in the city."

"As long as you're not alone, you shouldn't get into too much trouble. I'll run with you." He held out a hand. "Tyson Maxwell."

She shook his hand. "Emma Parrish, and thanks, but it's easier to come to the gym most of the time."

"Can I buy you dinner sometime? Unless you have a special someone who might object."

Emma took a second look. Tyson appeared to be a few years older than she was. Maybe thirty. His hair was on the thinning side with comb tracks, but he had a friendly face and warm brown eyes. He wasn't dressed to show off his muscles, but his calves were cut like those of a runner and he had some bulk around his shoulders. A month ago, she might have accepted.

Until that moment she didn't realize she was going to turn him down. "Another time," she said. "I'm..." what was she? The excuse seemed like a cop out, but she was taking it. "Sort of seeing someone."

"Lucky guy. If you decide you're sort of not seeing him, don't be afraid to cash in a raincheck."

"What if you're seeing someone by then?" she asked.

"Then it'll be my turn to take the raincheck, but something tells me you'd be worth waiting for."

Emma took a step back. Men didn't flirt with her. She didn't seek them out, and now, within a short time span, she had two men who wanted to date her? Check that. Liam hadn't mentioned a date, he'd only mentioned sex—well, not sex precisely, but that was definitely the inference, and Liam came with a host of complications. She reconsidered Tyson's invitation.

"Dinner?" she asked.

Tyson nodded.

She wasn't seeing Liam McCormick. In fact, once she'd taken him up on his offer, he'd run away. A date with another man might straighten out her wayward thoughts, get her to stop looking for a mythical selkie and bring her back to the real world. "Tomorrow night?"

Tyson smiled. "Sounds perfect."

They exchanged phone numbers and Emma headed to her condo. Life had a funny way of working things out.

LIAM SHOULD HAVE GONE to Rockford, should be working with Yosh on rehab. He should be preparing for the game tomorrow, assuming he'd get the promised playing time. He knew every nuance about the teams the Cowboys played, but not much about the Mustangs' competition.

Yosh had told him to limit his minutes on the field until he was stronger. He was strong enough, and he was the only one on the Mustangs who'd played on a big league team.

He'd get his minutes. He was tired of proving to everyone how hard he worked.

He was tired of putting in the work. For what? A game?

Right now family trumped soccer. He drove to the hospital, found a spot in the parking deck and phoned Kevin. "Amy okay?" he asked when Kevin answered.

"Looks like the real thing," Kevin told him. "We're going to be here a while."

"Where does an uncle go to wait?" Liam asked.

"You're here? At the hospital?"

"I was in town anyway. You need anything?"

Kevin gave him directions and asked Liam to bring a coke.

Five minutes later, Liam registered with the nurse, got a nametag, and found the birthing room. He stuck his head in the door. Kevin stood beside Amy, stroking her hair while she groaned.

Liam backed out.

He shouldn't have come. Amy looked like she was in a boatload of pain.

Kevin opened the door a minute later. "She's better now. For a few minutes."

Liam handed his brother the coke. "I can wait in the waiting room."

Kevin clapped Liam on the back. "I need to be with my wife, but it's good to know you're here."

Liam nodded.

"Come in for minute before you disappear. I'm sure she'd like to see you."

Liam backed away. "I don't know."

Kevin cocked his head. "C'mon. Say hello. Then you can leave."

Liam bowed his head and followed Kevin into the room. "Hey, Ame. Anything I can do for you?"

She gave him a weak smile. "Not unless you can coax this baby out."

She winced again and Kevin rushed to her side, holding her hand. A beeping monitor beside the bed sped up and Liam backed away. Amy panted measured breaths. Kevin held her hand and breathed with her. Within moments, she relaxed again.

"Pretty sure if I stay in here, I'm never going to want kids of my own. You'll excuse me?" Liam said.

Amy turned her head, exhaustion on her face. "Can you let everyone know what's going on? And make sure Kathleen is okay to watch Chloe until Kevin can pick her up?"

Liam nodded.

"You'd better let Ma know, too," Kevin said. "Did you stop by the house?"

Liam nodded again. "We can talk about that later."

Kevin straightened. "You okay?"

Liam chuckled. "Compared to this? Yeah. I'm fine. I'll be in the waiting room if you need anything, calling the family."

He backed out and wiped his forehead with his hand. He knew how these things went, how babies were born, but seeing Amy struggling with labor pains scared the life out of him.

No wonder Ma had taught them to respect women. He had a whole lot of respect for them right now.

Liam called his sister Kathleen first. She, in turn, offered to call the rest of the family, including Amy's mother, which left Liam with too much time on his hands and too many things to think about.

The last time he'd been in a hospital had been for his ACL surgery. Pain, but nothing like what Amy was going through, he was sure. How were women so brave?

Like Emma. She hadn't flinched when Cody threatened her. What the hell was wrong with Cody for imposing himself on her that way? Liam's anger flared, and yet, before he'd had a chance to react to Cody's inappropriate advances, Emma had flattened him. Next to Emma, Liam was a coward.

Was he any better than Cody, propositioning her the way he had?

And then there was the ghost. His father hadn't approved of a single thing any of them did, Liam and his siblings. They'd served as the nearest punching bag, the closest outlet for his rage.

Liam's phone rang with a call from Coach Clarence. "McCormick," he answered.

"Where are you?"

"At the hospital. My brother and his wife are having a baby." "Any reason you need to stay there?"

Liam's anger grew hotter. "Because he's family?"

"Yosh said you didn't show up for therapy with him."

Liam massaged his forehead. "Lost track of that in all the excitement."

"Gonna cost you minutes in the game," Coach told him.

Right now, he didn't care. In fact, he was surprised to find he didn't care if he played tomorrow at all. "I understand," he replied.

"I'm rescheduling you for first thing tomorrow morning. Be in the training room at seven a.m. and I'll reconsider those minutes."

Liam scowled. "Yes, sir."

"And McCormick—congratulations to your brother and his wife."

Liam disconnected the call and rose to his feet, pacing the small waiting room. He glanced at the clock and sat again, pulling out his cell phone and scrolling through his emails. How long did this baby stuff take?

Slouching into the chair, he opened a game and ran through his lives before he tucked his phone into his pocket. Another glance at the clock showed he'd killed a little more than an hour. What was going on in there?

"A grandson," a voice whispered inside his head.

Liam jumped to his feet, startled. "Why don't you go back where you came from? We were fine without you."

Kevin came out a moment later, a stupid smile on his face. "A boy," he said.

Liam checked the room for the ghost—nothing.

Kevin hugged Liam, and Liam absently hugged him back.

"Congrats," Liam murmured. "Everybody okay?"

Kevin broke away and swiped at teary eyes. "Yeah. She's beautiful. He's beautiful. It went so fast. They said the second one comes faster."

Liam smiled. "And the third. And the fourth. And the fifth."

Kevin laughed. "One at a time, huh?"

"Still going with Randall?"

"Randall Flynn McCormick."

Liam hugged Kevin again. "You need anything before I go?"

Kevin shook a finger at him. "One day..." He sniffled, "One day you're going to have babies, too."

"Cart before the horse." Liam laughed. "After what I saw—and that wasn't even the worst of it—I'm in no hurry."

Kevin ruffled Liam's hair. "Don't you have a game to play?"

"Yeah, tomorrow. I'm already in trouble for missing PT. I'll talk to you later?"

"Thanks for hanging around."

Liam scanned the waiting room one more time. Why had Da disappeared when Kevin arrived?

Chapter 17

While Emma wrapped his ankle, Javier Kruse chattered away about useless doctors who threatened to sideline him, but he knew he'd be fine, as long as he had trainers like Emma looking out for him. She was half paying attention, smiling at the appropriate times and getting him ready for practice. He was the last of the players to take the field, and when the training room was empty, she put away her supplies and headed for the sink to fill the water jug.

The quiet had her considering recent choices. Emma had done two of the most impulsive things she'd ever done. She blamed Portia for her spur of the moment trip to Rockford, although deep down she knew that wasn't fair. Portia might have made it sound more appealing, but Emma had gone after Liam on her own.

Liam hadn't followed through. He hadn't called. That was for the best. She had no business propositioning, or accepting a proposition, from one of the athletes she worked with, even if they didn't currently work together directly.

But her date with Tyson? She'd noticed him a time or two in the gym. Other than that, she didn't know the man. What had she been thinking, accepting a date after one brief conversation?

"Emma." Ray stood in the training room doorway. "Got a call from Yosh Tanaka."

Which likely meant something about Liam, but she was done with Liam McCormick. Emma folded her arms and faced Ray, waiting.

"McCormick missed PT yesterday."

"And you're telling me, why?"

Ray's forehead creased. Yeah, she knew she sounded like she didn't care. Her ego was bruised, and she needed a couple of days to get over it.

"They rescheduled him this morning, and Yosh said he thought something had changed in McCormick's attitude. Like he's given up."

She heaved an impatient sigh. "Again, you're telling me, why?"

One corner of Ray's mouth turned up in a half-grin. "Yosh got the feeling McCormick might be sweet on you. He thinks you can find out what's going on with him."

Heat rose up Emma's neck.

Ray held up his palms. "Not sweet like that intern, but you know how it is. Half of these apes see a pretty face and they forget you're there to assess their injuries."

"No," she said. "He was fully aware of why I was sent to Ireland. Sweet isn't the word I'd use."

"He give you trouble?" Ray asked.

Emma scowled. "No."

"The boys upstairs are waiting for Yosh to write his report on McCormick's progress. This isn't going to look good. He's trying to give the guy a break, thinking you could talk to him, or at least observe and give your take."

"When?" Emma set her hands on her hips.

"They have a game tonight. Yosh will be expected to report tomorrow." He raised his eyebrows. "Can you go?"

Emma groaned. "Can't you send one of the interns?"

"You've already established a relationship with McCormick."

Relationship. In the sense they had been working together, as far as Ray knew, but it had become so much more complicated. "I have a..." she started to tell him about her date, but he'd given her the perfect excuse to break it. "I can go."

Ray gave her a wink. "Excellent. You should have plenty of time to get there after practice."

After they'd gotten the aching muscles into ice baths and unwrapped wobbly joints.

"See you on the field," Ray called as he headed through the tunnel.

"Yeah," she muttered.

With the drink cart loaded, Emma took an extra minute to call Tyson.

"Hey," she said when he answered. "Turns out I have to work tonight. Sorry. I'm going to have to take a raincheck after all."

"What do you do?" he asked. "I was sort of saving that for dinner conversation, but since it came up..."

"I'm an athletic trainer with the Stockyard Cowboys."

"The soccer team? They don't have a game tonight, do they?"

He followed soccer? "No, but they're sending me out to Rockford to watch the D-league game. One of the Cowboys' players is getting back up to speed with them."

"Liam McCormick."

So he did follow soccer. "Yes."

"I'd love to go. I'm a big soccer fan. If you wouldn't mind the company. Are you allowed to bring a guest? Can I go into the locker room?"

So much for backing out of her date. She thought quickly. "As long as you're escorted by someone associated with the team." Emma exhaled slowly. "If you really want to go."

"I can meet you in the lobby at home, if that's okay. Or I can meet you. What time should I be ready?"

She gave him a time and wheeled the water cart onto the field. The soccer game should provide distraction if things went badly, but that was still a lot of time in the car together, either for awkward conversation or awkward silence. Why was she being so negative? It might be good get-to-know-you conversation. If nothing else, they could talk about soccer.

Time enough to worry about the rest later. After practice.

LIAM DID EVERYTHING he was supposed to. He went to PT at seven a.m. He did drills with the Mustangs. He'd showed up at call time for the game and went through the prescribed warm-ups for his knee. So why was Yosh asking him what was wrong?

"Pain?" Yosh asked.

He was sick to death of the 1-10 scale. "No." He'd write it off as Yosh being overly cautious with Liam's knee.

Liam sensed the change in the locker room. Emma? Was she back to check up on him? He fisted his hands and turned around.

She was dressed in typical trainer fashion, khakis and a polo with the team logo, but she wasn't alone.

Emma introduced the man she was with to the team. Who was this guy? He was built like a bodyguard. Emma didn't need a bodyguard. She was more than capable of taking care of herself. Stud service?

A new flash of irritation ran through Liam.

When the stud wasn't shaking hands, he put a proprietary arm across Emma's shoulders. His temper tweaked, Liam returned to lacing his cleats.

Her baby powder scent alerted him she was close before he heard her voice.

"This is Liam McCormick," she introduced, coming up behind him. "Tyson Maxwell."

Liam rose to his feet, forcing a smile and extending his hand as he turned around. He looked at Emma. "Business or pleasure this evening?" he asked.

Her cheeks pinked. "A little of both."

"Nice to meet you," the stud said. "I'm a Cowboys fan. Hope you're back on the team soon. I hear you're close to returning?"

"That's the game plan."

"How are you feeling today?" Emma asked.

Liam shot a glance at the man beside her.

Her tongue darted out to wet her lips. "Pain? Mental roadblocks? Anything that might get in the way during the game tonight?"

"Isn't that doctor-patient privilege?" he asked, cocking his head toward her *friend*.

Emma waved Yosh over. "Would you mind escorting my guest for a few minutes while I have a chat with McCormick?" she asked.

Yosh nodded and Emma grabbed Liam by the arm, pulling him into the trainer's office and shutting the door.

"Now you have more privacy," she said. "What's going on?"

Liam took a step closer, into her personal space. Her pupils dilated and telltale points poked against her polo. He allowed himself a satisfied smile and lowered his face to hers, his lips an inch away. "We have unfinished business."

Her lips parted, her breathing ragged. "I was under the impression you'd changed your mind."

He kissed her then, drawn into the haze she cast over him.

She took a step back, eyes flashing. "I don't know what game you're playing with me..."

He didn't either, except it wasn't a game. "Who's the stud?" he asked.

Her nostrils flared and she raised her chin. "Can we focus on what's going on with you?"

"Then he is your date?"

"Liam, I'm here because Yosh thinks you're dialing it in. He doesn't feel the effort. You want to tell me what's going on?"

Avoidance. As good as a confirmation. "I don't want to discuss my knee. I've already told anyone who'd listen I'm fine."

"Any more visits from your father?"

Liam stared at her. He didn't want to talk. He wanted to get lost in how she made him feel, but he couldn't. Especially if she'd already moved on to the next guy. "I have a game to get to."

"Liam," she called after him as he stormed from the trainer's office.

He joined the team in the locker room. Emma's stud took his place beside her, arm around her waist.

As the team jogged onto the field, Cody angled up beside Liam. "Thought you and the lady had an arrangement," he said.

"What made you think that?"

"I have eyes."

"Maybe you need glasses."

Cody shot a glance over his shoulder. "Lots of things can happen on the sidelines. Players have a tendency to drop their water. Would be a shame to ruin those soft, leather shoes of his. Or, you know, sometimes when a player is running to warm up, he might not be looking where he's going."

Liam fought a grin. "Yeah, but the guy looks like he could take care of himself."

Cody held up his hands. "Just sayin'. You're one of us until you're not. I'm sure the guys would be happy to help you out."

Liam patted Cody's shoulder. "Appreciate it, but don't waste your time. She's not mine." No, Emma was her own person, which was one of the things he admired about her.

Too bad she didn't like him quite as much.

Chapter 18

Tyson chattered throughout the drive to the city after the game. Emma smiled and nodded at the appropriate times, but her thoughts strayed to Liam, about the way he'd kissed her—again.

When Tyson kissed her goodnight, there was no spark. Not like the fireworks she felt with Liam. They agreed they'd see each other in the gym, but she wasn't ready to make a second date.

Alone in her apartment, she plopped onto her sofa and used her coffee table for a footrest while she analyzed what was different about Liam.

In Ireland, he'd played like the devil himself was after him. Tonight, he'd missed tackles. Made stupid plays. Been distracted while the opposition charged the goal. Yosh's assessment seemed accurate. Something was off with Liam. Was he afraid he'd re-injure himself?

At the end of the game, Yosh had said he'd report Liam as not ready to rejoin the Cowboys, and leave it at that.

Checking Liam's status was part of her job. He knew that. His refusal to respond to Emma's questions indicated a deeper problem. She'd mentioned a sports psychologist to Yosh since Liam had been so irritable.

The longer she sat there, the more irritated she got. Liam had told her he'd worked too hard to earn his spot on the team to quit, and yet that's exactly what he looked like he was doing—quitting.

"It's my job to find out what's wrong," she told herself as she pulled out her cell phone.

"Why are you calling me? Don't you have a date?" Liam said when he answered.

"What the hell is wrong with you?" she asked.

His sharp intake of air let her know she'd surprised him. He chuckled. "Can you be more specific?"

She smirked. He'd thrown a trainer question back at her.

"Are you afraid of re-injury?" she asked.

"No."

"Are you done playing soccer?"

"No."

Emma huffed. "You played like crap out there tonight. Why?"

"I did everything I was supposed to. Showed up everywhere they told me."

"Quit being so defensive. I'm trying to do my job here."

"If you were working, why did you bring a date?" he shot back.

"I couldn't get rid of him," she responded before she considered her words. Emma held her forehead and took a breath. "It was a first date. I told him I had to work, but he asked if he could come along—what was I supposed to say?"

"No?"

"Why do you care if I was on a date?" she asked, the rise in her blood pressure producing spots in her vision. "Aren't you the same mister-anywhere-you-want who changed his mind?"

He was quiet for a moment, which gave her time to regret speaking in anger. She was supposed to be a professional, not a groupie who'd been turned down.

"That was rude of me. I want more than that from you," he said quietly.

Her heart pinged in harmony with his statement, but she wasn't going to get tangled in his strings again.

"I should have asked you out instead of propositioning you," he went on. "Emma, can I buy you dinner?"

Every pore in her body cried yes, but she struggled to speak.

"But I don't want to talk about my knee," he added.

"Then what would we talk about?"

"My nephew? My brother and his wife had a baby. Or I could tell you how beautiful your eyes are."

A date? Her heart stuttered. "When?"

"All the time."

"All the time?" She shook her head to follow the conversation.

"Your eyes are beautiful all the time." He sighed. "This probably isn't going to work. I do a lot of traveling. So do you. We're two hours apart while I'm on the Mustangs, and Yosh told me he thinks I need more time to get strong. He said you agreed."

She laughed. "Are you trying to sweet talk me so I'll add my stamp of approval to your release to the Cowboys?"

"I don't know what I'm doing."

That statement she believed. Heaven help her, she wanted to see him again, and they didn't have many opportunities. "When I asked when, I meant when do you want to buy me dinner."

"I know."

She chuckled. "What time does the team practice tomorrow? The Mustangs?"

"Morning drills, afternoon team meeting."

"So if I come out after work tomorrow?"

"Emma..."

"Unless you've changed your mind again," she rambled. "Although dinner isn't quite the same as groping at your mother's."

"I can meet you in the city," he said. "And speaking of my mother, she's still at my place, so I can't invite you over. You should be safe enough from more groping. Just dinner."

Except for her place, but she wasn't going to tell him that. He sounded exposed. Beaten. "There's a steakhouse on South Michigan Avenue," she said.

"I know the one."

"Then I'll see you there. Tomorrow night." She hung up before she said anything else stupid, and then noticed she had a voicemail.

"Hey, it's Portia," the message said. "Checking to see how your date with the gym rat went. Call me tonight, unless you're *busy*, in which case I'll talk to you tomorrow."

Emma heard the understood "unless the date goes all night" in Portia's voice. She wasn't that quick to jump into bed, was she? At least with most men.

She wanted to jump into bed with Liam, though.

Emma called Portia. "Busy?" she asked.

"You're not?" Portia asked. "And you know what I mean by busy."

"You know it was a first date," Emma said.

"And you're calling me. That means it didn't go well."

Emma walked into the bedroom and sat on her bed. "It went fine, or at least as fine as a date can go while you're also working."

"A second date in the offing?"

"I don't think so." Emma stared at her reflection in the mirror. "He was nice and all, but there's something about Liam. I can't seem to get away from him, you know?"

"I don't know. Do tell."

Emma bounced to her feet to pace. "I don't know either. But I'm going to find out. I'm going to dinner with Liam tomorrow night."

"Tomorrow's Thursday? Hey, I'll have your dress back from the cleaners tomorrow. I can bring it by Friday and you can tell me about your hot soccer stud."

Emma walked into her closet and opened the top drawer in her three-drawer dresser. The one where she kept her fancy undies. "Yeah, okay. But Portia, don't stop by too early, okay?"

Portia laughed. "I'll call first."

"You do that." She disconnected the call and stared down a lacy red thong and red satin bra she'd never worn—gag gifts from Portia. Why did thoughts of Liam make her want to show those undies off?

———⁓☙⁓———

LIAM GLANCED AROUND the steakhouse. The hostess approached him and crooked a finger.

"Your guest has already arrived," she told him.

He didn't have to ask how she knew who he was. Hazards of the job. With a little luck, he and Emma would have enough privacy to talk for a while.

The guys on the Cowboys called Liam "The Virgin" because he didn't chase after the women who draped themselves on the players while they were on the road. He wasn't a virgin, but he liked to think he was discriminating. His mother had tried to teach him and his siblings morals, sometimes painting graphic pictures for Kevin and him about the trouble they could get into if they didn't treat the women they dated with respect.

He'd tried to make that clear to Emma when they'd visited Ma's house, that he did have some principles. How could she have interpreted that as changing his mind?

At the ripe old age of twenty-three, Liam had slept with two women in his life. He knew his count was below average, especially for a professional soccer player, but he wasn't interested in a quick tumble. He wanted a connection with his partners, wanted to know something about them.

He didn't know much about Emma, other than she was a sucker for a fairy tale, but the connection was definitely there. They needed to slow this truck up and not let it run out of control the way it had at Ma's.

Liam almost didn't recognize Emma as he approached the table. She'd tamed her hair so that it hung straight rather than in tousled tufts standing up on her head. She wore blue linen pants and a matching print blouse, not the polo and khakis he was used to seeing her wear. She offered a cheek, which he kissed, before he sat down.

"Why am I so nervous?" he asked, picking up the menu.

"Because you're afraid I'm going to throw you to the floor?" she asked, a mischievous look on her face.

So much for taking things slow. He did know something about Emma.

She held up her hands and bowed her head. "My bad. I take it back. How's the nephew?"

"Take what back?" he asked.

She shook her head. "I forgot how much you like when I talk tough. You gave me *that look* again."

He wanted to give her more than a look. "Nephew's great. My brother is over the moon."

"Does he have other kids?"

"One. A daughter." Liam smiled, thinking of Chloe and her inability to pronounce his name.

"You come from a big family?"

"There were five of us."

"Were? Oh, yeah, you told me your sister died. I'm sorry." She leaned over the table. "That must have been hard."

"What about you? Big family?"

She played with the necklace at her throat. "Military brat. My dad died when I was eleven, so it was just my mom and me."

That explained her toughness. "Where does your mom live?"

"San Francisco."

"That where you're from?"

"No."

Liam creased his brow. Her short answers indicated she didn't want to talk about it.

The waiter arrived to take their orders. When he left, Liam shook his napkin.

"Okay, let's see what other first date questions we can get out of the way," he said.

"Do we have to?" she asked.

"Then what do you propose we talk about?"

She narrowed her eyes. "I could reference the last time we quote-unquote went out for coffee, ask why you changed your mind, but I think I'll venture into safer waters. Are you worried you won't be able to play at the same level you were playing before the injury?"

"No shop talk. And for the record, I didn't change my mind," he said carefully. "Maybe you don't share the same moral compass I do."

Her eyes widened and her mouth tightened. Probably not the right thing to say.

He held up a hand before she could protest. "I know, I know. I'm the one who said anywhere."

"Except your mother's house."

"You can't understand that?"

"I can." She stared him down. "Do you think I do that with every man I meet?"

"Didn't take you long to bring another guy to the Mustangs game." He nodded to the necklace she'd been playing with. "He give you that?"

"No. It was a gift from my father. Are you giving up on soccer?"

She'd switched to professional mode, increasing the distance between them. "This was a bad idea," he said.

"You're the one who suggested dinner."

He held her gaze, not willing to let her off the hook. Not yet. Why was she so irritated? "What do you want to talk about? My post-soccer options?"

She raised her eyebrows, inviting him to continue.

He squirmed in his seat. "Most guys get ten years in the league. That gives me at least eight more." He looked away, checking the kitchen for a server carrying their food.

Emma reached across the table for his hand. "Something's changed in you. Last time I asked you that question, you told me you'd worked too hard to walk away. That fire's gone. I can see by the way you played last night. What happened?"

"Maybe I'm finally facing reality."

She sputtered. "You play better at eighty percent than most guys play at a hundred."

Now he was annoyed. "What if I don't want to play anymore?"

She backed away. "Is that true?"

Would she still like him if he wasn't a professional athlete?

This was Emma. If she wanted a professional athlete, she was surrounded by them every day, athletes who wouldn't hesitate to finish what Liam had chosen not to. What he still wanted to do. Especially with her looking gorgeous and out of uniform. He might not have paid attention to her when he was with the Cowboys, but why would he? Until the ACL tear, he'd have very little interaction with the trainers, and more often than not, he'd worked with Ray.

Since working with her, he'd noticed the looks the guys in the training room gave her. If she took the time to flirt with any of them, she'd have her choice of professional athletes to date—or do other things with.

She'd chosen him.

"Now what?" she asked.

"What?" he said, his voice coming from somewhere far away.

"You went from looking like you were ready to jump off a cliff to *that look* again. Honestly. Maybe I'm misreading *that look*, but it's the kind that would melt any woman into a puddle at your feet. Explain to me why the thought of me beating you up triggers it."

The waiter saved him again, imposing silence while he set their food on the table. "Can I get you anything else?"

A room? Why couldn't Liam get images of Emma beneath him, calling his name, out of his head?

"We're fine, thanks," Liam said. He glanced at Emma and she looked away. "What?" he asked.

"Will you quit asking me what?"

"Emma, talk to me."

She scowled. "It's *that look* again. I'm going to need to know exactly what you're thinking."

Liam picked up his fork. "You are strong and capable and independent, and I find those very attractive traits. You also smell like baby powder, innocent and clean. Have I mentioned I like your hair like that? I know I was crass that day in

Starbucks, but I can't say I've ever been so attracted to a woman before."

She blinked several times, studying her food. "Ever?"

"Ever."

She worried her bottom lip and he wanted to tug it between his teeth, to kiss her senseless and to hell with wasting more time. He knew everything he needed to know about Emma Parrish.

He needed safe topics.

"So my Ma is still at my place here in the city. I'm not sure how to convince her to go home, mostly because I don't know how to get rid of the ghost on my own. My brother-in-law..."

"We can go to my place," she said quietly, pushing her food around the plate.

He hadn't been looking for an invitation, but he was on board with that idea. Liam rose from his seat and held out a hand to help her up.

Emma giggled. "After we've eaten, hotshot."

He sat once more, praying she wouldn't rescind her offer.

Chapter 19

No pressure. Emma could make it through dinner without freaking out.

Liam appeared to be ready to leave the restaurant and go straight to her apartment. She might have thought she wanted that, too, but her trembling hands said otherwise. *You don't plan the first time*, and this was why. Too much time to think.

Had he actually said she had no moral compass? He thought she was a slut, and what did she do? She invited him to her place. There was the proof.

Liam carved into his steak and Emma forked off a piece of her fish. She didn't have to talk as long as she was eating. Working to find her inner Zen, she closed her eyes and tuned into the piped-in music. Muzak, instrumental. A classical arrangement of *Eleanor Rigby*. Wasn't the song about lonely people?

She was *not* lonely.

The song ended and she breathed a mental sigh of relief, until Liam started humming along with the new song.

"Danny Boy?" she asked.

Liam looked up from his plate and stopped with the fork halfway to his mouth. "What?"

"You are humming, aren't you?"

"I wasn't paying attention." He set his fork on his plate, raised his head and listened, then wiped his mouth and sang along—quietly, in a rich, tenor voice. His dark, soulful eyes held Emma's gaze while she listened, enraptured.

Who said sirens from the sea had to be women? Emma was right back to believing Liam was a selkie. Why else would she be so hypnotized by his charms?

When the song finished, the diners at the two closest tables clapped. Liam smiled and nodded to acknowledge them.

"The tune is Londonderry Air," he said. "Something we made many jokes about growing up, making sure to pronounce it London derriere."

"Where did you learn to sing like that?" she asked.

"As cliché as this might sound, Ma played the Irish Rovers for us to teach us the old folk tunes."

Emma slid her plate to one side and leaned on the table. "You could sell tickets. People would pay to listen to you sing."

"You telling me I'm washed up as a soccer player?" The crinkles at the corners of his eyes told her he was teasing.

"You know that's not what I meant." Why did he have to be so darn likeable? "In spite of the hardships you've told me about, it sounds like your mother did her best to make a good life for you."

"That she did." He took another bite of his steak. "Tell me something about you. What was your childhood like?"

Emma's hand went to her necklace while she stared at the steamed broccoli. "Before my dad died, we moved around a lot. After he died, we ended up here, in the suburbs."

"You said he died when you were eleven? Must have been hard on your mom, raising you alone."

"Your mom did it, too," she said with a smile.

"Tell me about your mom?" He set an elbow on the table and cradled his chin, studying her.

Emma lowered her eyes, stabbed her vegetables and took a bite. There had been good times, before her father died. "One of my favorite things when I was still pretty young, we'd go to the Museum of Science and Industry. Have you been there? The place is huge."

"I think everyone around Chicago does a school field trip to the museums," he said.

"Well, the night before, she'd make a list of things to find and we'd do a scavenger hunt. Find a submarine. Find an airplane. Find the walk-through heart. She'd give me the map and I'd lead her all over the place. Most days we got to everything on her list, but sometimes we wasted too much time. It's a big museum."

"Why'd she move to San Francisco?"

The emptiness gaped in her heart again. "She needed a change of scenery, I guess. She got a job there."

Liam held his glass of tea. "But you decided to stay here?"

"There was no reason for me to follow her." No reason to tell him she hadn't been invited to go. Her mother had left Emma behind without a job or a place to live. Thank heaven for Portia.

Liam set his glass on the table. "How old are you?"

She blinked and furrowed her brow. "Twenty-six. Why?"

"An older woman." He wagged his eyebrows.

He'd be turning twenty-four this year, if she'd read his bio correctly. "By two years."

He raised his tea and took another drink. "You said you didn't have brothers and sisters. You must be lonely without your mom."

There was that word again. "I'm not lonely."

He stared at her.

Emma made a conscious effort to brighten. "Must have been fun growing up with a houseful of siblings. Are you guys close?"

"Yes." He turned to his meal again, his expression closed off.

Touchy subject? Emma switched gears. "Did you have any pets?"

"No. Da wouldn't allow it, and after he left, Ma couldn't afford it."

"Same here. I always wanted a dog, but I travel too much." She took the last bite of her fish and set her fork down. "I'm not even home long enough to entertain a cat."

"I hear ya there. I picture myself with a chocolate lab, but I'm on the road—" He glanced at her. "I guess you know exactly how that goes."

"I do. You know what we should do? After dinner, we could go to the shelter and visit the animals. Someday, I hope to bring one of them home," she said.

"Bad idea. I'll fall in love and be depressed when I can't adopt one." He took the last bite of his steak, wiped his mouth and set his napkin on the table. "I have a better idea.

Let's walk around the city. Do a scavenger hunt. Play 'I bet you can't find.'"

There it was again, that warm feeling she got when she was with him. Yes, he made her hot and bothered, but there was more to Liam McCormick.

"You're not just a dumb jock, are you?"

HE HATED THE STEREOTYPE. "Is that what you think of me?" Liam asked.

Her cheeks reddened.

"I graduated near the top of my class." He folded his napkin and set it on the table while he glowered at her. "Got my Bachelor's Degree in three years, and I stayed an extra semester and a half to get my Master's."

"I didn't mean anything by it." She sighed. "My experience with soccer players leans more toward guys like Cody Voigt than guys like you."

"I'm not like Cody Voigt."

"I know that." She held his gaze as if to emphasize her point.

If he was honest with himself, he'd acknowledge her point. The guys on the team might not all be like Cody, but they weren't like Liam, either.

Liam settled the check. "C'mon, let's go for a walk."

He offered Emma a hand to help her up.

"Thank you for dinner," she said as she gathered her jacket.

He was still piqued. "Where to?"

She slid her arms into her jacket as they walked out. "How about we walk the Lakefront Trail? It's a nice night, and that way we don't have to worry about the car or finding a parking spot."

"Works for me. You plan to walk the whole trail?"

"How about a mile or two?"

"We've got all night." A night he'd had other ideas for, but he'd also promised himself to take things more slowly.

Emma jammed her hands in her coat pockets and bowed her head.

He hadn't meant to make her feel bad. She wasn't wrong about professional athletes, as a rule, but he hated being lumped in with the others. "What's on your mind?"

She looked up, a startled expression on her face. "Nothing, really." She offered a smile. "What did you get your degree in?"

He rested an arm across her shoulders as they crossed the footbridge toward the walking trail. "Bachelor of Science in business, Master's in finance. My ma always told me to have a back-up plan. She was supportive of my soccer goals, but there's that old saying, life doesn't always work out the way you plan."

"True enough. So what's the back-up plan?" she asked.

"Not ready to think about that quite yet."

"You must have done advance placement classes in high school to get your degree in three years." She walked sideways beside him. "There were books on the nightstand at your mother's. You're a bookworm?"

"No. Well, maybe. But I did other things. Soccer, for instance, Madrigals—yes, I was in the choir—and the swim team."

"You're making that up," she said. "The selkie coming through again?"

Lake Michigan shimmered in the twilight, the waves lapping gently against the shore beside the trail.

He shrugged. "Maybe it *is* in my blood, but then I should have been an Olympic swimmer instead of a soccer player, don't you think?"

She chuckled. "I suppose."

The Chicago skyline loomed on the horizon ahead of them, backlit by the setting sun. A chilly breeze flirted with Emma's hair. She took long strides, those of an athlete, and her trim figure indicated she did something to keep fit. Should he ask her about her training?

"How'd you become a triathlete?" she asked before he came up with a subtle way to ask.

"I like the variety. The different disciplines. Cross training."

"Your ACL should be fine," she said. "Don't count yourself out yet."

"Yeah, but once it's damaged, you're always at risk. At least that's what they tell me." A shiver ran through him, whether from the cooling night or from his uncertain future, he couldn't say.

"Why do you think we're all after you to work on your strength training? So you have the musculature to support your knee against re-injury." She punched his arm.

"Ow," he said playfully, rubbing the spot she'd hit. "So now you're going to beat me up?"

She took his arm, turned him to face her. "Why does that intrigue you so much?"

"I like a woman who can take care of herself."

She assessed him a moment, her eyes dark and inviting. "I like a man who doesn't feel like he has to take care of me."

Then why did she seem so nervous tonight? She hadn't been nervous at his mother's house, but there was something to be said for heat of the moment. Then again, she thought he'd changed his mind. Far from it. Time to lighten the mood, not frighten her away. "Then that settles it," he joked. "Let's get married tonight and be done with it."

Emma giggled, looped her arm through his and continued walking.

Except now that he'd said it, the idea appealed to him. He liked Emma. A lot. But married?

When you know, you know, Kevin had said when he'd married Amy after a very short courtship, and they seemed happy.

Not a topic he wanted to pursue tonight. Tonight he wanted to enjoy Emma's company for however long she was willing to share it.

Chapter 20

As the lighthouse beacon swept Lake Michigan, Emma stared at the breakwater that separated the harbor from the open water. The indigo sky reminded her of the late hour. "I should get back."

"Can I walk you home?" Liam asked.

He hadn't rushed her, hadn't made a move, hadn't kissed her once during their stroll along the lakeshore. Had he changed his mind about the 'anywhere you want me' thing again?

Why did that disappoint her?

"It's too far to walk, but yeah, since you drove, I wouldn't mind a lift."

When they arrived at his car, he opened her door before he climbed in.

"Where to, my lady?" he asked.

"Giving up on the selkie thing in favor of Prince Charming?" she teased.

"No Prince Charming about it. My mother taught me to treat a lady with respect."

Her heart did a leap. She already knew that, but his conduct was one more thing to like about Liam McCormick.

Emma gave him directions and watched the city pass outside her window as he drove her home.

Any way she looked at it, a relationship with Liam seemed like a bad idea, if not professionally, then personally. They both travelled, and in their current jobs, they'd be going opposite directions, although if he got back to the Cowboys...

No, she couldn't go there. Her credibility would be ruined if she dated one of the players.

Remarkably, there was a parking spot open in front of her apartment building. Liam stopped and looked across the seat, at the illuminated lobby.

"This the right place?" he asked.

"Yeah." The moment of truth. She could invite him up or send him on his way. After their date, she got the feeling he'd be fine with either choice. Would she?

Liam opened his door and walked around the car, opened her door and waited for her to get out. Emma hesitated.

"I wouldn't be a gentleman if I didn't see you safely to your door," he said.

Right. More of that Prince Charming stuff. Emma took his hand and rose to her feet. While she fished for her keys, Liam clicked the car locks and followed her into the building. His hand rested lightly at the small of her back.

She could still say no.

Emma led him inside, into the elevator. He laced his hand with hers after she'd pushed the button and they rode up silently, standing side-by-side.

At her door, she bowed her head and sorted through her keys, her fingers shaking.

"I won't ask to come in," he said. "Unless you want me to."

He'd been a perfect gentleman since that awkward moment in the restaurant when he'd been ready to leave before their entrees arrived. She slotted her key into the lock and opened her door.

"Can I kiss you goodnight?" he added when she struggled to know what to say.

She nodded. Why was she so nervous? He'd kissed her before.

Liam took a step into her personal space, looped his arm around her waist and drew her close. His lips covered hers and she sighed, caught in his spell once more.

"Would you like to come in?" she whispered breathlessly. She stepped back and allowed him to pass.

She followed him in, and once she'd closed the door and turned the lock, Emma draped her arms around his neck. "You're not going to change your mind again, are you?"

"Never changed my mind," he said, his voice low and sexy. "Only the place." He kissed her with more urgency this time, pressing his body against hers.

Her fingers itched to undo his pants, but their last encounter instilled in her a sense of restraint.

"Emma," he whispered against her lips.

That was all she needed. This man. Her bed. Now.

She tugged him toward her bedroom and he followed with a lazy smile.

Beside her bed, his hands went to the buttons on her blouse, releasing them slowly. He stepped back, taking in what he'd exposed.

She wished she'd given in to the desire to wear her fancy red underwear, but a cooler head had told her white was her better choice. Emma reached behind and unclasped her bra. Liam lifted it and bowed to her breasts, closing his mouth over each in turn and circling her buds with his tongue.

Fire raced through her. The time for restraint had passed. Emma reached for his pants and unbuckled him. Liam helped, unzipping and letting them fall to the floor. She'd seen the bulge before, tucked inside his briefs. Emma dropped her own pants before she slid her hand in to free the raging hard-on waiting for her. She checked Liam's expression. He was smiling, not backing away.

"You gonna drop me?" he asked. "I've seen you turn men down before."

Emma pushed him to the bed and he bounced. "Consider yourself dropped."

He took her hand and pulled her toward him. Kissing her as he dragged her down on top of him.

Emma kicked off her panties and Liam slid out of his briefs. She opened her bedside stand and pulled out a foil pouch. She ripped it open and retrieved the condom, throwing the foil wrapper before she sheathed him, kicked a leg over and mounted him.

God, he felt good. Her eyes rolled back and her muscles clenched.

Liam leaned up to kiss her, moving to her breasts again. "All yours, Emma. When you're done, it's my turn."

The thrill amped up her already racing hormones, bringing her closer to the finish line.

She moaned, taking him deep, leaning forward to get more friction.

Liam laid back and moved with her, his hands taking over where his mouth had been, and she continued to ride the wave, letting Liam do the work beneath her as her muscles clamped around him and fireworks clouded her vision. Her world exploded.

"Am I hurting you?" he gasped.

"God, no. Don't stop."

His hands flattened on the bed beside her knees and he growled, expanding with his own release. More fireworks behind her eyes as she leaned forward and tucked her hands beneath his shoulders, holding on as spasms continued to rock through her.

Liam relaxed into the bed, his body growing still. Emma waited for her breathing to return to normal before she pushed herself up again. Liam leaned up, kissing her.

"Holy hell," he whispered, pressing his forehead to hers.

"No kidding." She stared at the beautiful man beneath her, at his smooth chest. At his sleek black hair. At his soulful eyes. Just looking at him sent her stomach tumbling. "I guess your turn will have to wait," she said.

He had her on her back in one move, hovering over her. "The turns have only started, Emma." He withdrew from her and discarded the used condom in the wastebasket. "I assume you have another one of these?"

"You're going to need *some* recovery time. I did take biology, you know. I'm an athletic trainer."

"By the time you're screaming my name again, I'll be ready." With that, he slid down her body, kissing and teasing his way until he settled between her legs.

Liam had her writhing again in minutes.

LIAM'S PHONE RANG FROM a million miles away. He opened his eyes, face down in the pillow, and turned his head to where Emma lay beside him. The full moon shining through the window cast a silver light over the room.

"You going to answer it?" she murmured sleepily.

He did a push up to get out of bed, reached for his pants pocket, retrieved his phone and read the display. Kevin.

"Talk to me," Liam said, running a hand through his hair.

"Ma called. She wants to know what you did to cause Da to walk the earth instead of finding his eternal rest, wherever that might be. She's worried you might be practicing the dark arts, or some other heinous hobby. Apparently, he showed up at your place in the city."

"Then he must be looking for her, cuz I'm not there," Liam said with a yawn.

"Another reason she's so worked up. You got any ideas?"

Liam leaned over his knees, struggling to wake up. How long had he been sleeping? "We can try the house again. Da seemed pretty at home when I was there last, sitting at his desk. Did I mention he's pretty proud to be a Grandda? He was at the hospital."

"No, I think you left that out." Kevin sounded annoyed. "When can you get away?"

Liam glanced at Emma, who sat with the sheet draped across her breasts, showing off her impressive cleavage. The last thing he wanted to do was chase down a ghost.

"Traveling tomorrow," he said.

"Then we check things out tonight. Your apartment or Ma's house?"

Liam picked up his clothes. As much as he wanted to stay, he couldn't leave Ma to deal with a dead husband. He also didn't want to face Ma after spending the past several hours in Emma's bed. No sense making Kevin drive into the city. "Ma's house. Should take me about 45 minutes this time of night."

"I'll see you there."

The call disconnected and Liam stared at his phone.

"Your dad?" Emma asked.

Liam nodded. "Apparently, he showed up at my place, visited my ma." He leaned across the bed and kissed Emma. "I don't want to go, but I think I should."

The disappointed look on her face undid him, making him even less inclined to leave her warm bed. He cupped her cheek. "This isn't over, Emma."

She shook her head. "It probably should be. This doesn't make sense."

"It does to me. Can I call you when I get to Des Moines?"

She snorted. "Aren't you rooming with Cody Voigt? I think I'd rather not have him listening in to your conversation."

"I don't have to call from the room, you know." He straightened and pulled on his clothes.

"Liam."

He glanced over his shoulder.

"Can we talk about why you're holding back—on the field?" she asked.

The one thing she might say to make him want to leave. "Playing it safe until I feel solid again."

He finished dressing, kissed her again, and started for the door. "I'll call you tomorrow, after I get to Des Moines."

The lack of sleep was going to make the bus ride seem even longer.

A bus. One of the disadvantages of playing in the D-league. No, he didn't want to be a has-been or a wannabe. Plenty of guys were sidelined after injuries. If he couldn't reclaim his spot with the Cowboys, he'd rather quit.

When he got to his car, Kevin's words registered. He punched in Kevin's cell phone number.

"Yeah?" Kevin answered.

"So why'd she call you instead of me? What heinous hobbies are we talking about?" Liam asked.

"Did you tell her you thought Da had attached himself to you? That he followed you back?"

"It's a working theory," Liam said. "But heinous hobbies?"

"She's stressed out. She said she's going to call a priest. She wants to go home first thing in the morning to banish 'that demon' from her house."

Oh boy.

"I heard Duncan in the background asking her why she wouldn't move to a place that was theirs and she could leave the ghosts behind. Real and figurative. She proceeded to tell him about how it's her home. Where she raised her kids. Her kids' home. She told Duncan any time he wants to find his own place, he's free to move out."

Liam winced. "Trouble in paradise."

"I don't believe that, and hopefully Duncan won't either, but the guy's gotta be unnerved enough by having Da pop in. Ma, too. We gotta fix this, Liam."

"You think we should call Jared? Isn't this his area of expertise?" Liam asked.

"Eventually. In the meantime, Da seems to be interested in you. Maybe he'll talk to you."

Yeah, Da was too interested in him. As if Da was giving Liam his seal of approval, puffing up like a proud papa.

Liam didn't want his father's approval. In fact, Liam's deeply engrained response told him to do the opposite of what his father wanted him to do.

Something clicked. Emma said he seemed to be half-assing the effort at practice. Was that why?

He'd have to think about that more later. "I'm almost there. I'll see you in a few minutes."

Knowing Duncan wanted Ma to move was as troubling as everything else. That house was their home. Where they'd grown up. Where they still gathered for every holiday and for Friday night dinner every week.

What was the old saying? Home is where the heart is. The house was just a house, and if Da had moved back in, Liam was in favor of Ma moving out. Ma might have buried most of the bad memories, but with Da's reappearance, those memories were too easy to recall.

As Liam drove the street where he'd grown up, he checked the clock on his dashboard. Almost midnight.

Didn't ghosts come out at midnight? Or witches? Or something?

He shivered and steered into the driveway. Kevin was already there. He got out of his car when he saw Liam.

"Didn't want to go in alone?" Liam asked when he'd parked.

"Hell, no. I've had my share of haunted houses, thank you. If you're the one he wants to talk to, I'm good with that. Don't want to invite any unwanted attention."

"What happened to my big brother, the protector?" Liam asked with a grin and a punch to Kevin's shoulder. "Let's go."

"Fists I can block," Kevin said, his voice low. "Ghosts, I'm not so sure. You said he talked to you?"

"Sorta," Liam said, unlocking the back door. He flipped the light switch in the kitchen and looked around. "Like old times, don't you think? Coast is clear."

Kevin shouldered him further into the room. "No kidding. Ma's at your house, potato-head. You might have thought it was fun sneaking in late when you were a kid, but I was always the one got in trouble for covering for you. I should have let you get caught and explain to Ma why you were out 'til all hours of the night." Kevin set his hands on his hips. "So, what now?"

Liam drew a deep breath and faced his brother. "If you were looking for Da, where would you go?"

"The study?"

Liam nodded.

Kevin grimaced. "Old times. This time of night, going to the study used to be a bad idea."

"Aren't you the one who said a ghost can't hurt you?"
Liam cocked his head. "Come on."

Chapter 21

Despite Liam's unexpected middle of the night departure, Emma slept soundly after he left. He'd depleted her to the point of exhaustion.

She beat Ray to the training room late the next morning, where several members of the team sat on tables waiting for ankles and knees to be taped. The men were all attached to personal devices, either listening to music or scrolling through phones.

Emma approached the first table and pulled up a chair. "How's the ankle feeling?" she asked while she probed.

"Six today," Javier, the team's striker told her, giving her the 1-10 pain scale ranking.

"Take it easy during practice, and make sure you ice after." She looped pre-wrap around his foot and ankle, concentrating on her task. These guys were intensely competitive. That competitive edge was what got them where they were. The chances of him taking it easy were slim.

Ray took a seat at the next table, where another player lay on his back, holding his phone in the air. Ray spoke to the guy conversationally while he walked the guy through leg exercises to test his mobility.

Emma finished with Javier's ankle and gave him a nod. "Good to go."

As she rose from her seat, Ray looked up. "Can you check Novak? Concussion protocol. He should be clear to play today."

She saluted Ray and headed for the bikes, where Novak was warming up. As she passed the office, the phone on the desk rang.

"Cowboys training room," she answered.

"Emma? This is Yosh Tanaka. Ray busy?"

"He's taping an ankle right now. Can I help?"

"Yeah, it's your boy McCormick," Yosh said. "Ray wanted daily reports. McCormick's still walking through drills, the way he was last time you saw him. I'm thinking your idea about a sports psychologist is the next step. There's definitely something going on in his head."

Liam was going to lose his ticket back if he didn't apply himself. His knee checked out. "Maybe he needs more time." She rolled her eyes. Hadn't she taped Javier's sprained ankle for practice, knowing he'd work through the pain, because that's what professional athletes did, to their own detriment? "I'll talk to Ray and have him get back to you," she said and hung up.

She'd tried to ask Liam about his attitude last night, but he'd dodged the question and run. If she thought getting involved with him didn't have to affect her job, Yosh's phone call proved her wrong. Her first reaction after she'd rationalized Liam's response was to call him and tell him to get his head out of his backside. That approach would likely end any chances they'd repeat what happened last night.

They shouldn't repeat what happened last night, but now that she'd had a taste of Liam McCormick, he was her new favorite flavor.

Novak stood in the office doorway with a silly grin on his face. "Ray says you can clear me from concussion protocol?"

These guys couldn't wait to get back on the field after an injury, and McCormick was hesitating.

"Yeah, sorry. Had to answer the phone." She flashed a smile.

Liam's progress report would have to wait. She had a roomful of soccer players to get to the practice field.

Two hours later she filled ice baths and set out scissors to remove athletic tape when her cell phone vibrated in her pocket. She reached for it and answered, tucking it under her chin to hold it to her ear. "Parrish."

"Been waiting to hear your voice all day," Liam said.

Her phone nearly tumbled into the tub she was filling. She should have checked caller ID. "Hang on, I'm finishing something that takes more hands than I have." The excuse was real, and it would buy her a minute to regroup. What was she going to say to him?

She put the ice bucket in the icemaker, walked into her office and closed the door. "Hey."

"Last night was... outstanding," he said in that sexy, middle of the night voice. "How'd you sleep?"

Outstanding. Yeah. It was all of that and more. "I slept like a baby. Did you get any sleep after you left? Sounded like you were going to meet your brother."

"I did meet my brother, and no, I didn't get much sleep at the team hotel, but I did sleep on the bus."

Fatigue might account for his shoddy performance. "You must hate riding the bus to a game instead of a plane." She put the back of her hand to her forehead.

"More motivation to rejoin the Cowboys," he said. Emma closed her eyes and breathed a sigh of relief. "How's the knee?"

"Getting stronger every day, but Coach Clarence still won't let me start tonight."

Because you've been half-assing practice, no doubt. "He's probably giving you more time to heal." Subject change. She wasn't ready to ask him what the hell he was doing. Not yet. "So how's your brother? The new baby?"

"Baby's fine. Me and Kevin went to Ma's house," he said.

She glanced out the window in her door. "Did you find what you were looking for?"

"Bad memories?" Liam chuffed. "No. My da didn't show. He seems to be shy around Kevin." He was quiet a moment before he continued. "What if he turns up at the game tonight?"

"You can't let him distract you," Emma said. "Do your job and you can deal with your father later."

"You telling me not to gather daisies in front of the keeper?" Liam joked.

"That's exactly what I'm telling you. They're watching you very closely. You have to know that." Did she dare tell him about the sports psychologist? She looked up again and remembered she hadn't passed along Yosh's message to Ray.

"You know something I don't?" he asked.

"Only that Yosh is sending in daily reports." She grabbed a handful of hair and squeezed her eyes shut. "What's bothering you?"

He huffed. "Emma, can we not talk about this right now?"

"Sure." She couldn't force him to talk to her if he didn't want to.

"I'd like to see you when I get back tomorrow. We can talk more then?"

"The Cowboys have a game tomorrow night," she told him. Something he should know. "Don't you have curfew?"

"We can make this work," he said.

Was he trying to convince her? Or himself?

"Good luck at the game tonight," she told him.

"Can I call you after? It might be late, but I know you're at work now."

Maybe by then she'd figure out how to compartmentalize their relationship. "Yeah."

LIAM PLAYED THE SECOND half of the game, but didn't see much action. The Mustangs kept the ball on the other half of the field—they won six-nil.

Back at the hotel, Liam checked his phone for messages. The first one was from Kevin, letting him know he'd convinced Ma to wait until Liam was available to go to the house with her since Da seemed to be attached to Liam. "I told her if she wants to bring a priest then, at least we'll all be there in case something goes wrong," Kevin said. "Call me tomorrow. Good luck at the game tonight."

Cody's back was to Liam and the audible breathing told him Cody was asleep. Liam sat on the edge of his bed and pulled his shirt over his head, leaned over to unlace his Oxfords and kicked them off.

He hadn't called Emma. Would Yosh have sent in his report already?

He didn't want to talk about soccer with Emma, but he did want to hear her voice, to draw from her well of inner strength. When he picked up his phone to go into the corridor, he cast a quick glance toward Cody's sleeping form and froze.

Da sat on the end of Cody's bed. "That man's living in my house," the voice in Liam's head said.

"Why are you haunting me and not the rest of them?" Liam whispered. "Oh, except Ma. Haven't you done enough to hurt her?"

Da gave a mournful sigh that would have made Jacob Marley proud. Cody sat up, looked around the room, flipped Liam off and went back to sleep.

Liam wasn't afraid anymore. "Nice dramatics," he whispered. "You gave up your rights to the house when you walked out. You walked into the Celtic Sea? Not a very auspicious end to your life."

The ghost rose from Cody's bed and hovered over Liam, undulating like a cloud. "Don't you judge me, you little fecker. I had hopes and dreams like all of you, and I lost it all. My wife, my family…"

"Whose fault is that?" Liam asked, his voice louder than he intended. Cody stirred again and groaned.

"All I had left were the stories of me grandda, the tales that he was a selkie." The ghost slapped a hand to his ethereal chest. "I'd thought to find what peace I could with the seals, what family I had left. Ach, I knew it was a lark, but with a few drinks, the world seems a bit darker, d'you know?"

"Can't say that I do know." Liam scowled. "So because I was the one who went to Ireland, I'm the one you're bothering?"

The apparition floated until he appeared to stand on the floor. "Blood knows blood. I've much to atone for and I'm no longer able. Your sister Mary tells me I can't join her until I've attended to the business I've left behind."

"Somehow I doubt you're going the same way as Mary. Begone. We're better without you." The ghost vanished.

Liam shivered and wiped his arms as if shaking off cobwebs. So much for looking up relatives in Ireland. If he hadn't gone, his father might not have bothered looking for the family he'd left behind.

He surveyed the room, making sure Da had gone, when he spotted his phone.

Emma. He needed her normalcy in his life.

Phone still in hand, Liam retreated to the corridor.

Her voice was sleepy when she answered. "Hey."

The tension in his muscles let go. "Wish you were here."

"Something wrong?"

He smiled. "No. I played the second half. Didn't have to work too hard against this team. Six-nil."

She yawned. "I hope you weren't standing around while the team was on the attack."

"I did my part."

"Any more visits from your father?"

Tension tugged at his shoulders and Liam tried to shrug it off. "Yeah."

"And?"

Liam sighed. "He says he has business to take care of before he can move on."

"How does that make you feel?"

Why did she sound like a shrink? "It sucks. Why do you ask?"

She hesitated a moment before she answered. "Yosh suggested a sports psychologist. I'm worried this stuff with your father is screwing with your head."

She was right, but he wasn't about to tell her. "I've got it handled. That whole situation might have thrown me, but I'm over it. What I need is to start the next game. I'll prove to them I'm good to go, and if you have any influence, you might intervene on my behalf."

"Tangled web," she said. "I might not be objective."

"They don't know that."

"But I do."

He rubbed his forehead.

"How do we make this work without talking about soccer?" she asked.

In the short time he'd come to know her, she'd become important to him. He admired her strength, and the way she cared about him. "I'd like to at least try. Are you saying you don't want to?"

"I didn't say that."

Liam leaned against the wall and closed his eyes. His life had turned upside down. Maybe he did need a psychologist—sports or otherwise.

"I'll talk to Ray," Emma said quietly.

Liam nodded. Soccer was a retreat from his emotions. To hell with his da. This was Liam's life. "Do what you feel is right," he said. "I'll do my part. I promise."

Chapter 22

Emma slunk into the trainer's room like a kid coming in after curfew. She had to tell Ray about Yosh's call, had promised Liam she'd put in a good word.

Would Ray notice her lack of objectivity?

She tiptoed past Ray's office and had eased into the chair behind her desk. Ray leaned against her doorframe and said hello, nearly sending her through the ceiling.

He laughed. "Didn't mean to startle you."

She put her hand to her chest to still her pounding heart and forced a smile. "Sorry. I didn't see you when I walked in."

"Then you must not have been looking." His brow crinkled as he stepped into her office. "Everything okay?"

Couldn't he read the *I slept with Liam McCormick* sign on her head? The *I'm another loser groupie who slept with someone on the team* button on her shirt?

Ray had no way of knowing. Emma raised her chin. "Did you need something?"

"I don't have the paperwork on Novak's concussion assessment. Can you get that to me before the team arrives?"

"Of course. I've been tied up with running to Rockford and back." Did she sound angry?

Liam was part of her job. She had to discuss his progress with Ray. Emma plowed ahead. "Yosh and I discussed a sports psychologist for McCormick. Something's still not quite right, but when I talked to McCormick, he said he needs game time. A chance to prove himself."

Nothing incriminating there, right?

Ray sat in her guest chair. He steepled his fingers in front of his nose and studied Emma much too closely. She squirmed under his scrutiny.

"What do you think?" he asked.

Was it a trick question? Would he figure out she'd crossed the line with Liam? She'd worked so hard to be taken seriously, and one stupid Irish legend had turned her into the proverbial dumb blonde.

Ray set his hands beside him on the chair and leaned forward. "Ever since that day you went home sick from practice, I've been worried about you. Are you okay?"

The day she went to track down Liam in Rockford.

Emma straightened and lifted her chin. "McCormick thinks he can play, I think he should get the chance. If his stamina isn't there, they can pull him out at halftime, and if his knee isn't strong enough, we'll have our answer."

Ray nodded. "Okay, that answers that question. Back to you. What's going on, Emma?"

"Why do you think something's going on?" she asked, her voice pitching higher than normal. She was such a bad liar.

"Problems with the new boyfriend?"

Emma's eyes nearly popped out of her head. "New boyfriend?" Had someone seen her at dinner with Liam, or going into her apartment?

"Yosh said you brought a date to the locker room when you went to Rockford. Or am I mistaken?"

She nearly giggled with relief. "Well, I did try to tell you I had a date that night, but when I called to cancel, he asked if he could go along." She smiled. "A first—and likely last—date."

Ray nodded again. "You're very dedicated. I hope you know the Cowboys appreciate that." He rose from the chair. "Do you have someone you can talk to? You know, in case there's something personal going on."

"Yes," Emma answered. Thank heaven for Portia.

"Emma, I've come to think of you as a daughter. I know I'm just a dumb guy, as my wife likes to remind me, but if you need a sounding board, someone you need to vent to—or, my wife is a pretty good listener, and she gets this job. If you need someone to talk to, that is."

If she told Ray about Liam, he wouldn't think she was so dedicated. He'd look at her differently. The whole team would look at her differently.

"Gotta be hard to be on your own in this city," he went on.

"I'm not lonely," she told him.

Ray furrowed his brow again. "That's not where I was going."

She might have overreacted. Emma rose from her chair. "I appreciate the gesture, but I'm okay. I promise."

He took her hands in his. "Offer stands," he said before he left her office.

She'd done what she promised. She'd talked to Ray about Liam. She'd also lied to Ray.

Emma *was* lonely. She ached for Liam.

He had to be a selkie. Why else would she be so obsessed with him?

LIAM MOVED WITH CODY, defender against striker, as Cody tried to dribble past him. A one-on-one drill designed for Liam to prove he was game-ready. Liam feinted, tried to tackle the ball. Cody redirected. Liam adjusted. Cody looked ahead to the goal and in that moment, Liam tackled the ball away from him.

Liam grinned and sent the ball across the field to the waiting assistant coach. "Lapse in concentration," he told Cody. "You telegraphed your intent."

The coach passed the ball to them. "Again," he called out. This time Liam intercepted the ball and dribbled it toward the other end of the field with Cody in pursuit.

"You've got to control the ball better." Da's voice echoed in his head, pulling him up short.

Cody stole the ball and headed to the goal. "Lapse in concentration," Cody parroted. He lined up and took a shot on goal, but Liam was there to divert it.

While the coach retrieved the ball, Liam checked the field for ghostly distractions. Da stood in the goal box.

"I don't need your help," Liam muttered.

"I think you do," Cody said.

The ball came toward them and Cody got there first.

"All those times I wasn't there," Da said. "All the games we should have played together. I mean to make it up to you."

The ghost hovered in Liam's path and Liam pulled up to avoid running into him.

Cody darted around Liam and took a shot on goal.

"What are you doing, McCormick?" the coach called out.

"I got here without your help," Liam whispered to the ghost. "I'll thank you to get out of my way now."

Da feinted, as if to tackle the ball.

He was a ghost. Insubstantial.

Liam ran through him. "Let's go again," he called to the coach.

Chapter 23

The plane to Boston had landed late Thursday night. When the shuttle arrived to take the team to the stadium early Friday morning for field time, Emma was only half awake. Everyone seemed to be dragging except Ray.

With the players prepped and on the field, Ray paced the sidelines. Emma sat on the bench sipping her coffee, eyes on the action for any missteps or hitches.

When the team broke for lunch, Emma had a couple of hours to herself before the afternoon call. Back to the hotel? Or venture into the city?

The city option was the more appealing, somewhere away from the players and accusing eyes. Even if they didn't know about her and Liam.

"Want to catch a bite?" Ray asked, startling Emma out of her insecurities. "There's a great little sandwich shop out on Boston Fish Pier."

Emma always found peace beside the water. The pier sounded like just what she needed. "Sounds great, but I don't know if I'm in the mood for fish."

Ray chuckled. "Funny thing about this place. The only fish they have on the menu is a tuna sandwich. Surprised me, too, first time I went."

"Then, let's go."

They left the locker room together. When they reached the street, Emma raised a hand and let out a shrill whistle to hail a cab.

"Where'd you learn to do that?" Ray asked.

"The one ability I inherited from my father," she said. A cab stopped at the curb and they ducked in.

"Thanks for keeping me company," Ray said after he'd given the cabbie their destination. "It also gives me the opportunity to talk to you about something."

Emma tensed. Did he know? "Oh?"

"Listen, I know you told me you had someone to talk to, and legally, it's none of my business, but some of the guys mentioned you seemed different. Not as talkative. Not joking with them. They asked me what was up and all I could tell them was it's none of our business." He held up his hands. "It isn't, but I'm going to repeat my offer. If there's anything I can do."

The looks weren't her imagination then. "It's something I'm working through," she said. "I appreciate your offer, but I don't feel comfortable talking about it. I wouldn't want people to judge me, or view me differently."

Ray's eyes widened. "I can't imagine anything that might change the way they see you. You're professional. You're good at your job. The players respect you. Half of them want to date you, but you've made your position clear enough that all they can do is admire you." He tilted his head. "One of them hasn't acted inappropriately toward you, has he?"

Emma burst into laughter. His guess was too close for comfort. "No, and I can handle myself when it comes to unwanted attention."

He held his hands up again. "I'm not prying, I swear. You said you don't want to talk about it, so I'll let it go, but as your boss, I sincerely doubt there's anything bad enough to change the way our little family feels about you."

She wanted to believe that, but her relationship with Liam felt unethical on so many levels.

The cab stopped at the end of the pier. While Ray settled the fare, Emma wandered to the waterfront to find her Zen gazing across the ocean.

A boat floated in. Fishermen rushed around the deck preparing to dock. As it grew closer, black heads bobbed in the water alongside the pier. Seals? One poked its head out and barked before it dived under.

Emma leaned across the wooden railing, searching out more seals. Were there selkies in the United States? Why did the legend make her feel so lonely?

If her tears fell into the ocean would another selkie come to her?

"Emma?" Ray put a hand to her shoulder.

Liam was not a selkie. Why was she being so silly about a stupid fairytale?

"You look like you've seen a ghost. I'm going to say it again, I'm worried about you."

She tried to laugh it off. "I was watching the seals. When I was in Ireland, the locals told me a legend about them."

Emma needed to pull herself together. She would not become a simpering wimp of a woman pining after a man.

Not just any man. Liam McCormick.

Benches lined the pier railings, some occupied by people eating their lunches.

Emma put on a smile. "That's the restaurant over there? Come on. I'll fill you in on the story."

The walk-up counter inside showed a menu overhead. No tables.

"Nowhere to eat inside?" Emma asked.

"Folks generally sit on the benches outside, unless you'd rather take it back to the stadium?"

"The pier sounds great."

Five minutes later, they sat overlooking the ocean. Emma related the story she'd heard and joked about how the Irish had taken advantage of a foreigner. She left out the part about watching Liam and Shane emerge from the sea and her misguided fantasies.

"I'm beginning to wonder if I should have sent someone else to Ireland," Ray said. "Feels like that's when something changed in you. You haven't been the same since you've been back."

"You might say I've been facing down some ghosts," she said. The nugget of truth was as near as she could explain her fascination with Liam and the run-ins with Liam's father. "To further complicate things, I'm also having relationship issues, but I don't want to bore you with girl talk." That should end his questions. Men hated talking to women about relationship issues.

"I hope the trip didn't add to those complications, or sending you to Rockford the other night." He raised his eyebrows. "You could have said no."

"It's my job to go," she said.

"Your dedication is admirable, but don't forget to take time for yourself sometimes, Emma."

The last time she'd done that, she'd met a selkie.

In the harbor below, a herd of seals barked their approval when the fisherman who'd come in threw scraps overboard. The seals dived and played as they went after their snacks.

There were plenty of other selkies in the sea. Liam McCormick wasn't magical. She didn't need the complications that came as a result of a relationship with him.

She'd put an end to it next time she saw him.

LIAM STALKED INTO THE hotel room. Satisfied that Cody wasn't there, he faced down the ghost.

"I'm trying to win back my place on the team. I can't do that if you're in my way every time I run down the field. Why can't you leave me alone?"

Da's thundering expression mirrored the one that had them cowering when they were children. But Da wasn't real anymore. Liam had run *through* him on the soccer pitch. "You can't beat me anymore."

Da swung a hand to slap Liam—a hand that passed painlessly through Liam's face.

"Leave me alone," Liam repeated.

The shocked expression on the old man's face didn't provide Liam the satisfaction he thought it might, having finally faced down his tormentor.

Da's weary voice echoed in his head. "Give me a listen. Please. I'm only trying to be the father I should have been."

"It's too late for that," Liam said. "Why me? Why not the others? You said it's because I was the one who went to Ireland to find you, but that's not why I went to Ireland. I went for a soccer match. Ma deserves better than to be driven out of her own home."

The ghost seemed more substantial, more of a man. "I was the one driven from my home."

"As I remember it, you walked out of your own accord. Had enough, if I recall your exact words."

Da hung his head. "Drunk at the time, and too proud to apologize. I had nowhere to go, so I went back to Kinsale. To my people."

"And left your family behind."

"Can you not forgive me?"

Liam scrubbed his face with his hands. "I can thank you," he muttered. "For marrying a woman strong enough to raise a brood of kids on her own. If forgiveness is what you need to move on, then you have it."

The ghostly aura shimmered and Da's face screwed up as if he was in pain. He howled like Liam imagined a banshee would and flew through the ceiling.

Liam exhaled his relief. Could his forgiveness, however grudgingly given, send his father on his way?

His phone chimed a notification in his pocket. Liam checked and found an email from his cousin Moira.

"Was out to the cemetery today," it read. "You'd mentioned you wanted to see Frank McCormick's headstone. I took a picture for you. Next time you visit, we can go together to pay our respects, if you think you're able."

Able. To visit? Or to pay his respects?

He wanted to write off the ghost as a psychological demon. Hadn't the trainers told him an injury could mess with his head?

No, Emma had seen the ghost, too. And Ma.

Their father had been gone ten years when Ma told them he'd died. He'd become little more than a bad memory by that time, so the news held little impact. Seeing the stone that marked his grave drove his father's death home.

He had to call Emma. Liam punched in her number before he stopped to reconsider.

"Ready for the game tonight?" she asked as she answered the call.

He closed his eyes and a tear slid down his cheek. More than anything else, he wanted to hold Emma right now. Draw on her strength.

His voice was rough when he spoke again. "He was here. The ghost. I told him to go away."

"You're not sorry about that, are you? Telling him to go away?" she asked. "From what you've told me about him, no one would blame you."

"He's dead, Emma."

Her breath hitched before she asked, "You okay?"

"When do you get home?"

"The game is tomorrow. We fly back the day after," she replied.

"I need to see you. Can I see you?"

Her voice caught a second time as she hesitated. *Please say yes.*

"Yes," she said.

His muscles loosened as tension slid away. "I'll call you after my game tonight."

"Good luck."

He disconnected the call and stared at his phone for several minutes.

Liam should have called his mother. Or Kevin. Or one of his sisters. He still needed to call one or all of them.

But Emma's voice was the one he'd wanted to hear. He had to find a way to make this relationship work.

Chapter 24

At midnight Boston time, Emma had given up on the promised phone call from Liam. She moved her phone from the pillow beside her to the hotel nightstand, not sure if she was relieved or disappointed. She didn't want to end things over the phone, which left her wondering what to say to him.

As she rolled over, her phone rang. Wasn't that the way the universe worked? As soon as you stopped waiting, something happened.

"Hey," she said. "How'd the game go?"

"We won, two to one." His voice was breathy with the adrenalin high he was obviously riding, much better than the sadness she'd heard from him earlier. "I played the first half, but Yosh didn't want to push things, so he said to wait until next week to play the whole game."

"That's great," she said. "How does the knee feel?"

"It's sore, but nothing I can't manage. I think I was more worried my da would show up to screw with me like he did at practice, but I think he's moved on."

"Wait. What?" Emma sat up and scooted to lean against the headboard. "I know you said you'd seen him again. He was at practice?"

Liam laughed. "He wanted to teach me how to play. Actually, he said he was trying to be the father he never was, but playing soccer with a ghost isn't very competitive. I told him to stop distracting me."

"That's when you told him to leave?"

"Yeah. Everyone already thinks I'm not trying. I don't need a ghost getting in my way on the field." His voice grew quiet. "But it *was* nice to have a cheering section."

In his position, she would have been distracted, too. "You okay?"

"Yeah. Sorry about earlier. My cousin sent me a picture of his grave. Somehow that made his death more real, you know? I hope he was able to find his peace." Liam's tone when he talked about his father seemed reflective, not annoyed, the way he had been previously when the ghost appeared. "But hey, then my ma can move back home. I learned something I didn't know before through all of this. Her husband wants to move to a place of their own, but my ma is holding firm. She doesn't want to leave the place she raised all of us. When I heard that, I was on Ma's side, you know? After all, it's home. The family gets together for dinner every Friday night, or at least everyone who can. Tomorrow's Friday. I wonder if she'll change where we go since she's staying at my place. Doesn't matter. The more I thought about the whole moving to a place of their own thing, the more I think Duncan—that's her husband—might be right. I mean, we're all grown and gone and there's no reason for her to stay there. She should get on with her new life. I'm happy she found someone to care for her, a second chance at love. Is that weird? Thinking of your mother in love?"

Emma smiled, listening to his scattered thoughts. "I think it's sweet." More than sweet. His sense of family was endearing. She reached for a neutral topic. "How's your new nephew doing? Everybody okay?"

"Kevin's so excited that he has a son," Liam said. "Not that he wasn't excited about having a daughter." He chuckled. "Although he says it's a bit messier. Says changing a diaper is more challenging. He's already been sprayed."

Emma laughed in response. "Well, points to him for changing a diaper."

"My mother taught us we're just as responsible for those we bring into the world as our spouses are. There were no divisions between men's work and women's work in our house."

"I like your mother already."

"She's going to like you, too."

Talking to Liam, she wanted to see him again. *Craved* seeing him again. But meeting his mother?

"What's happening in Boston?" he asked.

She went on to tell him about the Cowboys' practice, how Novak had been cleared from concussion protocol, how she'd wrapped Javier's ankle—except he hadn't been limping before she wrapped it, only after.

"I'd bet there's nothing wrong with his ankle," Liam said. "He has a crush on you. A lot of the guys do, you know."

Heat rose up Emma's neck. "No, they don't."

"Oh, yes they do. If you showed anyone so much as an inkling of interest, you'd have dates all year. Don't show them any interest, will you? I'd like to keep you to myself."

The room was too warm all at once, and her heart thumped heavily. "I have no intention of dating anyone on the team," she said, her voice breathless.

"Hey, Cody's back. I think I'm going to let you go for now. Dinner when I get back?"

She nodded before she answered. Her fingers tingled to touch him and the ache of longing tugged deep inside. "Yeah."

Was she a coward for not breaking things off with him? She told herself the decent thing was to do it face to face, but after talking with him, ending what they'd started might be harder than she'd expected.

LIAM SLEPT THROUGH the night without the aches in his knee waking him up. Progress.

Yosh had cleared him to play the whole game next week, assuming the coach agreed.

He was ready.

The Mustangs gathered in the hotel bar to watch the Cowboys game. Liam had plenty of time before the trading deadline to be recalled to the team. In the meantime, he'd keep current on the Cowboys' roster as well as the competition so he'd be ready when the call came.

His phone rang and he moved to the back of the bar.

"Busy tonight?" Kevin asked.

"Watching the Cowboys game, so yeah."

"Can you swing a trip to the house? Ma's fussing that she can't have Friday dinner with the ghost haunting her house. She's determined to call Father Kelleher. I talked to

Kathleen, and if you're available, I thought we'd all go over."

Liam took a deep breath and walked out of the bar. "Yeah. I can go. By the way, in case you're interested, our cousin in Kinsale sent me a picture of Da's gravestone. Made his death more real for me. Thought it might do the same for you, unless you don't need that sort of thing."

"I don't need it, but I'd be interested to see, just the same."

"And another thing," Liam went on. "I had another visitation, and I pretty much told Da to go away. He vanished pretty quickly, so maybe he's finally decided he can move on."

"We can only hope. Meet you at Ma's in half an hour?" Kevin asked.

"On my way."

So much for watching the game—for doing his homework—but sometimes family was more important. If Da didn't make an appearance, Ma would move back home and Liam would be free to take Emma out tomorrow night the way they'd planned—and invite her to stay the night at his place.

He couldn't wait to see Emma again.

The detour his life had taken seemed to have reconnected with the main road. Things were looking up.

When he arrived at Ma's house, Kevin was waiting outside, along with Ma and Duncan.

"Why didn't you go in?" Liam asked when he got out of his car.

Ma's lips were fixed into a tight, thin line. "Waiting for you. You're the one what's brought him home." She crossed her arms. "You can see to it that he's not there, and if he is, I'm going straight to Father Kelleher."

Liam hugged his mother in spite of her crossed arms. She let them drop to her sides.

"Did Kevin also tell you my theory that he's moved on?" Liam asked.

"But we can't be sure," Kathleen added, closing her car door.

"No spouses," Liam said. "They didn't want to come?"

"Amy just had a baby, potato-head," Kevin said.

"And Sebastian has had his share of ghosts," Kathleen added.

Ma cocked her head. "Go on then. You'll check for us."

"When I'm done, I think we all need to have a talk," Liam said. "And I think we should call Siobhan and include her."

Ma gave him a shove toward the house.

"All right, all right." Liam unlocked the back door and walked into the kitchen. He flipped on the light and glanced around the room. So far, so good.

The family huddled behind him.

"It's a ghost. He can't hurt us anymore," Liam said.

"If you'd met the ghost I did, you might not be so sure," Kathleen told him.

Liam scowled. The last time he'd swept the house for signs of his father's ghost, Emma had been with him.

A twinge of guilt tugged his shoulders from his last encounter with Da, the one where Liam told him to go away. Emboldened, Liam raised his head. "Come out, come out, wherever you are."

Ma swatted at him. "Stop."

Liam turned and gave her a cocky grin. "He's not here, Ma."

"You'll check," she told him, pointing toward the living room.

Liam inched toward the living room, the dread that accompanied walking into Da's study as strong today as when he was a kid.

"I've got your back," Kevin said quietly, a step behind him. Just like the old days.

Liam flipped on the light in the study. Ma's sewing machine. The easy chair in the corner. Magazines stacked on the table beside it. Kinder memories than the ones hidden in the dark. The only reminder of Da was the heavy desk.

No sign of Da.

"He's not here," Kevin reported.

"How do you know?" Liam asked. "You didn't see him before, did you?"

"Is he?" Kevin asked.

Liam shook his head. "I'll check upstairs, just to be sure." Turning on lights as he went, Liam crossed the living room and took the steps two at a time. He followed the same path he'd taken with Emma, from Ma's room to the girls' room. No ghost. He paused outside his boyhood bedroom one more time, remembering how close he'd come to getting Emma naked. He glanced over his shoulder, afraid his mother could read his thoughts.

He hadn't violated the rule. Not really. Yes, she'd gone upstairs, but they hadn't done anything. Not much, anyway. Not here.

"I'm sorry I didn't make dinner," Ma said when Liam returned to the living room. "But at least we're all together now." She wrung her hands. "Do you think he's gone to his reward, then?"

"I'd like to think so," Liam said.

"What did you want to talk about?" Duncan asked, a protective arm across Ma's shoulders.

Liam shot a glance toward Kevin. How much should he let on that they knew about Duncan's wishes? "How about we sit in the kitchen?"

They all took a seat and Liam looked to Kevin for support once more. Kevin had been the one to overhear the conversation. It was his place to speak, but since he wasn't...

"I got to thinking. You and Duncan should consider selling the house and find a place of your own. Somewhere your family isn't always walking in at unexpected times or imposing on you."

"Whatever gave you such a notion?" Ma asked, leaning forward.

"No," Kevin said. "He's right. You don't need this big house anymore. We're all out on our own. You need a place to build new memories. To let the past go."

Kathleen leaned back and crossed her arms. "Wait a minute. What about Friday night dinners? We haven't called Siobhan to get her feelings on the matter."

"It's Ma's life," Liam said. "She deserves a fresh start. Home isn't a building. It's wherever we're all together."

Duncan didn't say anything, but the smile on his face conveyed his thanks to Liam for bringing up the topic.

"But—" Kathleen started.

"You want your family barging in on you and Sebastian?" Kevin asked. "Ma deserves the same respect, doesn't she?"

"But she's Ma," Kathleen replied weakly.

"She'll always be there for you," Duncan said.

Tears spilled down Ma's cheeks. "The memories here, they're not all bad ones, you know. If I don't want to move?"

Kevin leaned across and took Ma's hands. "We want you to be happy, Ma."

"You don't think I am?"

Kevin looked to Duncan. "It's your life, Ma. We thought since you decided to move on, you might like to go all in."

Kevin had been the one to hear the argument between Ma and Duncan, so he'd had time to think it through, too. Kathleen would come around.

Liam's cell phone rang. He checked the number. Coach Clarence. "Gotta take this. Hang on." He moved into the living room and answered the call.

"You watching the game?" Coach asked.

"No," Liam said. "Family meeting."

"Adrian Crane went down. Looks like a broken leg. They want you to report to the Cowboys first thing Monday morning."

Chapter 25

The bay in the emergency room smelled of oranges and antiseptic. Emma waited with Adrian Crane for the on-call orthopedic doctor to fit Adrian into the surgical schedule. Adrian's speech slurred, his eyes half-mast. The pain meds were kicking in.

"Go big or go home," he said. "No sprained ankle or pulled hammie for me. I had to go for the compound fracture."

"I guess that means your ankle doesn't hurt anymore— the one I've been wrapping for you all week," she joked.

"Huh?" He struggled to look at her, and then rewarded her with a silly smile. "Anyone ever tell you you're pretty? I probably shouldn't tell you this," he leaned across the bed and lowered his voice, "but there's nothing wrong with my ankle. I was hoping you'd notice me. Would you go on a date with me? Then I won't have to wrap my ankle anymore."

She laughed. "I'm flattered, but no, I won't go on a date with you."

"Do you have a boyfriend?"

Did Liam count?

"I prefer to keep my personal life and my professional life separate." She reminded herself to break things off with Liam next time she saw him, next time they were both in the same state. Her body warmed, and she considered asking for "one more time" before they parted company. Was that selfish?

Adrian didn't seem to have heard. "We could see a movie, or go to dinner. Do you like musicals? I'd even take you to a musical. Is this Friday night?" What do you usually do on Friday nights?"

"I sit with injured soccer players in the emergency room. Rest. The doctor will be in soon. Do you have anyone you want me to call? The team will have notified your family."

"My family. They're in Oregon. They're not going to fly here on account of a broken leg."

"I wouldn't be so sure." Since he'd asked Emma out, he probably didn't have a girlfriend to call. "I'm sure the team will be in and out to see you," she told him.

Family. Friday. Emma straightened. Liam mentioned his family had dinner together every Friday night, or those who could. All those brothers and sisters, and a mother who gathered them together once a week as a family. What would that be like, surrounded by people who loved you the way his family obviously did? Emma pictured a scene from The Waltons and chuckled.

Emma hadn't spoken to her mother in more than a month. Even before her mother had moved away, they'd rarely had dinner together. Her mother was too busy, either working or taking care of one of her social responsibilities.

She'd never had five minutes to sit and talk with Emma, not without being simultaneously distracted. When the promotion and transfer to California came through, her mother accepted and left without a backward glance, the reminder of which produced a stab in Emma's heart.

You don't need me anymore. You're all grown up. Time for you to be on your own, anyway. It isn't like we'll never see each other again, and these kinds of opportunities only come along once in a lifetime.

Except they hadn't seen each other since. Emma called when the team traveled to the west coast, but her mother was always too busy for dinner or a cup of coffee. Seven years her mother had been gone. Oh, she called from time to time, once every couple of weeks when she had "five free minutes."

No, Emma was sure she hadn't heard from her mother in a month.

The doctor breezed into the room, reading his chart. "You're the AT?" he asked Emma.

Emma nodded, swiping at her eyes.

Adrian issued a loud snore.

"We'll keep him overnight. I can't get an OR until the morning." He smiled. "You did a great job stabilizing the leg."

Emma cringed, unable to shake the sense the doctor was being condescending. "That's my job."

The doctor shot a look at Adrian. "Right. I'm sure you have your own paperwork to fill out. We'll keep you posted."

Now he was dismissing her. Emma drew a deep breath and forced a smile. "Then I'll leave him in your capable hands." She slipped sideways past the doctor and headed to the waiting room to finish filling out her report.

Except she was still thinking about family. Adrian's. Liam's. Her mother.

Emma pulled out her phone and dialed her mother.

"Emma, I was just thinking about you, but I'm right in the middle of something. Can I call you back?"

Emma's standard response was 'sure,' but tonight Emma needed that connection. "No, Mother. You've been going to call me back for nearly a month. You can't spare five minutes?"

"Now don't be like that. You know how busy I am," her mother said. "Don't be such a child. What's the matter? Another break-up? That's part of life, you know. Now I really have to go."

"Of course you do." Emma's free hand curled into a fist. "And you know what? You were right when you left. It isn't as if I need a mother anymore. It isn't as if you ever provided more than a roof over my head and food on my table. I should be grateful to you for that, at least. I'm sorry to have bothered you."

"Emma! What has gotten into you?"

All these years she'd waited for her mother to love her. To be part of her life. Adrian's family might be in Oregon, but she'd met Mrs. Crane at least once when his family had come to watch the Cowboys play. No, not everyone was as close as Liam's family appeared to be, but was it asking too much to have a relationship with her only family?

Her phone beeped with another incoming call. "Hang on, I have another call," she said.

"I'll call you later," her mother said.

Emma rolled her eyes and switched to the other call.

"Emma, one of our instructors has the flu," the scheduler at the health club told her. "Are you available to teach a self-defense class in the morning?"

"I'm sorry, I'm out of town," she said. "Maybe next time."

That's what she needed. A strenuous workout. Throwing someone to the ground.

She tucked her phone in her pocket and cradled her forehead in her hand.

Unbidden, she pictured Liam, his dark eyes searing her as he asked her if she was going to throw him to the ground.

"Can you make him listen to me?" a quiet voice whispered in her ear.

Emma raised her head, gooseflesh popping up on her skin. Liam's father.

"I'm not accustomed to being wrong, or to apologizing," he said. "I can't move on until they know, all of them, how sorry I am."

She was done with absentee parents. Done with excuses that came too late. "Then shouldn't you be talking to them instead of trying to reclaim a life you left behind?" she asked.

"I don't know how it is that Liam can see me, and more, you. I'd thought Eileen would hear me out, but she's gone and found herself a new husband."

"Which she's entitled to do when her first husband walks out on her. She's entitled to a life."

Liam's father hung his head. "And mine is ended. You're right enough. What am I to do?"

Emma shook her head. Why was she involved in this? "You need to apologize?" she repeated. "To all of them?"

"Yes."

Tears pricked her eyes and her throat tightened. "They have dinner together every Friday, as many of them as can make it."

The ghost brightened. "Sure?"

Emma nodded, and the ghost vanished.

Even Liam's father wanted to do right by his family. Why couldn't her mother spare her even five minutes on the phone?

She needed a gym, somewhere to work out her frustrations. Surely there was one in the team's hotel.

She'd muscle through this bad mood on her own.

She didn't need anybody.

LIAM REPORTED TO THE Cowboys' locker room on Monday morning for the team meeting ahead of practice. He stopped, closed his eyes and drew a deep breath. Sweat. Leather. The air freshener in Novak's locker. Familiar smells.

He got a pat on the back, and then another, along with greetings of, "Hey, slacker." This was his team. His friends.

They jostled and shoved each other as they made their way to the meeting room to review the last game. When Coach Simmons walked in, the room grew quiet.

"McCormick, report to the trainer. Once he's cleared you, you can join us."

Liam nodded and walked out.

Emma would be in the training room. She hadn't answered her cell phone all weekend, hadn't returned his calls. He was worried something might have happened to her, but he didn't know who to call to ask. If she wasn't at work, he'd ask Ray if she was okay.

Two assistants bustled around the training room, but no Emma.

Liam knocked on Ray's door. "Checking in."

Ray rose from his chair to shake Liam's hand. "Welcome back. You ready?"

"As ready as I'm going to be."

Emma stopped outside Ray's office. She stared at Liam as if she'd seen a ghost.

Liam glanced around. Was his da hovering in a corner?

"McCormick." She looked to Ray. "Problems on the Mustangs?"

"I hope not," Ray said with a smile. "They've recalled McCormick to take Crane's place. Figured he's close enough in his recovery that he can continue here."

"Let me know if you need anything from me," she said, and ducked into her office.

Ray walked Liam out to the training room and patted a table. "Hop up."

Liam complied, making a conscious effort not to look toward Emma or ask about her. She'd told him she was worried about perception, and he was determined not to make her uncomfortable at work, but her silence worried him. Had she been avoiding him?

Ray ran down the checklist with him, starting with the inevitable pain scale and ending with Liam doing squats. He reviewed Yosh's reports with Liam, including the recommendation that although Liam might play all of his next game, his condition would be evaluated at half time. He relayed what the team would be watching for and what Liam needed to do.

When Ray asked if he had any questions, Liam shook his head. He knew what he was supposed to do. Knew what the team expected from him.

"Are we done?" Liam asked.

"I hope that's because you're eager to join the team and not because you're not paying attention," Ray said.

"I'm paying attention. To you, to Emma, to the coaches. I know what you need from me, and trust me, I'm eager to prove to all of you that I'm up to the challenge."

"Then get going." Ray tucked Liam's chart under one arm and extended the other toward the door.

With one last glance to Emma's office, Liam headed for the meeting room.

Yes, he wanted to talk to Emma, but he'd been given an opportunity with the team, and he wasn't about to screw it up. For now, knowing nothing untoward had happened to her was enough. Liam would find a way to talk to her later.

After the meeting, the team returned to the locker room to prepare for practice. A handful of guys, Liam among them, headed for the training room to have joints wrapped or kinesio tape applied. They each took a trainer's table to wait their turn. Would he get Emma or one of the other trainers?

He got his answer when Emma took a seat in front of him. He leaned back on his elbows.

"How's the knee?" she asked.

"Good. Don't need the pain scale today," he replied.

She lowered her voice. "We need to talk."

"Agreed."

"Your father was here again. Have you seen him?"

"No." Liam straightened. "I thought he'd... you know... moved on."

"Apparently not. He seems to be struggling with how to apologize. He said he needs to make peace with the family. All of you."

Her shoulders rose and she grimaced. Was she in pain?

"You okay?" he asked.

Emma forced a smile. "Worked out yesterday. I might have overdone it." She wound pre-wrap around his knee and reached for an elastic bandage.

Liam glanced around the training room. No one appeared to be paying attention to them. As much as his hands tingled to touch her, to pull her to him, he didn't dare.

"I told him what you said about Friday dinner." She met his gaze. "Is your mother back home?"

Liam nodded. Emma's eyes were glassy. Something was bothering her. "Emma..."

She shook her head. "Not here. Not now."

"My oldest sister will be coming home this weekend." He leaned forward. "Come to dinner with us Friday night. You're part of this, after all."

"I don't know," she said. "It's your family. I'd feel out of place." She fastened the elastic bandage and sat straight.

"They won't bite." He grinned at her, but she had a look on her face he hadn't seen before. She was afraid. "My da?" he asked.

She surveyed the training room.

"Right," he said. "Not now, not here. Lunch?"

She gave him a barely imperceptible nod.

"Thanks," he said in more normal tones.

"Take it easy on that knee, McCormick," she said loudly.

He smiled at her once more. She returned the smile, but her eyes showed a wariness that left him wondering what was wrong.

She turned to Novak, who waited at the next table.

She'd said she'd talk to him at lunch. Until then, Liam had to focus his energy on his job.

Chapter 26

Emma dropped the pre-wrap. She dropped the scissors. Every time she tried to put something into her fanny pack of medical supplies, she missed.

An hour later, a student doing a clinical rotation tended to the last of the team in the trainer's room. Emma breathed a sigh of relief.

She slipped outside to the parking lot. Portia stood beside her BMW, arms folded, waiting.

"You sure you want to break up with him?" Portia asked.

Emma laced her fingers into her short hair. "I thought I could. I thought I wanted to. Oh, Portia. I'm not over him. Not by a long shot."

Portia grinned and dangled the key to a luxury box on one finger. "You know, in an empty stadium, the box provides privacy for a whole lot more than talking," she said.

Emma shook a finger at her. "Don't. Don't even get me thinking about that." She snatched the key from Portia's hand.

"Just a reminder. The stadium also has a key to the box. There isn't an event tonight, and while I doubt anyone will miss this key, I'd like it back sooner rather than later so I don't get into trouble. *Capiche?*"

"Got it," Emma said. She hugged Portia. "I told him I'd meet him for lunch. If you need the key later, I can slip out. Otherwise, I'll give it to you tonight?"

"Text me when you're done and we'll figure it out," Portia said, getting into her car.

"He invited me to dinner with his family," Emma said, hands on the roof of the car. "What if they don't like me? My own mother doesn't like me."

Portia reached through the open window to take hold of Emma's arm. "Your mother's loss. Relax. You've got this."

"What am I doing, Portia? Once people find out we're seeing each other, they'll see me as a love-struck groupie. I'll lose credibility."

"You underestimate yourself, my friend."

"Hey, Emma." One of the students called across the parking lot. "Ray wants you on the field."

Emma waved to the student, then turned to Portia again. "Thanks."

"Good luck."

Emma closed her eyes, drew a breath to compose herself, and trotted toward the stadium.

No one had to know.

She bypassed the locker room and ran through the seats to the stadium floor. Ray stood at the end of the bench, watching the team finish their warm-ups. When Emma stopped beside him, he gave her a cursory glance.

"I figured it out," he said, still scanning the field.

"Figured what out?" she asked.

"What's bothering you."

Emma stiffened. Time to deflect. "You mean how my mother is pissing me off again?" she joked.

"Nope. Not your mother, although if that's true, I'm sorry."

The team ran in to huddle around the coach in preparation for a scrimmage. Shirts and skins. Liam peeled off his jersey and Emma's mouth watered. She grew uncomfortably warm. She turned her attention elsewhere and found Ray watching her.

"You said no one had acted inappropriately," he said. "I'm guessing that means you actually want to date him."

"P-pardon me?"

Ray smiled. "Remember when I told you it's okay to have a life?"

"I have a life," she said.

He stared at her, reading her like the open book she knew she was. "What are you afraid of?"

No point denying it. "The team will see me differently. They won't respect me."

"You've earned that respect," Ray said. "You aren't going to lose it because you made a choice to date... I'm assuming you made the choice."

"But that PT intern—"

"Whatever's going on between the two of you, it seems to be having positive results." Ray nodded toward the field. "He looks stronger than ever. I should have seen this sooner. Wouldn't have guessed until I saw your reaction to him when you walked in this morning. The way he looks at you. The way you blush around him." He shrugged.

"I won't let it affect my work," she said.

"I didn't think you would." Ray waved Liam to the sideline. "How's the knee?"

"So far so good." Liam glanced at Emma, a heated gaze that reminded her she didn't have the strength to walk away from him despite her resolve to do just that.

Ray glanced between them and shook his head. "Honest to God, the sparks flying between you could light a campfire. Get back out there before you *really* make me uncomfortable."

"Yes, sir," Liam said. He slanted a smile at Emma, winked, and took his place on the field.

"MCCORMICK." EMMA COCKED her head for Liam to follow as the team came in from the field for lunch.

Liam glanced around the locker room.

"Sounds like you're in trouble," Novak teased. He leaned closer. "I'm friends with Parker, on the Mustangs. He told me she decked Cody Voigt in Ireland. I'd watch my step if I was you."

"Don't I know it. I was there." Liam grinned. "Probably more endless tests on my knee. Nothing but respect for the lady."

Novak nodded.

"See you in the weight room after lunch." Liam threw on his shirt and followed her into the hall.

She stood by the staircase, and when she saw him, she surveyed the area to see who else might be lurking. He didn't see anyone, and when she seemed satisfied, as well, she motioned up the stairs.

They climbed to the luxury box level of the stadium, where Emma produced a key from her pocket.

"I can't get away for more than a few minutes," she said, "but I wanted to talk to you about your dad. I saw him again." She opened the door and pulled him into the box. "But first..."

The minute the door closed and locked behind them, she pushed him to the wall and kissed him. Any thoughts of the conversation she might have wanted to have fell away, along with his shirt, and then her shirt. He fumbled with her pants while she tugged at his shorts.

"Condom," he said, coming up for air.

"You do know there's a supply in the First Aid kit in the locker room, don't you?" She pulled one from her pocket before her khakis pooled at her feet.

"Is this all you brought?" he asked.

Emma giggled. "I wasn't sure if you had rules about boxes at the stadium."

He reversed their positions, his hands on either side of her head as he backed her to the wall. Liam covered her mouth and dropped a hand to sheath himself. He helped her slide her panties down and then he hoisted her. Using the wall to brace her, he slid into her with a sigh.

This was where he belonged. With Emma.

He took a moment to feel her warmth surrounding him. "I missed you," he sighed. He moved slowly at first, kissing her neck, her ear, her cheek, and back to her lips. Her legs wrapped around him and she held tight.

"The seats," she gasped. "Let's move to the seats."

He set her on her feet. She pointed him to a leather chair, and as soon as he sat, she straddled his lap. Emma's head tilted back when he cupped one of her breasts and lavished it with attention. She moaned her approval.

No one would look for them here. No one would hear them, but knowing someone might heightened the experience. Emma was in his hands, in his mouth, in his head. She felt so damn good.

One or both of them cried out, he wasn't sure. His heart pounded like he'd run wind sprints. Emma was draped over him, her pulse keeping pace with his.

"I'm thinking you should have brought more condoms," he whispered as he kissed her ear.

She giggled again. "I wasn't sure we'd use the one. I didn't mean to jump you like that."

"Are you kidding? You? Me? A private room? Pretty sure if you hadn't, I would have made an effort." He hugged her before he kissed her again. "I think you should stay with me tonight. You haven't seen my apartment yet. Pack a bag."

Emma kicked a leg over the chair to stand before she leaned down to kiss him again. "Why can't I get enough of you?"

"Is that a yes?"

She smiled. "Yes."

She cupped his face, leaned in and kissed him once more. When she pulled back, he darted his tongue to a still-pebbled nipple.

A shadow of concern creased her brow. "I'm not sure I'm good at casual sex. I don't know how this works." She reached for her clothes.

His heart cracked. "This isn't casual sex, Emma. This is an expression of my feeling for you." She wouldn't meet his eye. "I don't do casual sex, either. We can dissect all this later, but Emma," he shook his head. "This is not casual to me."

She nodded.

Casual? Did that mean she wasn't feeling the same things he was? Liam was pretty sure he'd fallen in love with Emma Parrish. Her adventurous spirit and the aggressive way she'd let him know she'd missed him reinforced his opinion. Something deep inside told him if he said the words, he'd scare her away.

They'd have plenty of time to talk later.

Chapter 27

Emma checked the clock. Three a.m.

The physical pull was stronger than she remembered, a distraction she hadn't planned on. Oh, she knew it was there, but she thought she'd be more in control. After the first round of lovemaking, she'd promised herself she'd tell Liam this couldn't go on. Tell him she couldn't go to Friday night dinner with the family. But he'd dropped off to sleep. Next thing she knew, he'd woken her for a second round. That was over an hour ago. They still hadn't had that conversation.

"I can hear you brain churning from here," Liam said sleepily. He turned to face her and leaned on one elbow. "Why aren't you sleeping?"

So many reasons, but she started with her visit from his father.

"Then I suppose he'll show up Friday night," Liam said. "Which works well. Good timing with my oldest sister coming home. We'll all be together." He leaned over to kiss her. "I can't wait for them to meet you."

She hadn't accepted his invitation. Not officially. He must have taken her lack of response as an affirmative. Was it? As much as she thought she wanted to, Emma couldn't break off their relationship. She had a few more days to come up with a reasonable excuse for missing the family dinner, or to suck it up.

When his lean body covered hers once more, she got lost in those dark eyes, smoothing his sleek, black hair. He gave her *that look*, the one that reflected her desire, and she wanted him again. Was the conversation, the one where she said she couldn't go to his mother's for dinner, so important?

Surely they'd have time to talk in the next couple of days.

Except the time never seemed right.

They both worked long hours at the stadium before going home to collapse into bed together. One day turned into three, until it was Thursday. His first game back with the Cowboys.

The development league games were one thing, but in the big leagues, the players were more ruthless. They were all highly competitive athletes who had something to prove every game. Including Liam. Would his knee withstand the test?

Thursday night. Which meant tomorrow was Friday.

The more time Emma spent with Liam, the more time she wanted to spend with him. But his family?

She didn't have to report until after noon on game day, so she took the opportunity to call Portia for an emergency lunch, not nearly enough time to talk through her misgivings. She either had to meet Liam's family, or explain to him why she couldn't.

When Portia walked into the restaurant wearing a pencil skirt, frilly blouse and heels, Emma felt underdressed in her polo and khakis. She hugged Portia tight.

"Glad you could come up for air," Portia teased. "Things must be going well." Her smile slipped. She tilted her head. "Oh, honey. What did you do?"

Emma released a sigh. She started talking the minute they'd both taken a seat. "Tomorrow's Friday." The words spilled out. The feelings she didn't want to have for Liam. The worry about what his family would think of her. People didn't tend to stick in her life.

She was midsentence when Portia grabbed her hands and tugged.

"Stop."

Emma swallowed her next words, closed her mouth and took a breath.

"You have to trust me on this," Portia said. "No one knows you better, huh?"

Reluctantly, Emma nodded.

"I think you should go. Meet the family. They're going to love you, by the way."

"But..."

Portia waved a finger at her. "Even if you sit there all night and don't say a thing. You need to go. I've never seen you like this with a man before. You've never second-guessed yourself. Why are you so twisted up inside? Unless it's because, for the first time in your life, you're in love. Am I right?"

Tears pricked the corners of Emma's eyes. "What if it's the selkie thing? A predisposed impression. Honest to God, what I feel borders on obsession. It isn't normal."

"Quit blaming it on the legend. You've had plenty of time to get to know him. You also don't have his sealskin, and if what you told me holds true, he wouldn't still be around without you holding that true part of himself. Consider that when you insist on clutching a legend as an excuse."

"Okay, but love? Lust. It's lust, right?"

The waitress interrupted them to take their order. Emma composed herself with a drink of water while she waited for the waitress to leave and Portia to answer.

Portia lowered her voice when they were alone again. "Every relationship goes through that 'can't keep your hands off each other' phase, but I gotta tell you, that part gets old pretty quick without something substantial to back it up. One of you gets tired, isn't in the mood. You start getting antsy that sex isn't enough. On the other hand, when you connect with someone like that, the sex never gets old."

Emma sputtered. "What are you? An expert all of a sudden?"

"On the getting old part? Yes. On the connecting part?" She shrugged. "There's always the one that got away, you know?"

Emma did know. She'd held Portia's hand through more than one breakup after a man Portia thought had long-term potential had called it quits.

"But I'm not like you," Emma countered. "I've never met a man with long-term potential."

"Until now. Don't wreck it because you're afraid. Give him a chance." Portia rested her elbows on the table and leaned forward. "I'm worried about you. I hate that your mother's done this to you, made you doubt yourself so much. Since she's been gone you've been kicking ass, proving to everyone you've got this on your own, and you do. Including Liam. You need to allow yourself to be happy, my friend."

Wasn't she happy?

No. She was miserable. She'd never had so much at stake before. Her heart had been broken when her father hadn't returned from his last deployment, but she still thought she had her mother, even if her mother had grown too busy to make time for her.

When her mother had moved away, Emma thought she'd understood. Every child needs to learn to fly on their own—but she hadn't expected never to see her mother again.

The waitress set their food on the table. Emma stared at it, old wounds stealing her appetite.

If Liam walked away from her, she wasn't sure she could recover.

LIAM HAD PLAYED THE whole first half without so much as a twinge. He'd challenged the forwards on the opposing team, stolen the ball a dozen times, stopped half a dozen shots meant for the goal.

Coach Simmons gave him a nod, as close as he'd get to an 'atta boy' and, at halftime, asked for Ray's opinion on if Liam would be strong enough for the second half.

"Never felt better," Liam told them both. "I'd love to give it a go if you'll let me."

"Ice?" Ray asked.

"Doesn't hurt," Liam told him.

Ray shot a glance at Coach Simmons. "I'll put him on a bike to keep his muscles warm."

Liam was going to play the whole game.

He was back.

The Cowboys won the game three-nil. Liam went out with the team afterward to celebrate. He excused himself early for a more private celebration with Emma. Everything was right with the world tonight.

She fed off his euphoria, adding an extra element to their already incredible chemistry, and in the afterglow he considered declaring his feelings for her.

Until she turned her back to him.

"Tired?" he asked.

She nodded.

He spooned behind her, kissed her ear and let out a contented sigh. "Emma."

She sniffled. Something wasn't right.

"Emma?"

"Tired," she repeated.

He kissed the back of her neck, a perfect end to a perfect day. Nestled against her backside, she roused him once more. Would he ever grow tired of loving this woman?

She arched into him and he slid inside once more.

"Emma," he said on a sigh, moving more slowly this time, feeling every inch of her body against his, the heat inside her. "Emma, I love you."

She froze, not meeting his strokes the way she had been.

He hadn't meant to say it, but once he had, he wasn't about to take it back.

He kissed her shoulder and Emma's body responded, moving with him once more.

She'd said she was tired. He shouldn't have taken advantage of her warmth, and yet she'd invited him in.

"Do you want to sleep?" he whispered in her ear, even as he rocked into her, not withdrawing.

"Don't stop," she replied. "Don't ever stop."

Liam closed his eyes, wrapped his hands around her to hold her breasts and gave in to the way she felt. The way she made him feel.

When his body surrendered once more, he didn't pull away. Not wanting to break their connection. Liam closed his eyes and fell asleep.

Chapter 28

"What if they don't like me?" Emma asked. "What if they think I'm a bad influence and I'm somehow responsible for this thing with your father? Liam, what if..."

"Stop," he said.

But she couldn't. Emma was cold, even though the weather had taken a pronounced turn toward summer heat.

"First," he said, steering onto the street where he'd grown up, "they're going to love you."

Love. It sent prickles of panic all over, including stabs to her heart.

"Second, and don't freak out when you hear the stories around the table, which you undoubtedly will," he shot her a quick glance before he veered into the driveway, "my family has experience with ghosts. They're not going to blame you for my father's sudden reappearance." He threw the gear shift in park, turned off the engine and faced her. "Third, they're going to know I'm crazy about you, and that's going to make them very happy. Most especially my ma."

"No woman is ever good enough for a mother's little boy," she muttered.

"Ma wants to see us all settled, and wouldn't you know it? Everyone is. Except me. She's going to try to talk you into putting up with me if she sees any glimmer of interest on your part." He grinned, leaned over and kissed her. "I hope there's at least a little glimmer."

Emma punched Liam in the shoulder.

"Foreplay. I like it," he teased.

He'd allayed some of her fears, but he had no idea how afraid she was she'd like his family, that she'd want to feel a part of them, only to have them ripped from her life like everyone else she'd loved.

There was that word again.

Emma shot a furtive glance at Liam as he got out of the car. She was in love with him.

The panic was back.

"Wait," she said, leaping from the car. "Did you say they have experience with ghosts?" She took hold of his arm to stop him from walking toward the house. "What aren't you telling me?"

Ghosts. Fairy tales. Legends. Her flight response made her itchy to run, to get away from the tension that held her in a vise.

Liam took her in his arms and laughed. "I guess that sounded worse than it actually is. It's not like we're mediums, or fortune tellers, or any of that, although Amy might be. My brother's wife. And Jared." His brow creased as his words seemed to soak in. "Wow. I never thought about it that way." He chuckled. "Maybe we are a bunch of kooks and you should be running for the hills. Wait a minute. You've seen a ghost, too. That makes you part of the club."

Emma took a step back, ready to bolt.

"I'm joking. Look, you decide. You're afraid they won't like you? What if you don't like them?"

As if.

The selkie thing continued to haunt her. What if she was entranced and none of this was real?

She'd never been such a bundle of nerves, always been in control of her life. Red flag warnings popped up all around Liam.

"This is a bad idea," she said quietly.

"Too late to back out now," he said, pulling her in for a hug. "It'll be okay. I promise." He kissed her forehead. "You're always so brave. So strong. I guess I never considered you might have a vulnerable spot, but it seems as if I might have uncovered one." He cocked his head toward the house. "Come in with me? They're pretty normal. I promise."

With a deep breath, Emma nodded. She was here. She could do this.

Liam took her by the hand and led her into the kitchen, which was filled with people.

A woman with flaming red hair, who had to be his sister based on what she knew of his siblings, pointed a finger at Liam, walking toward him before she pulled him into a hug. "I saw your post-game interview on television. Looks like you're back, eh?"

Liam shrugged out of her embrace with a silly grin. "I do try, you know."

A man with copper colored hair shook Liam's hand and then embraced him. "Congratulations, slacker. Good to see you back in the game." A little girl clung to his pants leg. The brother. Kevin?

Emma glanced around the kitchen, at the saying scrawled on the fascia over the cupboards. At the other faces in the room. Another woman with copper colored hair. A man with bronze skin. A small woman with white hair standing at the stove with her back to them, and a distinguished-looking man sitting at the table. Another woman walked in from the living room carrying a baby. Kevin's wife?

Liam's arm went around her shoulders. "Let me introduce one of the people responsible for my rehab, Emma Parrish. Emma, my sister Kathleen and her husband, Sebastian. My sister Siobhan and her husband Jared. My brother Kevin and his wife, Amy. That little urchin clinging to Kevin's leg is my niece Chloe. My mother's husband, Duncan."

The woman by the stove still hadn't turned around. Her way of saying Emma wasn't welcome? Emma swallowed down the lump in her throat.

"Ma?" Liam said.

The tiny woman bowed her head, wiped her hands on her apron and turned to face him, tears streaming down her face.

"Ma," Liam said more gently, taking her into his arms.

"It's that happy I am for you," she said, traces of Irish in her voice. She peered around Liam at Emma. "I'm sorry to burden you with our distasteful family business. Liam tells me you've seen him, too?"

Emma nodded. "I have."

His mother pushed Liam away and stood before Emma. "I'm pleased to meet you, and I'm very sorry. He has no right to trouble a stranger, nor yet his own family—the family he left behind." Anger flashed in her watery eyes. She shook Emma's hand. "I'm Eileen Phelps."

Liam's brother and sisters nudged each other, sending what appeared to be meaningful glances at Liam. Was that a good thing or a bad thing? The intimate interaction made Emma smile. The sense of family that bound them together was tangible.

"Thank you for having me," Emma replied.

Emma glanced around the room once more, checking the dark corners, the reflections in the windows. Liam's father didn't appear to be in attendance. Then she looked at the woman with the baby, Kevin's wife, Amy. She looked normal. What was her history with ghosts? Liam had mentioned Siobhan's husband—one very good looking man. What ghostly secret was he harboring?

Liam appeared at Emma's elbow and whispered in her ear. "I haven't told them what you told me. About Da wanting to apologize to the whole family. Maybe he won't show up."

"What are you whispering about, Liam?" his mother asked.

"Telling her it's not too late to run away," Liam joked. "Meeting the McCormicks can be an overwhelming ordeal."

Duncan rose from the table. "They're not so bad as all that," he told Emma. "Liam tells me you're an athletic trainer. If you ever get tired of working for the Cowboys, we can always use a talented trainer on staff at the hospital. You let me know if you ever want a job, will you?"

"Duncan's a doctor," Liam said. "Siobhan's a nurse."

"Nursed me back to health after a car accident," Jared said. "So much for not getting involved with the patient."

"I never got involved with my patient," Siobhan protested. "Not until you'd healed and moved back home."

"And came back to carry her away from her family," Kathleen added. "Still not sure I forgive you for that." Her smile said otherwise.

"You're always welcome to visit," Jared said in a slow, lazy drawl.

"I've had my fill of New Orleans," Kathleen said with a laugh.

"Good thing we live in Vacherie, then," Siobhan said.

Good-natured ribbing continued, the casual conversation showing how comfortable they were with each other and the "married-ins."

Emma settled into a chair beside Amy. "It always feels weird to congratulate someone on having a baby, but I suppose that goes more toward surviving the ordeal with a healthy infant. Congratulations. He's beautiful."

"Thank you. Would you like to hold him?"

Emma's heart tugged. Another bond she couldn't afford. "No, thank you. I don't have much experience with babies. He looks content where he is."

"Kathleen, love, can you get drinks for everyone?" Eileen asked.

Emma jumped to her feet. "Can I help with anything?"

Eileen waved a hand across her face. "Don't be silly. You're a guest tonight. Now if you were family..." She speared Liam with a look. He pointed to his chest with a questioning look that made Emma laugh.

Emma sat again.

"Liam said you've seen their father," Amy whispered.

Emma nodded. "He wants to make amends. That sort of thing seems to be difficult for him."

"He's actually spoken to you?"

"I suppose you could say that." Emma faced Amy. "Liam said you have some sort of ghostly connection?"

The wrong thing to say based on Amy's grimace.

"I didn't mean to pry."

"It's something I was born with. I hear things other people don't. That's all."

"And Jared?" Emma asked.

Amy smiled then. "He's from New Orleans, where ghosts are a way of life. Helping ghosts move on is a family business for them."

"Then he can help their father move on?" Emma's mood lightened. A professional, if such a thing existed.

"I hope so."

Eileen sat at the table. "Shall we say grace?"

"Grace," Siobhan responded.

"For that, you'll lead us," Eileen said.

They said a short prayer and conversation continued as plates of food were passed around.

"I hope you don't mind my asking," Amy said, her voice low. "Kevin tells me you're more than Liam's trainer."

Amy's eyes were an odd sherry color. Something about them seemed otherworldly, unsettling. She seemed to look straight through Emma. "We're, uh, sort of dating, I guess." Why was she equivocating? Easy. It sounded better than telling Amy they couldn't keep their hands off each other, or that she was over her head where her feelings for Liam were concerned.

"He's a good guy. He's been so focused on his career, and then getting better. It's nice to see him relaxing a little bit." Amy shifted the baby to one hip, took a couple of pieces from a plate of pork, and passed the plate to Emma.

Emma took a portion and passed the plate to Liam.

"What are you two whispering about?" he said, also whispering.

"Getting to know each other," Emma replied.

"Emma. How do you feel Liam's knee is holding up?" Duncan asked.

"Judging from this last game, I think his prognosis is good."

More plates of food traveled around the table.

"You're a doctor?" Emma asked Duncan. "What's your specialty?"

"These days? Bossing people around. I'm on an administrative rotation."

Conversation lagged as the family dug into the meal.

"The food is very good," Emma told Eileen. "Thanks again for inviting me."

"Liam insisted," Eileen said. "I'm glad he did. Thank you for joining us."

Silverware clanked on china, providing a musical background for the occasional comments being exchanged between the family.

Beside Emma, Amy went still. She set her fork on her plate and shifted the baby to her other side. "Kevin."

Kevin accepted the baby and Amy hunched over.

"Are you okay?" Emma asked.

"Duncan, I hate to impose on you, but could you...?" Kevin began. "Chloe, can you show Grandpa Duncan where Randall's diaper bag is?"

Duncan furrowed his brow, glanced at Amy, and nodded as if he'd gotten a secret message. He pushed away from the table and held his hand out to Chloe. "Let's take Randall into the living room for a bit, shall we?" He dipped down to gather the baby in his free arm and they left the room.

"Amy?" Emma asked again.

"Paper," Amy said.

"Is she okay?" Emma asked Kevin.

"She doesn't need paper," Jared said, rising from the table. His eyes were focused behind Emma.

Emma looked over her shoulder. Her blood froze when she saw the specter.

"Leave my house, demon," Eileen said. "I'll call Father Kelleher to cast your soul straight to hell where you belong if you don't leave us be."

Kevin rose from the table and stood between the ghost and his family, a defensive posture? Liam had mentioned how Kevin had tried to shelter the rest of them when they were children.

Emma stepped beside Kevin and lay a hand on his shoulder. "He's a spirit," she said. "He's come to make his peace." She turned to the ghost. "Isn't that right?"

The ghost wavered, an angry frown on his face.

"Isn't that what you told me?" Emma repeated.

The wavering slowed, the specter taking on a more-defined shape.

"No," Siobhan growled from her end of the table. She threw her glass through the ghost and it shattered on the floor. "You're not welcome here."

The spirit took his cap from his head. The hollow voice echoed from the corners of the room. "My time here is short. Siobhan. My heart. I drove you away and for that I'm sorry. Kevin. I thank you for being the man I never was. For helping your Ma raise your brother and sisters. Kathleen, oh my Kathleen. Always a beauty, and such fire." He turned toward Eileen. "I didn't know how to be a father, how to provide for our growing brood nor yet to discipline five children. I lost myself working long hours, and then felt inadequate to head my family for the time I was with you. We'd left *mo mhuintir*— my people—in Ireland and I didn't know who to turn to, so I turned to the drink and lost whatever control I might have had. I don't blame you for kicking me out, and then I was too proud to ask for forgiveness. Too bull-headed to admit I'd done wrong. Too lost in the drink to find my way back.

"Our Mary has sent me to beg your forgiveness. All of you. My soul cannot rest until I've made amends."

"What of Liam?" Kevin asked. "You've not apologized to him."

"I have. He's forgiven me. Not willingly, I'll admit, but he has granted me his forgiveness that I might move on."

Kevin turned to Liam. "Is that true?"

Liam nodded.

Siobhan rose to her feet, accusing eyes fixed on the ghost as she placed her hands on the table. "You called me a whore," she shouted. "Because of you, I left my family. I blamed them for what you did."

Jared rose beside her. "Let him move on," he said gently.

"He can go to hell for all I care," she said between clenched teeth.

"He can't go anywhere. Not without your forgiveness. Let him go."

Her hands fisted. She stared at the ghost for what felt like an eternity before she turned away and made a sound of disgust. "I'll accept your apology."

Not forgiveness, Emma noted.

"Kathleen?" Kevin said.

She nodded.

"Ma?"

Eileen refused to look at the ghost. "I loved him once. It's why I married him, before he became..." She closed her eyes. "It's that man I'll remember, and not the one who lost his way. Frank McCormick is gone." She crossed herself. "May his soul rest in peace."

"And you?" the ghost asked Kevin.

Kevin crossed to Siobhan and unfurled her hands. He spoke to her rather than the ghost. "Forgiveness is something we give without someone's asking. It's how we move on. To hold onto the anger does no one any good." He turned to face the ghost once more. "I will not forget the horrors you put us through, Da, but I will forgive you for them."

"It's all I ask." The ghost wavered in front of Eileen. "You've done well by them. Better than I could have done had I stayed. You did right in sending me away." He passed through her, the ghostly equivalent of a hug? He vanished as his words trailed behind him. "I never stopped loving you, Eileen, merely lost my way."

Kevin walked to each of them, took their hands in turn, and gave each a nod. He stood before his mother last. "*Teaghlach.*"

All of them repeated the word.

Liam slipped his hand in Emma's. "It means family," he told her.

Chills coursed through her. The word was like buddytaping fingers, their sense of family stronger than anything she'd ever witnessed.

For one night, she allowed herself to be a part of Liam's family. Embraced. Included. Loved.

Chapter 29

Liam stared at Emma. As nervous as she'd been to meet the family, she'd been the one to stand up to the ghost. His brave Emma.

Kathleen nudged his arm.

"What?"

"I see the way you're looking at her, potato-head," Kathleen said quietly. "'This is my athletic trainer,'" she said in a mocking tone. "Anything you'd like to add?"

He nudged her back and surveyed the rest of the family standing around the table. "I don't want to scare her off. You know how family can be. Case in point, a certain policeman you never invited over?"

Kathleen's hands went to her hips. "You knew about him, too?"

Liam waved a finger at her. "You can't keep secrets from family." He nodded toward Sebastian. "Turns out there was a reason you never brought the other one home."

"Is that the end of it?" Ma asked, her face chalky-white.

Kathleen hugged Ma. Kevin and Siobhan and Liam exchanged glances and joined her for a group hug.

Ma broke free and crossed to Emma. "I'll thank you."

"I didn't do anything," Emma said.

"You were the voice of reason he often lost." She glanced around the kitchen. "Has he moved on then?"

"I wish I knew," Emma replied.

Ma looked to Jared. "But you'll know."

"I believe he has," Jared said. "But I've been fooled before."

Ma nodded. "I believe he has."

Amy handed a piece of paper to Kevin. He read it, smiled, and handed the paper to Liam.

"What is it, then?" Ma asked.

"Jared was right," Amy said. "I didn't need a piece of paper. He didn't need me to pass along his final thoughts, but I thought it was appropriate."

Liam handed the paper to Kevin, who read the blessing she'd written.

> *May joy and peace surround you,*
> *contentment latch your door,*
> *and happiness be with you now*
> *and bless you evermore!*

Duncan leaned around the living room wall to peek into the kitchen. "Is it safe to come back?"

Ma walked to him, took his hand and drew him into the kitchen. Chloe dropped his other hand and hurried to Amy's side.

"Where's Randall?" Kevin asked.

"I put him down in the playpen," Duncan said. "He fell asleep."

"Thank you," Amy said, hoisting Chloe into her lap.

"You might be right," Ma told Duncan. "It's time to leave my old life behind." She motioned to the family surrounding them. "This brood is likely to follow wherever we end up, and that will always be home."

"Are you sure?" Duncan asked.

His mother backing down? Liam glanced at Kevin. They exchanged a surprised look.

Ma shot a nervous glance toward Kathleen.

"What about you?" Duncan asked Kathleen.

She held up her hands. "Don't ask me. I'm not the one has to live with you." She smiled, conveying her acceptance of the idea.

Duncan nodded. "We'll talk more."

"Sounds like our cue to leave," Kevin said. "I know Amy needs her rest, and frankly, so do I."

As everyone said their goodbyes, they included Emma in hugs with promises to see her again.

Liam and Emma climbed into his car and headed into the city. Liam was so wrapped up in his own thoughts he almost forgot he wasn't alone.

"Lot to take in," he said.

Emma didn't answer.

"You okay?"

"Mmm hmm."

Except she'd freaked out right before they'd gone inside. Something was off. His strong, brave, Emma had been a wreck. "Want to talk about it?"

"No," she said.

"I get it. You hate my family," he joked.

"They're lovely," she said wistfully.

Why did she sound so sad?

Her cell phone rang.

"Hey," she said. "Listen, we're in the car right now. Can I call you later?" She hesitated. "It was fine." She shot him a glance.

"Anyone I know?" Liam asked.

"Portia," she said. "My best friend."

Liam held out his hand for the phone.

"What?" Emma asked.

"I want to talk to her."

"You don't know her." She twisted away, talking into the phone. "But..." She glanced at him again and then handed the phone over.

"How come I don't know about you, Portia?" he asked.

"Because our friend doesn't share much of herself. I, on the other hand, know everything about you. What happened at dinner that she's not telling me?"

"Nothing much. A little family, a little food, sending a ghost on its way."

Emma reached for the phone. "Give me that."

Liam switched the phone to his opposite ear, gripping the steering wheel.

"It's the family part," Portia said. "You and me should talk, Cowboy. You are a Cowboy again, aren't you?"

"Yeah."

"But it would be better if she doesn't know about our conversation. At least not yet. On the QT. On the down low."

"You're not trying to proposition me, are you?" he asked light-heartedly.

"Give me that," Emma repeated, making another attempt to get the phone away from him.

"I'm going to guess she'll want to be alone tonight," Portia went on. "If I ask you to meet me at a bar later, will you?"

Liam glanced at Emma. She looked scared to death. Right now, he'd take whatever insight into her he could get. "Yeah."

After Portia gave him a place and time, Liam handed Emma's phone back to her.

"What did she tell you?" she demanded.

"Nothing much. She told me to be nice to you," he lied. "How come you've never mentioned Portia before if she's your best friend?"

"It hasn't come up," she said.

"So tell me now. Is it because she knows your deepest, darkest secrets?"

"Yes."

The answer was so quick and so short, it caught Liam by surprise. "I'm pretty good at keeping secrets, too," he said.

"Liam, can you take me home tonight? Alone? I'm pretty tired and I'd like to catch up on some things there. By myself."

Portia was right then. "You sure you don't want to talk?" he asked.

"Please. I need some time to myself."

"Okay."

THE NIGHT COULDN'T possibly get any weirder.

Liam sat in the bar, not knowing what Portia looked like. Waiting for her was worse than waiting for a blind date, or so he assumed. So far, he'd signed three autographs and turned down two propositions. For all he knew, Portia had been one of those women, but he'd wait five more minutes. As he nursed his ginger ale, a shapely blonde tapped one shoulder, then appeared on his opposite side.

"Even better in person," she said.

Portia. He recognized her voice.

"So what do you need to tell me?" he asked.

"Buy me a drink. Better yet, we should find a quiet corner to talk."

Liam hailed the bartender. When Portia got her drink, they crossed the dark room to sit at a table.

"I was right, then?" she said.

"About?"

"She wanted to be alone."

Liam nodded.

Portia leaned over the table. "So this is what you need to know. That girl is like a sister to me. We're close." She twisted her fingers together to demonstrate how close. "I'm the only family she has."

"What about her mother?"

"I'll get to that." Portia took a sip of her drink. "First. What do you want with her?"

Liam straightened. "What do you mean?"

She rolled her hand. "A roll in the hay? A good time? White picket fence and happily ever after? Fun for now?"

He considered his answer. If this was Emma's best friend, she was likely to relay anything he said. Why did he feel like he was on trial?

"Okay, okay." She held up a hand. "I'm asking for me. Not her. She's had a rough go of it and I don't want to see her hurt anymore, so I want to know. Do you love her? Do you think you might be in love with her?"

Again he hesitated. "I don't really know you."

"She's in love with you, whether she's told you or not. She's scared to death you're going to break her heart."

"She hasn't told me," he said, somewhat angrily. "How do I know she won't break *my* heart?"

Portia sat back and smiled. "Then you *are* in love with her. How bad is it?"

"Can we get to what you wanted to tell me?" he asked impatiently.

"She tell you her dad died?" she asked.

He nodded.

"What'd she tell you about her mom?"

"They visited museums when she was a kid, before her dad died. Her mom moved out West? San Francisco, I think she said."

"That's right." Portia sized him up. "What I'm sure she didn't tell you is her mother moved without her."

Liam cocked his head. "I'm not following."

"Here. Let me play it out for you. 'Hi honey, I'm moving to San Francisco. The lease is paid until the end of the month, but you're on your own after that. You should be able to find a nice apartment before then, don't you think? Hey, let's keep in touch.'"

The statement hit him like a brick. Emma's mother had done that? Something didn't fit. "Emma is a grown woman. That doesn't sound so unreasonable."

"Emma was still in college. Working while she was struggling to pay her tuition. Living at home so she could conserve her money." She leaned over the table for emphasis. "Emma was nineteen, so yes, technically, she should have been a self-supporting adult, but she had no forewarning.

"We've been friends since junior high, me and Emma. Emma says her mother changed after her father died. She resented having to get a job, having to raise a daughter by herself, and she didn't pretend otherwise. Suddenly, her job became the whole focus of her life. It was all about the promotions and the recognition. She didn't have to move to San Francisco, she chose to. She said it would be character-building for Emma to be on her own."

Cold. "You're saying she abandoned Emma."

"She hasn't seen her in seven years. Emma was out there with the team and asked her mother if she'd like to get together for dinner. Her mother was too busy."

The picture was coming together. No wonder Emma was so brave. She had to be.

"Let me spell this out for you, Cowboy. Everyone Emma has ever loved walked out on her. I'm not even going to bore you with the boyfriend details." Portia leaned over the table once more. "Are you going to walk out on her? Because if you are, do it now before she gets in any deeper."

"What makes you say she loves me?" he asked, searching for something to say.

She looked at him, studied him. Took a sip of her drink. Studied him some more. The silence grew uncomfortable. "You told her you loved her. She didn't say it back."

Suddenly, Liam wished he had something more than ginger ale in his glass. "She told you that?"

Portia shook her head. "No, but that would be par for the course. Don't let her get away with it, Liam. I've never seen her so twisted up about a man before. If you really do love her, make sure she knows you mean it."

"I don't want to scare her off."

Portia beamed at him then. "You really do love her, don't you?"

"White picket fence and happily ever after."

She scooted around the table and side-hugged him. "Tell her. Every day. I'm pretty sure she'll come around eventually." She shook a finger at him. "But if you mess her up any more than she's already messed up, you'll have to deal with me. You got it?"

Liam grinned then. "Loud and clear. Want to help me pick out a ring? If I give it to her now, she can have a year or so to get used to the idea."

Portia chuckled and finished her drink. "No, I think you've got this." She reached up and set her glass on a server's tray. "I like you. I can see why she's infatuated with you, but tell me the truth. You aren't really a selkie, are you? You aren't going to disappear back into the sea someday?"

He cocked an eyebrow. "You never know."

She shook her finger again. "You'd better not." Portia rose from her seat. "Get your sleep while you can. After she's talked herself off the ledge, she's likely to want more slumber parties." She leaned down and said in a loud whisper. "The chemistry must be off the charts. I don't see it, personally, but been there, done that, if you know what I mean."

Liam laughed as she walked away.

Emma's brave front was a matter of survival. Apparently, he wasn't the only one afraid of screwing this relationship up.

Chapter 30

Along the walk from the parking lot to the practice pitch, Emma reminded herself she was overthinking. Dinner with the McCormicks was just that—dinner. Liam might have whispered those three little words in a moment of passion, but as long as she didn't say them back, he didn't have to feel bound by them, and she didn't have to feel like she'd given that part of herself away.

Even though she had.

She huffed a sigh as she pushed into the stadium. Could she enjoy this thing with Liam while it lasted? When the newness flamed out, one or both of them might be looking for an exit strategy. *She* might be looking to end things. Until that happened, she could take advantage of the extra warmth in her bed—or his bed. Relationships happened all the time. People survived when they ended. She'd survive.

She passed through the weight room, where early arrivers warmed up their muscles. In the training room, two of the team members were already perched on tables, waiting to get taped before practice.

"Hey, Emma," Javier said.

With one last fortifying breath, she dove into her job. "Javy. How you feeling today?"

"The ankle's pretty good, but I don't want to take any chances. I figure a couple more days. What do you think?"

"Can't hurt." She pulled up a stool and rooted around her fanny pack for the roll of pre-wrap.

"Can I ask you something?" he asked while she tried to focus on her job.

"Shoot," she invited.

"Are you going out with McCormick?"

Her heart skipped a beat and she dropped the pre-wrap. "What makes you ask?"

Javy grinned. "I guess that's a yes. I know I got no business asking, but these guys are like a bunch of women the way they gossip."

She retrieved the pre-wrap and continued winding. "They're gossiping about me?" she asked, fighting to appear cool.

Javy held up his hands. "Nothing bad. Mostly about how it's their own fault for not asking you out first. Liam's one lucky S.O.B. Unless it's only gossip, and if it is, would you go to dinner with me?"

Emma relaxed and smiled. "That's sweet of you, Javy, but I prefer to keep my professional life and my personal life separate." She cut the pre-wrap and ran the elastic bandage around his ankle.

"Yeah, I get that."

Her skin warmed and her nerve endings prickled. Emma didn't have to look up to know Liam had walked into the room. Head bowed to her job, her suspicions were confirmed when he greeted Javier. She finished her task and gave Javy a smile. "Good to go."

An intern sat in front of the table Liam occupied, with Ray watching over his shoulder.

"How you doing today?" Liam asked Emma.

"Great, thanks. How's the knee?"

He cocked an eyebrow.

Ray cleared his throat. "Newkirk, run to my office and get an ice pack," he told the intern bent over Liam's leg.

"Ice pack?" the intern repeated.

Ray cocked his head and the intern shrugged.

"Two minutes," Ray whispered to Liam and Emma before he walked away.

Liam lowered his voice "I missed you last night."

"Me, too," she said.

"Tonight?" he asked. "We're heading out of town tomorrow, and I'll have a roommate then."

The attraction hadn't flamed out yet. She nodded.

"Who's the ice pack for?" Newkirk asked her, stopping beside the table.

"You'll have to ask Ray." She gave Liam one more glance. "Let me know how the knee feels after practice, McCormick."

"Yes, ma'am."

LIAM DIDN'T WANT TO challenge Portia's assessment of Emma's response last night, but his warrior woman was back tonight.

Emma had walked out of his bedroom wearing nothing but a smile and helped herself to a bottle of water from his refrigerator like she owned the place. She took a sip, set the bottle on the nightstand, then slid into bed to snuggle in the afterglow.

"Javy asked me if we were dating," she told him.

For someone who had been so afraid of the team finding out, she sounded pretty casual. "What did you tell him?" Liam asked.

"That I keep my personal life separate from my private life."

He'd been hearing from the guys all day, too, getting shit because he was the one who'd had the guts to ask her out when half of them wanted to.

Emma sat up and tugged the sheet with her, turning to face him. "You said something the other night."

"I'm sure I said a lot of things. Which one merits your attention?"

Her lips twisted into a crooked smile. She dropped the sheet and swung a leg over him, positioning herself on his lap. Emma in charge. This was the way he liked her best. While his body responded to her heat, he grazed his fingers across her nipples. Would he ever get enough of her?

"Something you said in the heat of the moment," she said huskily, squirming into a more receptive position.

"As I recall, it was after the heat of the moment, and I thought you were sleeping. Not that I wouldn't tell you when you were awake."

"Oh," she said, sliding him inside once more. She closed her eyes and sighed.

His body tensed in response, his pleasure center lighting up. "Here I thought you wanted to talk." Liam held her hips and pushed deeper. She moaned and leaned forward, clutching his shoulders.

"I love you," he whispered into her ear. "Even when you're awake."

She straightened and met his gaze. "I love you, too."

If she hadn't been riding him, he would have taken the opportunity to go to his dresser and show her the ring he'd bought for her right now instead of waiting for the off-day, Monday after the game. She did a shimmy and instinct took over. With a growl, he gave up trying to be gentle, gave up going slow and drawing this out.

Emma was his, as surely as he was hers. The connection they shared went deeper than their joined bodies. She loved him, too. They were going to spend the rest of their lives together. Raise a family together. Now that he was whole again, he could buy her anything she wanted, give her the kind of life she deserved. Give her a family of her own to love.

A family of their own. The idea was like a detonator, catapulting him toward his vision of heaven on earth.

"That was amazing," Emma said breathlessly.

He struggled to open his eyes, to look at her, perched on top of him. Her grin was back. She giggled as he flipped her to her back, leaned over her and kissed her.

"You ever think about kids?" he asked.

Her eyes opened wide. "Who's?"

"Little black-haired selkies, or mop-tops with crazy hair." He ran a hand across the top of her head. "For the record, I like it better straight, but I love you no matter what you do to your hair." He watched her face for signs of panic. He knew he was pushing the boundaries of her comfort zone, but he had to show her he was in this. All the way. So far, so good.

"I'm still getting used to the idea of being in love." She sobered, holding his gaze. "If I ever thought about kids, which I haven't—" she toyed with the ends of his hair and another smile lit up her face. "You'd make a great dad."

"You think so?" He nipped her nose with a kiss. "Hey, we could have a whole soccer team."

"Whoa, there." She pushed him away and sat up. "Ten kids? Are you serious?"

"How many would you want? If you thought about it."

She shrugged. Had he pushed her too hard?

"Three?"

"Six," he countered.

"One at a time."

Liam shot a glance at his dresser. Was this his opening? The perfect time to propose? Except he'd planned a whole romantic scenario. On the other hand, the subject was open, she seemed receptive...

No. He didn't want to overwhelm her, and yet she'd overwhelmed him. She was perfect. That she'd even consider being the mother of his children brought him near to tears. He leaned across and kissed her again, cupping her face.

Whatever disappointments she'd had in her past, he was going to make it up to her. He vowed to give her everything she ever wanted and make her forget about the hurts and the heartbreak.

She stared at his face, studying him as if trying to read his mind. "We should get some sleep," she said. "Travel days are always long."

"I need one more thing before we go to sleep," he told her, kissing her.

"What's that?"

He glanced down, to where he'd grown hard once more.

"Again?" she asked, gasping for breath.

"Slow and easy. I want to make love to you, the way you deserve to be loved." Liam kissed her neck, her throat, suckled at her nipples, and dipped a hand between her legs. She gasped as his fingers slid across her most sensitive spots.

She was so beautiful. How had he never noticed her before she'd come to Ireland?

Within moments, she flailed with her release, took a moment to catch her breath, and pulled him on top, giving him control.

He'd prove himself worthy of her trust.

Chapter 31

The weather in Columbus didn't affect practice in the indoor arena, but when a warm, gentle rain continued to fall on game day, the players donned their rain cleats for the outdoor stadium.

Emma envisioned pulled hamstrings and fresh cuts and bruises from sliding—and falling—on the turf.

Like little boys playing in puddles, the starters laughed and splashed in the grass, acclimating to the weather rather than huddling under the team's canopy.

The coaches, along with Emma and Ray, were wrapped in rain slickers to keep dry, which were much too warm on an early summer evening. The occasional spray of rain carried on the wind was a welcome relief.

Emma folded her arms as the game got underway, her nerves wound tight. She and Ray watched intently. Every stride, every tackle, every slip.

The atmosphere on the field was that of a high school game. Slippery balls made passing difficult. Challenges for the ball were more deliberate. Shots on goal stopped short of the keeper in the wet grass.

The first Cowboy didn't go down until almost twelve minutes into the game.

Ray leaned toward Emma. "Novak."

Emma prepared to run onto the field. "I see him."

Novak came up limping, but waved off attention from the sideline. The referee restarted the game and the moment passed, but Emma watched him closely.

Liam went down next and Emma's heart stopped. His leg slid forward and he ended up seated in the wet grass. She took one step toward the field and hesitated when Liam took Novak's hand and rose to his feet laughing. No limp.

"I hate this," Emma whispered.

"Boys will be boys," Ray said.

The team made it to halftime without any significant injuries. Half a dozen players spent the break in the training room re-taping or getting massages on hyperextended muscles.

Liam wasn't one of them.

Emma stopped him in the tunnel on the way to the field for the second half. "You okay?"

"Never better," he said with a smile.

The sun had come out, glistening off the wet grass. The humidity made the air too thick to be sure the rain had stopped. Emma held out a hand to check. Hot and sweaty, she peeled off her raincoat.

Both teams continued to slip and slide.

The opposing striker took a shot on goal, flipped onto his back and stayed down. The Columbus trainer rushed to the field with the stretcher bearers. In a matter of minutes, the striker walked off on his own. Play resumed, and the other team kicked the ball out of bounds toward where the striker stood beside the referee. The referee waved him in, and the game resumed.

"If that's the worst thing that happens, we can count ourselves lucky," Ray said.

"Right?" She glanced at the clock. "Ten minutes to go."

The striker advanced the ball, dribbling directly at Liam. Liam met him, challenged him, dodged left, then right. He made a play for the ball and missed. The striker dribbled past him. Liam took another step and went down.

And didn't get up.

A frisson of fear buzzed through Emma. The referee waved to the sideline.

"Let's go, guys," Ray said to the stretcher bearers.

Emma wasn't hot anymore. She wrapped her arms around herself to ward off a chill that came from deep inside.

The stretcher came to the sideline. Liam draped his arm across his head, turned away from Emma.

They took him into the training room, Ray trotting alongside the stretcher. "You got this?" he called to Emma over his shoulder.

She nodded, turning to the game. She had a job to do—a job that required her to concentrate on the rest of the team instead of the missing defender.

LIAM COULDN'T LOOK at Ray.

Déjà vu. He knew what came next.

"What happened?" Ray asked, going through all the joint tests.

"Cleat got stuck. Tried to move and my leg didn't come with. Twisted funny."

"There's a gap," Ray told him.

Liam heaved a sigh. "I heard it pop."

"I'm sending you to the hospital for an MRI, but I think we can both take an educated guess here. It doesn't look good." Ray wrapped an ice pack around Liam's knee.

This was it. The end of his career. Yes, they'd patch him up again, but the fact his ACL had blown up a second time meant he'd be facing this same scenario again. The doctors had told him his knee would never be the same, even if the surgery was successful. It had been successful, but every successive surgery would diminish his function further.

"You want me to get Emma to go with you?" Ray asked.

How was he supposed to support a family? His contract ran another year, but after that, his income stream would depend on what came next. All the things he wanted to give Emma were suddenly out of reach. He wouldn't subject her to an uncertain future. She deserved so much more.

"No. Get me out of here before the game ends," Liam said. "No one needs to see me like this."

Ray folded his arms and studied Liam. "The ambulance should be waiting outside. You sure you don't want..."

"No," Liam repeated. He closed his eyes, shook his head. "She's got enough to do here. I don't want her at the hospital."

Ray raised his arms in the air. "Okay. Your call, hotshot, but if she insists, I'm not going to try to stop her." He crossed to Liam's locker and picked up Liam's duffle. "In case you miss the flight home." He chucked the bag and it landed on Liam's gut, making him grunt for air.

"I'll find my own way," Liam said, struggling to find his voice.

Ray shook a finger at him. "She's like a daughter to me."

"Every time I see her, I'm going to remember she's still part of the team, and I'm not." Liam's tempered flared.

"You can come back from this."

The paramedics pushed a cot into the training room.

"That's what I thought last time," Liam muttered.

"Don't you give up."

Liam glared at Ray. "Another year? How many games can I play next year before we go through this all over again?"

"You need help moving to the cot?" one of the paramedics asked him.

Liam turned away from Ray. With one paramedic on each side of him, Liam hopped off the table onto his good leg to transfer to the gurney.

"What about Emma?" Ray asked.

The paramedics waited, wanting to hear what Liam had to say. The injury was a dark hole that threatened to swallow him up. "She's brave. She's strong. I'm not any of those things. You know where I'm going? Back to my mother's house to recuperate. Just like last time. I hid from PT after that incident with the intern. I doubted myself in the D-league and screwed around, and now that I'm finally where I want to be..." He shook his head. "She deserves better than I can give her."

Ray waved a hand at the door. "Get him out of here."

THREE COWBOYS FOLLOWED Emma into the training room under the guise of needing help taking tape off. Ray pointed each of them to a table, not meeting Emma's eye.

"What hospital did they take him to?" she asked.

"Why don't you take Javy. I've got Novak."

Avoiding the question? "Ray?"

"We have work to do," he said. He glanced around. "McCormick won't be flying home with us. He'll join the team later."

"I can stay behind. Fly home with him."

Ray pulled her to the side and lowered his voice. "He doesn't want you to."

"His ACL again?" she asked.

Ray nodded.

"He can't walk through the airport on his own. I mean he can, but he shouldn't."

"He doesn't want you there."

Emma studied Ray's face to read what he wasn't saying.

"Give him a couple of days," Ray said.

A couple of days? She considered storming out of the facility, going to the hospital and damn the consequences. Except Liam had given her the space she needed after dinner with his family. The new injury had to be a blow. She owed him the same courtesy of time to think it through.

"A couple of days," she repeated.

Again Ray nodded. "He's feeling frustrated. Defeated. Give him time."

He'd said he loved her. He wasn't going to run away. Wasn't going to leave her because of an injury. She had to believe that. Reluctantly, she walked to the training table where Javy waited for her.

"He okay?" Javy asked.

She forced a smile. "I guess we'll find out."

Chapter 32

Portia sat on Emma's sofa with her feet on the coffee table. "So how long has it been?"

"Has what been?" Emma asked, knowing full well she was about to get another earful on the deficiencies of the male species.

"Since your Cowboy faded into the woodwork."

"I haven't been paying attention," Emma lied.

"Well, I have. Unless you're holding out on me, he hasn't called you in what? A month? Dumb jock," she muttered. "I'd like to take that guy into a dark alley where the bikers hang out and tell them he pushed over their hogs."

Thirty-eight days, but she wasn't going to encourage Portia. "Why are *you* so mad at him?" Emma asked, hands on hips. "I'm the one he's ghosting."

"Because I believed him," Portia told her.

"About what?"

Portia's eyes widened. She pressed her lips together.

"Portia?"

Portia's voice turned to a whine. "You're my best friend. I had to know what his intentions were."

Emma dropped into the chair beside the sofa. "What did you do?"

Portia studied her fingernails. "I may have told him about your past."

"Why would you do that?"

"Because he convinced me he was in this thing, that it wasn't just 'fun for now.'"

Emma's skin crawled. "You had no business telling him anything. I was perfectly willing to try to be in the now this one time."

"That's why you've been moping around your apartment instead of going to the gym? That's why you hate your job? The job you've always loved? Emma, I'm trying to look out for you."

"In case you haven't noticed, I've been looking out for myself for a long time." She jumped to her feet and paced to the barred living room window. On the horizon, a lighthouse beacon crept across the dark expanse of Lake Michigan.

Emma cast a glance at her bedroom. She might not have believed she was lonely before, but Liam's conspicuous absence from her life highlighted that she was lonely now. "You're right. I should go to the gym. Hey, I might run into Tyson again. If he's still interested, I could suggest a second date. If I didn't totally piss him off after the last time."

"That's not the answer and you know it." Portia approached and draped an arm across Emma's shoulder. "Honey, I love you. I hate to see you like this. Hey, I have an idea. We could drive over to my mother's. I told you she's been asking about you. She'll insist on feeding you something high calorie and fuss over you. What do you say?"

Emma forced a smile. "I'm fine."

"You sure?"

As much as she loved Portia's mother, she didn't want to be fussed over. "Maybe next weekend."

"I really thought he was the one." Portia shook her hands at her side. "I believed him, Emma. I can't begin to tell you how pissed off I am about that."

"Then stop trying to mother me and go back to being my friend. I don't want to talk about him anymore." Tears stung the corners of her eyes. "I just want to get past this. By myself."

Portia chortled. "Stop trying to mother you? This is when a girl needs her mom the most, not that your mother ever stepped up to the plate."

Emma rubbed her forehead. "Speaking of, she called me yesterday."

"Will wonders never cease? What's the occasion?"

"The last time I called her I thanked her for making the effort and essentially told her she was right, that I don't need a mother anymore, and she didn't need to bother calling me back. When she called yesterday she said it was time to clear the air—she said she'd booked a flight. She's going to be here in an hour."

Portia grabbed Emma's arm. "Here? Your mother?"

Emma nodded.

"Thanks for the warning. I think that's my cue to leave." Portia narrowed her eyes. "Unless you're making it up. You know, if you want me to go, all you have to do is say so."

Emma traced a finger over her heart and held up two fingers. "Scouts honor. I'm sure she'd love to see you."

"You were never a scout, and you know how I feel about your mother." Portia eased her grip and stroked Emma's arm before she took a step away. "Her timing is impeccable, showing up when your life is falling apart."

"There's nothing wrong with my life, thank you." Emma turned toward the window once more. "You know I'll be working ten and twelve hour days this week ahead of the game Friday night. I'm not going to have time to see her."

"Then she'll know what it's like being on the receiving end of 'I'm too busy.' That's not necessarily a bad thing."

Emma shook her hands. "But she's my mother."

"Exactly. Is she expecting to stay with you?"

Emma shook her head. "She's staying at the Ritz."

Portia rolled her eyes. "Of course she is. At least it will give you something else to think about. Maybe she can help you move on from Liam."

"I don't need her to do that." Emma hugged Portia. "And I know. A month is long enough to wait by the phone. If I expect things to change, I'm the one who has to change them. Right?"

Portia narrowed her eyes. "Like?"

"Everywhere I look, I see him. Everything I do reminds me of him. I've been sleeping on the sofa because I can't bear to sleep in my bed alone. I go to work and I'm looking for him. I stand on the sidelines watching practice and I look for him. The whole damn team looks at me like I'm going to burst into tears at any moment, and you know what? I might."

"How do you change that?" Portia's brow furrowed.

"Liam's stepfather mentioned the hospital is always looking for an AT. Imagine. Regular hours. I might even be able to have a real life instead of working all the time. Do you know why I liked working so hard? So I wouldn't have to think about how alone I was. You can see how that worked out."

"You're going to ask Liam's stepfather for a job?"

"No," Emma said. "I don't even know what hospital he works at. I don't want any favors from Liam or his family. But I have been applying for hospital jobs, on my own merits. It's time I lived my life instead of hiding in my job."

The knock on the door had Emma nearly leaping through the window.

"She's early," Portia said. "I'll let her in on my way out."

"You are not leaving me alone with her."

Portia shook a finger at Emma. "She scares me. For that matter, you scare me. Which means you should scare her." She pulled Emma into another hug. "You've got this, and if you need to get away, I'll even go running with you tomorrow."

Portia opened the door. "Mrs. Parrish. I was just leaving."

"Portia. Nice to see you again," Emma's mother said.

Portia cast a last glance over her shoulder and mouthed 'call me later.'

Emma's mother hadn't changed much. Her hair looked freshly colored, her trim figure unchanged. She wore blue silk pants and a fashion-forward top, and her face—the subtle make-up hid any signs of aging. She looked ready to head to the Museum of Science and Industry.

Emma felt eleven years old. The memory destroyed whatever fight she had left.

"Mom."

"Emma."

A fragile smile creased her mother's face. Her chest rose and fell with a slow breath before she passed through the door and closed it. "Cozy."

Emma folded her arms. "Plenty of room for one person. It works."

"Portia looks well. I'm sure she thinks I've been a bad mother."

"Funny. I was thinking about our scavenger hunts at the museum."

Her mother relaxed with a smile. "There. I knew you'd understand."

Emma raised her chin. She'd been silent all these years. She was done putting up with dismissal. From anyone.

"Like the time you couldn't see me when I was in San Francisco? Like not returning my calls?"

"Emma, I've been busy."

"Too busy for your daughter."

Her mother surveyed the apartment. Looking for an escape route?

"My career—" her mother began.

"Was more important. I get that. You had a life to get on with. You'd done your job as a mother."

"Don't say it like that." Her mother's eyes flashed.

Emma raised her eyebrows, daring her mother to challenge the truth.

Her mother cradled the necklace at Emma's throat, the heart her father had given her. "Do you have something to drink?" she asked as she let the necklace rest against Emma's skin.

"Have a seat." Emma clutched the necklace as she hurried to the kitchen. "Water?"

"Yes."

Emma handed a bottle to her mother and sat opposite.

"Rather than recriminations, why don't we get caught up? Tell me about your job."

"I'm considering a change," Emma replied.

Her mother opened the bottle and looked around. "Don't you have a glass?"

Emma sprang to her feet. "Sorry. I guess I'm used to the athletes who take it straight from the bottle." She grabbed a glass from one of her cupboards and set it on the table beside her mother.

"All those fine male specimens and you're still single?"

Her mother's words hit her like a one-inch punch to the chest. Emma gasped for breath. "I don't have much time for relationships."

Her mother shook her head. Was she going to judge Emma's life? Emma's nerves prickled and she tightened her fists.

"I loved your father very much," her mother said softly. "So much that when he died, I was lost without him."

Not what Emma expected to hear. "You had me," she reminded her.

"I did. But it wasn't the same. I never wanted to be a single parent. I knew the risks of marrying a military man, knew there was a possibility he might not come home one day, but I loved him so much." Her voice faded and she took another drink. Her eyes filled with unshed tears. "I buried myself in work so I wouldn't have to think about sleeping in a cold bed.

Waking up alone. Not knowing if I was doing everything I needed to do to raise a child."

Emma eased into her chair, surprised by her mother's admission.

"Work was where I found validation after he died. The only thing I did right. You hit your teen years, when every kid hates their parents, except I didn't have anyone to share the angst with."

"I never hated you," Emma said.

"Every kid does. Even if you didn't show it, I was sure you did." She shrugged. "So I stuck with where I got my feels. Work. I was good at my job and I got recognition for it." She took another drink and leaned forward. "Emma, if I've made you feel like I don't love you, I'm sorry. I didn't know how..." She pursed her lips.

Emma didn't want more heartache. She'd been as crushed by her father's death as her mother. "We don't have to do this."

"I'm afraid I do," her mother said.

Tears slid down Emma's cheeks. "I missed Daddy, too. What do you think it felt like losing my father and having my mother disappear right before my eyes?"

"Unbearable," her mother whispered. "And there you are. Bearing it. Look at you. You are so strong."

"Why did you come?" Emma asked, wiping her face.

Her mother rose from the chair and sat beside Emma on the sofa. Head bowed, she took Emma's hands in hers. "Hasn't enough time passed?" She raised her face and smiled. "I met someone."

"Met someone?" If her mother had a boyfriend, someone new to love—now, when Emma had lost the man she'd given her heart to—she was sure she'd break into pieces.

"I learned something when I met him, Em-Gem."

Emma cringed at the familiar endearment, the one she used to bask in.

"I've been hiding myself away. From you, from myself, from life." She drew another deep breath. "If there's one thing I've learned in the last several months, it's that there's a whole lot of life out there waiting to be lived. It's okay to grieve, but I'm not dead yet, and neither are you. There's so much yet to experience, including love."

Emma chuffed. "Yeah, well, I lost my chance."

"I don't believe that, and neither should you."

Emma ground her teeth. "So now you're going off to live happily ever after. Does he even know you have a daughter?"

"Of course, he does. He can't wait to meet you."

Years of resentment bubbled up. "Someone else you can introduce me to and then hide me from?"

"What do you mean?" Her mother reached for Emma, but she backed away.

"You think I know you didn't tell any of my grandparents where we moved after the funeral? You took away all the family I had left except you. And then you left me, too."

"Is that what you think? That I did it to hurt you?"

Emma pressed her lips tight. She might have thought she'd moved past the resentment, but the tears sliding down her cheeks said otherwise.

Her mother folded her hands in her lap and stared at them. "As to my parents—Emma, my mother smothered me.

She never believed I could take care of myself, much less raise a child. Moving around with your father was a blessing. It was a way to get away from them and the helicoptering. I swore I'd never do that to you, and it seems I went too far the other direction." She raised her eyes, overflowing with tears of her own. "You were always so independent. So self-sufficient. You didn't need me." She hiccupped with a sob. "I never considered you might feel orphaned. I'm so sorry."

Sorry wasn't enough. "What about Daddy's parents? At the funeral you promised them they'd still see me, spend time with me, and then we moved away. You didn't tell them where we went, did you?"

Her mother shook her head. "I was afraid they'd try to take you away from me. My own mother threatened as much." Her shoulders tightened and she winced. "Even after all the years I was married—and you were eleven years old, for heaven's sakes. She completely discounted all that time, everything I'd done on my own, without her help. In her eyes, I was still five years old and incompetent." She reached for a tissue and blew her nose. "Oh, Emma. I never thought about what my actions would do to you. You could still contact your Parrish grandparents. I know they'd love to hear from you. The letters they sent me..." She bowed her head again, then buried her face in her hands.

Emma reached over and cupped her mother's shoulder. "You should have told me. All of it. You should have let me make my own decisions. I would have stayed with you, Mom. They wouldn't have been able to take me away from you." She wiped her face and reached across to hug her mother. "If I try to contact any of them now, after all these years, they're going to wonder what I'm after."

"No." Her mother shook her head. "They're going to think I'm dead." She chuckled. "And if you want to contact my parents, I'm sure you could hold your own against my mother. You're so much stronger than I ever was."

Her mother smoothed Emma's hair. "I like the highlights, by the way. Is this how you normally wear your hair?" Emma laughed, shocked at the abrupt change of topic.

"Actually, I usually go with the tousled look, although I've been told straight is preferable."

"By your boyfriend?"

Fresh tears rolled down Emma's cheeks. She nodded.

"I won't say he's right, but I will say I agree."

Her mother touched Emma's face. "I miss you. I want things to be different. I promise to call you more often. I'd like it if we could see each other more. Will you still be traveling with your new job?"

Emma smiled. "No. I've been applying for hospital jobs. Regular hours and no more traveling."

"Then I'll have to come to you."

Emma sat back, dumbfounded. Her mother crossed her heart and smiled, then handed Emma a tissue.

The mother who used to take her on scavenger hunts and buy her ice cream and read her bedtime stories.

"Now, tell me about this man. Is it serious?"

Emma found herself talking about the trip to Ireland, about how she thought Liam was a legend come to life. All the years fell away and she was a little girl again, talking to the most important person in her life. Her mother.

She wasn't alone. Not anymore.

Chapter 33

Liam worked the controller to get Mario to jump to the top of the wall. He'd beaten the game a dozen times over, and still he struggled with that damn wall.

The front door opened and he turned to greet his ma.

Except it wasn't Ma, it was Kevin.

"Where's Ma?" Liam asked.

"She's busy." Kevin walked into Liam's kitchen and set down a bag of groceries.

"What's up?" Liam asked.

Kevin bowed his head, turned slowly. "She's tired of hauling ass into the city to take care of you."

"I thought she'd prefer it to me lying around on her couch."

"She'd prefer you taking care of yourself." He glared at Liam. "How long are you going to sit on your ass this time? Three months since the injury, or am I wrong? And you've finished eight weeks of physical therapy?"

Liam tossed the controller onto the coffee table. "What's eating you?"

Kevin waved a hand at the television. "Is this what you're planning for your future? Playing video games?"

"Now you sound like her." Liam shut the game off. "I'm not just sitting here all day every day. I've been going to the health club. Swimming. Trying to get back to triathlon shape, if nothing else. You got a better suggestion?"

"I've got plenty. Let's start with what happened to the woman you brought to Ma's? I think her name was Emma?"

Liam drew a deep breath. "Why all the questions?"

Kevin leaned both hands on the counter. "You really going to quit the Cowboys?"

Liam nodded slowly. "Even Duncan says my knee will never be the same."

"That doesn't mean you can't come back from your injury."

"Did. Got hurt again."

Kevin bowed his head. "Liam, you worked hard to be a professional soccer player. You achieved what a lot of other people couldn't. You're going to throw that away?"

"Things can change in an instant," Liam said. "Just like Ma used to say. One injury, and your career is over."

"But it doesn't have to be," Kevin said, an impatient tone creeping into his voice. "So what's Plan B? To sit around and feel sorry for yourself?"

Liam's shoulders sloughed. He had the degrees, but he didn't know what to do with them. "Damned if I know."

Kevin crossed the room and settled into the chair beside the sofa. "What happened to Emma?"

Liam shrugged.

"This is me you're talking to. We all saw how much you liked her."

Liked. They didn't know the half of it. "You know me. I'm the man with the plan," he said. "The problem is I don't have one right now. I can't start a family without regular income," Liam said.

Kevin let out a quiet whistle. "Family, huh?"

"I'll get paid through the end of next year, but after that? What I have coming is equivalent to a severance package. What do I do when the money runs out? This is exactly the type of scenario I talk to the high contract players about, except they get more money." He bowed his head. "They have more years in the league. Their paychecks give them the cushion to fall back on, as long as they're smart about their money."

"You're smart about your money," Kevin said. "You must have some tucked away. A rainy day fund. The man with the plan."

When Liam didn't respond, Kevin folded his hands and leaned over his knees. "Did you talk to her about it?"

"Until I get my life straightened out, I've got no business screwing up someone else's."

Kevin straightened. "You're giving up on her? The same way you're giving up on your career?"

Liam winced. "C'mon, Kev. Aren't you supposed to be making me feel better?"

"No, actually. I'm here to make you stop whining. To make you stop taking advantage of Ma, who feels guilty about abandoning her son in his time of need, even though you can take care of yourself." Kevin scowled. "I know this whole situation has to hurt."

"Hurt?" Liam said. "Leg cramps at three o'clock in the morning hurt. That's nothing compared to how I feel right now."

"Then do something about it."

"I'm all ears, big brother."

Kevin scowled. "Get over yourself. You had to know this might happen. Why the hell did you get a Master's degree if you didn't intend to use it?"

"Because I could? Because the whole finance thing was easy? Because six more semesters at State University gave me a better chance at getting drafted?"

Kevin's face brightened. "Wait a minute. Liam. How many of the Cowboys come to you for financial advice?"

Liam shrugged. "A few."

"Do they pay you?"

Oh.

Liam met Kevin's eye, the light dawning. "No. But they would. I gave them my advice as a friend."

Kevin nodded.

Liam rolled his eyes. "I'm such a dope."

"No argument."

Liam grinned then. "I could get certified."

"I have no doubt. You're the one with all the brains in the family."

So why didn't he feel smart?

"You still look like you have leg cramps," Kevin said.

"I screwed things up with Emma."

"No surprise there."

Liam scowled. "No, I mean I *really* screwed things up. I did the very thing I told her I'd never do." He glanced at Kevin. "I disappeared on her."

"Plead stupidity. Or tell her you've been concentrating on getting better. Lead with an apology."

Liam bowed his head again. He'd avoided her calls for almost three months. "It's too late for that."

Kevin chuffed. "You really are a potato-head. I take back that comment about you having brains."

"Hey." Liam reached across to swat at Kevin.

Kevin held up his hands. "It's your life."

"Don't you have a family to take care of?"

"You're family, too. Now get off that couch and make me some dinner since I came all the way into the city to take care of you. Ma says you told her you know how to cook."

Liam eased to his feet and threw a fake jab at Kevin. Kevin jabbed back and caught Liam in a hug.

"Women like a man who'll cook for them," Kevin suggested. "Unless you already have. Am I going to regret asking you to make my dinner?"

"I already told you. I screwed up royally. Emma's one tough cookie, and me? Haven't I proven to everyone that I collapse at the first sign of trouble?"

"Not hardly. You've spent the last year rebuilding your knee, and you made it all the way back. Not your fault your body had other plans. Give her a call. What do you have to lose?"

Liam shook a finger at Kevin. "Not your life to run, and while I'm grateful to you for pointing out the obvious to me,

I've got a long road ahead of me once again. Going a different direction, but a long road, just the same."

"I'm here for you," Kevin said.

"Always have been." Liam led Kevin into the kitchen. "You know, it occurs to me. Da might have been a poor example of a parent, but we're all stronger because of him. Closer, too, I'd wager. I'm that glad to have you as a brother," he said, slipping into his ma's way of speaking. "And glad that they had a brood of us to be there for each other."

A luxury Emma didn't have. No, Liam had betrayed her in the worst possible way. He'd done exactly what Portia warned him not to do, all in the name of his own pride. Emma deserved better than he'd given her.

Chapter 34

"You sure you won't reconsider?" Ray asked Emma while she cleaned out her office.

"You're the one who said it was okay for me to take some time for myself." She surveyed her office one last time.

"Since when do you listen to me?" he asked. Everything okay with you and McCormick? You haven't said much about him since the injury."

Liam's name hit her like a punch to the gut, but she wasn't about to tell Ray she'd been ghosted. "Why wouldn't it be?" Emma smiled and gave him a hug. "Thanks for everything. Really. If you want to blame someone for my mood, blame my mother. It's time to make room for something in my life other than work. Regular hours, a regular schedule..."

"McCormick's a lucky guy."

Liam was lucky, all right. Lucky Portia didn't lure him into a back alley where Emma herself would be more than happy to go a few rounds with him.

"You're a good trainer, Emma. If you ever change your mind, you let me know, huh?"

"You'll be my first call." She picked up her box of personal effects and offered Ray one more smile. "Thank you. For everything."

"I expect to hear from you," he said, his voice husky. "Bunny will probably call you to invite you over for dinner."

"We'll keep in touch. I promise." She nudged him with her shoulder. "Now let me get out of here. I'm supposed to meet the scheduler at the hospital."

Ray held out his arms. "I can carry that for you, you know."

"I know you can, but as you see, I already have it."

"Then I'll hold the doors for you." He led the way from the practice facility to the parking lot, giving her a clear path.

When she'd loaded her box and climbed into the car, Ray stood beside her, hand on the roof. "You take care, Parrish. You hear?"

"You haven't see the last of me," she told him.

He nodded, patted the roof and took a step back.

Emma drove away from the arena for the last time. Her heart twisted with the bittersweet end of her job with the Cowboys, and the excitement of starting over. She'd have patients at the hospital who wouldn't take the fact she was a woman into account, unlike a male soccer team.

To be fair, she could count on one hand the times she'd been patronized based on her gender, but it was enough to make her defensive.

While she drove from the city to the suburbs, her cell phone rang.

"Emma Parrish," she answered.

"Hey, Emma. It's Bobbi from the health club. You aren't by chance in town are you? I need a self-defense instructor tomorrow morning. Can you fill in?"

"As a matter of fact, I can," she said. "What time do you needme?"

"We have a nine and a ten. Want to do both?"

"Can do. I'll check in around 8:30."

"Fantastic. I'll see you then."

Unbidden, an image of Liam giving her *that look* whenever he asked if she was going to drop him popped into her head. The difference now was if he made a pass at her, she *would* put him on the ground.

What went wrong? Was it because she didn't want ten kids? He couldn't have been serious. Had they gotten too close too fast? He'd obviously had second thoughts about something. He might have had the courtesy to tell her what those second thoughts were.

She exited the expressway at Edgarville, and for half a second considered stopping by Liam's mother's house. Emma had an extra half hour to kill.

Not productive. His family didn't have to answer for Liam. They probably didn't know or care what had happened. For all Emma knew, he brought a different woman home every Friday night.

The hospital was on the outskirts of town, half a mile off the expressway. Was this the hospital where Liam's stepfather worked? She hadn't run across him during the interview process, which meant if he was there, he wouldn't be part of her day-to-day duties.

Emma wound her way through the lot to visitor parking. When she walked inside, she took notice of the coffee shop and the cafeteria on her way to the elevator. She'd interviewed in the administrative offices on her last visit, and had a tour of the orthopedic floor, including the post-surgical rehab area. She hesitated a moment, trying to remember which floor was which. A map in the elevator sent her to the sixth floor for administration.

She was still early. When she stepped off the elevator, windows lined the corridor overlooking the town. The Chicago skyline shimmered in the distance like an oasis in the desert.

"I was hoping to run into you," a man said, walking toward her.

Liam's stepfather. Question answered. Emma's pulse raced.

"Duncan, right?" she said. "I didn't realize this was your hospital."

"Well, it's not really mine, but I do work here," he said with a smile. He took her hand between both of his. "I would have given you a reference, you know."

"You hardly know me," she replied. "I didn't want to impose."

"Nonsense. We're glad to have you on board. When I saw your name on the new hire list, I wanted to greet you in person. Would you care to step into my office?"

Emma surveyed the corridor. "I have an appointment with..."

"Yes, I know. We'll let her know where you are. What do you say?"

Emma's skin prickled. What was this about? "I'm not sure..."

"Please?"

Against her better judgment, she agreed.

"Funny story," he said, leading her to his office. "Liam's sister used to work for me. She's the one who introduced me to Eileen. She took pity on me and invited me over for Thanksgiving one year, and the rest, as they say, is history."

What was she supposed to say? Emma gave him an uncomfortable smile.

He waved her into an office, invited her to sit, and continued to his chair on the other side of the desk.

"I wanted to talk to you about Liam," he said.

"I'm not sure I can help you," she replied. "He and I haven't spoken in a few months."

Duncan frowned. "Which makes it worse than I thought."

Worse than what? "Excuse me?"

"The first time he had ACL surgery, he laid around my wife's house playing video games all day letting her wait on him hand and foot. It's different this time."

Emma shifted uncomfortably in her seat. "I'm not sure what that has to do with me."

"It's different this time," Duncan repeated. "I suspect part of that is because of you."

Be careful what you wish for. Wasn't she entertaining going to his family for answers? "As I've mentioned, I haven't heard from Liam since his injury."

"That's likely because he's holed himself up in his apartment in the city. Eileen has been going to him instead of him coming to her, but that's more because she feels she has to care for him than because he expects it. With that being said, I'm sure he's glad she does. She spoils those kids."

Emma fought a smile. The McCormick children were hardly kids.

"He's been like a lost puppy," Duncan said.

"I don't want a dog," she replied.

A small part of Emma did a fist pump. He should be suffering. He'd made her suffer, but she was over it. This job was meant to be a fresh start, a chance for her to leave the old insecurities behind and make a life for herself, one that didn't involve hiding in her work, the way her mother had.

Duncan sat back and steepled his hands in front of his face. He studied her a moment before he leaned forward again, lowering his hands. "I'm not trying to interfere. I had hoped things were better between the two of you. They seemed to be when he brought you home for dinner." He exhaled loudly. "I'm making a muck of things. Whatever happened between you and Liam—" He frowned. "No. That would be interfering." Duncan gave her a smile. "Impinging on your personal life is a poor way to start a new job."

"Thank you for understanding." Emma rose from her seat to leave.

Duncan stood behind his desk. "Whatever's going on between you and Liam, it won't affect your job. You have my assurance on that."

"Thank you."

"But Emma..."

She met his gaze, got suckered into his sheepish smile. "As his mother's husband, I can't seem to help myself from interfering. If he should reach out to you, can I ask you to give him a chance? Hear him out?"

"As that seems highly unlikely..." Emma's muscles bunched. "I'm sorry. I can't promise."

Chapter 35

Liam had the pool at the health club to himself. This time of the morning, most people were already at work or, he supposed, unwilling to go to work smelling like chlorine. It wasn't the same as training at Foster Beach, but he wasn't ready for the triathlon course yet.

He would compete again, but not until next summer. He could get certified to coach other triathletes along with building his financial advisor practice. For now, he'd stick with the rehab, work on getting stronger. Again.

He climbed from the pool and headed to the locker room, showered, and packed his duffle.

He had a few hours before his pitch to the Cowboys at their afternoon team meeting. When the front office had accepted his proposal, he'd spent the week preparing. The project energized Liam for the first time since tearing his ACL again. The horizon didn't look quite so bleak.

He threw his duffle over his shoulder and left the locker room, winding his way through the hall toward the exit and stopped dead before he reached the registration desk.

Emma.

Awareness woke his nerve endings. He'd acted like an idiot, and he wasn't sure how to recover. Seeing her brought back a host of emotions, none of which he was prepared to deal with.

She laughed with the woman at the desk and, as if she sensed him standing there, halfway down the hallway, she looked up. Their eyes locked for a moment.

He should say something, but he didn't know what. "I'm sorry" seemed wholly inadequate, and "I love you" would sound false.

He did love her, and seeing her again reminded him how much.

Emma nodded to the desk clerk and walked away.

Liam berated himself for being such an ass. She deserved an apology, at the very least. He couldn't let her walk away, not without saying something.

He followed her down another of the hallways, into a room filled with women.

The look in her eyes—accusing and filled with hurt—undid him.

Liam cleared his throat. "Can I have a moment?"

She raised her eyebrows. "You can have several if you'll allow me to use you for demonstration."

That sounded ominous.

One of the women seated on the floor whispered his name loudly to the woman beside her. A soccer fan?

"Ummm," he stammered.

Emma turned to the class. "How many have you been to a self-defense class before?" she asked.

She was going to throw him down. Repeatedly, from the sounds of things. He deserved that, and more. Liam dropped his duffle, put his hands together and bowed before her.

A couple of women raised their hands.

"Would you mind showing everyone what you know?" she asked, inviting a woman who'd raised her hand to the front of the room.

"Mr. McCormick," Emma said, her voice deceptively sweet. "Would you stand behind...?" She nodded to the woman in search of a name.

"Iris," the woman provided.

"Iris. Would you stand behind her and put an arm around her neck, as if you meant to choke her?" Emma glanced at his knee. "Unless you're worried about getting hurt again."

She was the trainer. She knew better than he did if he was in danger of getting hurt. "Worried?" he replied. "Not if you aren't." He positioned himself behind Iris, striking the pose she'd asked for.

"Now, Iris, can you walk the others through what you're doing?"

Iris tittered nervously, shot a look over her shoulder at Liam. She grabbed his arm, blushed, and giggled again. "I don't know if I can," she whispered.

"Liam," Emma said, giving him a nod.

Right. He was supposed to be an attacker. He tightened his hold, reached for Iris's arm and was promptly tripped painfully to the ground, a knee in his back and one arm twisted behind him.

"Very good," Emma said. "Thank you, Iris."

Iris blushed furiously as she returned to her seat.

Emma extended a hand to help him up. "Did you all see what she did?"

"Can I try?" another too-eager student asked.

Emma smiled. Liam hung back, listening as she lectured the class on techniques for threats who approached from behind and from threats who came at them head-on. She invited him to come at her for another demonstration.

"For the record, I'm not in the habit of attacking women," he told the class.

"Our volunteer is worried about his reputation." Emma narrowed her eyes once more. "I think they understand you are here to demonstrate rather than threaten, but it also helps to know they can overpower someone who might be stronger than they are. Now, would you come straight at me as if you meant to hurt me?"

"I don't want to hurt you," he said quietly. "I never meant to hurt you."

She pressed her lips together. Her throat bobbed as she swallowed hard. "For the benefit of the class," she said, a break in her voice.

He stepped inside her personal space, the same way he had on the beach in Kinsale. He'd challenged her then, but he was fairly certain he'd meet the ground if he tried to kiss her this time.

Why not? He wanted her back more than he wanted his next breath.

Liam took her by the arms, cupped her face, leaned in and kissed her. Like the beach on Kinsale, she stepped between his legs, took hold of his arms and, like the beach in Kinsale, she melted into the kiss.

The class applauded, pulling them out of the moment. In an instant, he was on the floor.

"I want to try," one of the ladies said, raising her hand.

Emma stared at him, pain in her eyes. She reached down to help him up and pointed to the door. "Ladies, will you excuse us a minute?" She snatched his duffle from the floor and followed him into the hallway.

She tossed his bag at him and, hands on her hips, glared at him. "Why did you walk into my classroom?"

"I wanted to learn self-defense?" he said innocently.

Her tight expression conveyed that she wasn't amused. "What do you want?"

So many things. The white picket fence. The three—for starters—kids. With her. But he didn't know how to fix this. "I need to apologize," he said meekly. "There's no excuse. When I got hurt, all I saw was an end. To everything."

"Clearly."

"I panicked, but Emma, I made a mistake. I don't even know how to make it up to you, but I'd like to try. Can we get dinner tonight? Or if that's asking too much, a cup of coffee at Starbucks."

Her nostrils flared, hands firmly planted on her hips. "I don't see the point."

Except she'd kissed him. Again. Like she had in Kinsale. This wasn't over. "You kissed me back."

"You embarrassed me in front of my class."

"You invited me in."

She threw her hands at her sides and turned away.

"Please?" He took her arm and she yanked it back.

"Coffee," he said. "Thirty minutes tops. I owe you an explanation."

"Then you'll leave me alone?" Her eyes took on a glassy sheen.

"If that's what you want, yes."

She nodded once.

"When is your class over?"

"I have another one after this." Emma took a deep breath and raised her chin. "What about lunch in the cafeteria here?"

He started to agree when he remembered his proposal to the Cowboys. "Um, I'm giving a presentation right after lunch. Can we have coffee this afternoon? Or, if you'll agree to dinner..."

Her nostrils flared again and she smirked. "I'll tell you what. Why don't you *call* me and let me know?"

Judging by her tone of voice, she didn't think he would. "All right."

She stormed into her classroom.

He had another presentation to prepare, the one where he pled his case to Emma to win her back.

Chapter 36

Emma tapped her foot while she studied her phone. Portia continued to text her, even after Emma had arrived at the restaurant to meet Liam.

I'm only ten minutes away, not too late to be your second, if you need one.

Her second. As if this was a duel. Emma texted her reply, the same one she'd expressed verbally two hours before. Liam might have gotten to her at the health club, but he'd caught her by surprise. She'd spent the better part of the day rehearsing potential conversations in her head. No pretty boy, dumb jock logic was going to get him out of what he'd done to her. He'd destroyed her faith in him. She had this. She was prepared to shut that door between them. Closure.

Until she watched him walk into the dining room. The smile on his face looked as if he'd won the lottery.

This was going to be harder than she thought.

He's just a man. He's just a man.

Liam stopped at the table, leaned over to kiss her cheek and pulled out his chair.

"You're never going to believe the day I had," he started. "I pitched my services as a financial advisor to the team. Half of them signed up right away. Of course, three of them were already getting my services free of charge, but even they signed up."

The waiter stopped by to take Liam's drink order. He asked for water, then pointed to Emma's glass of wine. "You need a refill?"

She shook her head.

Financial advisor?

"And then," he went on, "the General Manager got me an invitation to address the rookie class for the NFL team, the NBA team and both MLB teams."

"That's great," she said softly. Cross off dumb jock, although she'd already known there was more to him. She cleared her throat. "So you're not going back to the Cowboys?"

"I'm listening to what my body's telling me," he said, repeating an oft-repeated phrase used by the AT's. "I came back from the injury once. I'm sure I could do it a second time, but how many times do I want to try? How long before no one wants to sign an injury-prone defender? No, my ma always told me to have a Plan B. I think it's time to pursue that."

The hostess led a large group into the dining room. One woman had fiery red hair, and another man in her party looked suspiciously familiar.

No. It couldn't be.

Emma's phone buzzed with another text.

I know you're going to hate me. I'm in the bar. Send me a signal if you need me.

She didn't want Portia's help. She glanced toward the bar. Portia sat at a table, her side to the restaurant. She made the

"I'm watching you" sign with two fingers, turning Emma's wince to a scowl. She texted back.

I've got this.

The woman with the red hair, Liam's sister, waved as his family took a seat two tables away. Did he know his family had arrived? Or were they following him the way Portia had followed her?

"They tell me you left the Cowboys, too," Liam said.

Emma lowered her eyes and fingered her wine glass. "That's right."

"Why?"

She did not want to explain herself to Liam McCormick.

Emma lowered her voice. "I needed a change of scenery. A change of pace."

"It wasn't because of me, was it?"

"It was not."

He sobered, the excitement he'd walked in with falling away.

"Emma, I know I've been an ass these last few months. I screwed up. I don't know how I can make it up to you, but I'd like to try."

Emma's eyes darted to his family, who seemed to be engrossed in their own conversation. "What's the point?"

"I told you I'd be there, and I wasn't. I've had some pretty life-changing decisions to make and I didn't want to drag you into my problems. All I can say is I'm sorry, and I hope you'll forgive me."

"Oh, I might," she said. "Portia, on the other hand, wants to take you into a dark alley and beat the crap out of you. There's no coming back, as far as she's concerned."

"She's not the one I'm trying to make it up to." He raised his eyebrows. "Should she be?"

Emma nodded to the bar. "When I told her I was meeting you for dinner, she followed me. I can't be responsible for her actions."

He turned in his chair to look. Portia bent forward, letting her hair cover her face, and pretended not to notice. Liam sent her a finger wave and she turned away.

He did a double take when he noticed his family. He rolled his eyes and seemed to consider for a moment. "We could go somewhere else."

"I'm guessing they'd follow us. It's only dinner."

Liam seemed to come to a decision. He held Emma's gaze. "I told Portia I was in this, and I meant it. I didn't expect the rug to get yanked out from under my career so quickly, and when it was, I didn't know what to do. I didn't feel like I could give you the life I'd envisioned for us together. My ma—and no, I didn't know they'd be here," he cocked his head to where she sat at the table behind him, "told me to have a Plan B, but I never thought I'd have to revert to it so soon, and when the time came, I wasn't sure how to put it into action."

"Life can change in an instant," Emma murmured.

"Yes, it can. Before they carried me off the field on a stretcher—Emma, I had plans. I had intended to spend the next day, the off day, convincing you I was going to be there for you. Forever." He pulled a box from his pants pocket and thumped it on the table. "I was going to give you this." He opened the top and a diamond ring glittered against a blue velvet background.

Emma struggled to take a breath. "You were going to," she managed to say. "Until you changed your mind." She forced a smile. "Good sex doesn't necessarily translate to happily ever after."

"It was more than good sex, and you know it." He glanced over his shoulder and lowered his voice. "It was phenomenal sex, but that's beside the point."

Her heart ached, her nose tickled and her eyes burned. "Then what's the point? To show me what I might have had if life hadn't changed in an instant?"

"To show you I'm sincere. That this is still what I want. I went into a dark place with that injury. I wasn't good enough anymore. I didn't have the bright future I thought I had. My brother was the one who shook me out of my funk."

"You're lucky to have family," she said, sparing a glance at the other table.

"The point, Emma, is that I love you. Probably from the moment you stormed into that pub with my wetsuit. I had a speech prepared for you, before I went down." He slid off his chair and went to one knee—his good knee—with a grimace. "It went something like this. I'm not asking you to marry me tomorrow, even if that's what I want, because Emma, I know you're the one I want to spend forever with. I'm asking you to trust me. To love me back. To consider being my wife and the mother of my children."

Kathleen and Kevin jumped from their table to stand behind him with an expression akin to panic.

Liam shrugged them off. "Do you mind?"

"You look like you need a little help," Kevin said.

"I don't."

When they didn't leave, Liam scowled and went on, ignoring the siblings hovering over his shoulder. "Take as long as you need to decide. I'm not going anywhere. There isn't another person in this world I want to be with." He paused. "I know I've proved myself untrustworthy by wallowing in self-pity, but I'm over it, and one thing remains. I want to spend my life with you, Emma. When I asked you how many kids you wanted? This was why. I'm yours to command, even if I don't have a sealskin for you to hide."

"Kids?" Kathleen asked Kevin.

"Shut up," Liam said without turning.

Tears crept down Emma's cheeks. She shifted her gaze from the ring to his eyes—those dark, soulful, selkie eyes which also welled with tears.

"Give me a chance to make it up to you. I love you, Emma."

"That's all you got?" Kevin asked. "Good thing we're here to pick you up off the floor."

"Oh, Emma," Portia said, snatching the ring box off the table.

"Can we have a moment?" Emma asked the spectators.

"His knee," Kevin said, reaching for Liam.

"I'm an athletic trainer," Emma told him. "I think I can help him up."

Portia spoke in a loud whisper as she set the ring down again. "Say yes."

Emma speared her with a look. "You were the one who wanted to beat him to a pulp."

"Yeah, but honey, look at him. You know he probably shouldn't be kneeling. Listen to what he's saying."

Kevin cocked his head toward Kathleen and they returned to their table. The whole family leaned toward the center as the two apparently relayed what was happening.

Emma shot Portia another withering look.

Portia raised her hands and backed away. "Right here if you need me."

Liam leveraged his weight against the table and pushed to his feet. "You going to take me out back and rough me up now?"

Emma rose to help him and he shrugged her off. When Liam regained his seat, his mother approached the table.

"I don't know what he's done to destroy your trust in him," Eileen said, "but I believe he means to make amends, if you'll let him. That night you came to dinner, I knew you were one of us, and nothing would make this mother happier than if you'd at least give him a chance. He's a good boy, my son."

"Ma, please," Liam said. "Can we have a little privacy?"

Emma laughed while she swiped at her eyes.

He looked around the restaurant, at cell phones pointed their direction. "I'm sorry. I didn't know they'd be here."

"Like I said, my guess is they would have showed up no matter where we went," Emma said. "I know Portia would have. And the cell phones? You're still a celebrity, and you're making a scene."

He didn't meet Emma's gaze. He seemed crestfallen.

"I didn't think you'd call," she said.

He spared her a glance. "I know, but I couldn't let you go again. Not after I saw you. I had to at least try to make it right. I wanted to give you everything, and in the blink of an eye, everything I had to give was taken away from me."

Liam McCormick was lethal at close range. She'd always known it.

Her mother's words rang in her ears. Emma had been hiding herself away, trying to protect herself from this very situation. She'd gone to the Celtic Sea in search of a selkie, and she'd found something better.

She glanced at his family, all eyes watching. Emma checked the bar. Portia placed a dramatic hand to her heart.

"Explain what you think 'everything' entails," she said to Liam. "Because there isn't much I truly want."

"A future. A family of our own to love and to love you back. How was I supposed to give you that when I'd lost my paycheck? My future?"

"How about you stop trying to take care of me and we do this as a team?"

Liam looked up slowly, a confused look on his face.

"I've been taking care of myself for a long time," she said. "I don't want someone else to take over."

He cocked his head, his brow still furrowed.

Emma smiled then. "Liam, the only thing I want is you."

"Is that a yes?" he asked cautiously.

She shrugged. "Who can resist the charms of a selkie?"

Liam turned to his family. "She said yes."

Kevin motioned for him to turn around.

"Yes?" Liam asked Emma again.

"Yes," she replied.

Kathleen ran over to give Emma a hug. "Welcome to the family, although what you see in this potato-head is beyond me."

Family.

Emma had regained a mother, and she'd been embraced by Liam's clan.

Something told her that, far from being lonely, it might be a challenge finding time to be alone again.

Dear Reader:

Thanks so much for reading this book. If you enjoyed the story, I hope you will encourage others by "liking" my books on Goodreads.com and everywhere the option is offered, and by posting an honest review to the site where you bought this book and/or at other book blogs/reading sites so you can help other readers decide whether it's worth their time. Authors like and need to get feedback to make each new book as good as it can be.

—Karla Brandenburg

Also by **Karla Brandenburg**

The Epitaph Series
Epitaph
The Twins
The Mirror
The Architect

The Northwest Suburbs Series
Cookie Therapy
Return to Hoffman Grove
Living Canvas
Touched by the Sun

The Mist Trilogy
Mist on the Meadow
Gathering Mist
Rising Mist

Other Novels
Intimate Distance
Heart for Rent, with an Option